T0209560

Prey of the Falcon

An International Thriller

Len Camarda

authorHOUSE

AuthorHouse™
1663 Liberty Drive
Bloomington, IN 47403
www.authorhouse.com
Phone: 1 (800) 839-8640

© 2020 Len Camarda. All rights reserved.

www.lencamarda.com

No part of this book may be reproduced, stored in a retrieval system, or
transmitted by any means without the written permission of the author.

Published by AuthorHouse 05/29/2020

ISBN: 978-1-7283-6149-9 (sc)
ISBN: 978-1-7283-6147-5 (hc)
ISBN: 978-1-7283-6148-2 (e)

Library of Congress Control Number: 2020908551

Print information available on the last page.

This book is a work of fiction. While there are some references to historical persons
and events in selected chapters, these are used to establish background for the fictional
storyline. Other names and characters, while associated with actual places, organizations,
countries and their leaders, are the product of the author's imagination and are used
fictitiously. Any resemblance to actual persons, living or dead, is to be construed as
totally a work of fiction and not related to their actual beliefs, policies nor activities.

Cover, Falcon training in the desert near Dubai
Photo by Robert Haandrikman via flikr

Map of the Middle East from pixabay.com with license from Adobe
Camel caravan with Dubai skyline by Adrian_ilie825, from Adobe
Midnight at the Oasis. Song written in 1973 by David Nichen and recorded by Maria Muldaur

This book is printed on acid-free paper.

Because of the dynamic nature of the Internet, any web addresses or links contained in
this book may have changed since publication and may no longer be valid. The views
expressed in this work are solely those of the author and do not necessarily reflect the
views of the publisher, and the publisher hereby disclaims any responsibility for them.

For my daughter Georgeann—George—the alter ego of Frankie. Always dependable, reliable and a tremendous sounding board, and much more.

"Let your tears roll tonight, but tomorrow you will start the battle again. What defeats us, always, is just our own sorrow."
—Amin Maalouf, *The First Century After Beatrice*

Chapter One

"*Ya voy, ya voy,*" Paz said as she lingered near the steps of the building's entrance. Looking back into the hallway beyond the front doors, she very slowly made her way toward her friend. The sun was setting and the parking lot would soon be dark. At that time of year—late November—the lights in the parking lot were always about twenty minutes late in illuminating the area with their pale yellow glow.

"Javier isn't coming out now," yelled Frankie. "I saw him talking with Carmen, who is much prettier than you are."

"Bitch," muttered Paz, hopping down the steps and walking briskly toward Frankie, who was laughing.

The two girls were like sisters; both were attractive brunettes, about five-three with shoulder-length, wavy, chestnut hair. Paz's eyes were deep brown and Frankie's were piercing emerald-green. They had outgoing, strong, and friendly personalities.

While the two women walked to Paz's white BMW—a birthday gift from her father—their movements were closely observed by two young men who were softly talking to each other through sophisticated headsets. One—Zayed Falaj—was crouching behind a red Peugeot about thirty meters from Paz's BMW. The other—Rasid bin Seray—was even closer.

"The two are together again, Assad," whispered Zayed in Arabic.

"Shit," replied Assad al-Amin, leader of the *Saqr* unit—a word meaning "falcon" in Arabic—observing the women through powerful Zeiss binoculars about a hundred meters away. "Ali assured me that the American was going to leave early today."

"Do we abort again, Assad?" asked Hazem al-Sawai, who was at the wheel of a black Volkswagen van. Assad did not reply; he remained fixated on the images in his binoculars.

"Assad, they will soon be at their car," Zayed said, making eye contact with Rasid, who shrugged while waiting for orders from their leader.

"Damn that little shit, Ali," said Assad speaking mostly to himself. He watched the two women talking and laughing as they drew closer to the BMW. When he saw Paz fishing for her keys in her handbag, he put down the binoculars and unconsciously lifted his hand and spread his fingers. He looked toward Hazem and said into his mouthpiece, "Move now—slowly. Zayed, Rasid, we take both of them. Go."

"Both of them?" Rasid exclaimed touching the microphone extending from his headset.

"Both," ordered Assad. "Rasid, take the American. Zayed, you take the Cruz girl. Move. We will be at the car in twenty seconds." He nodded to Hazem to move out.

The two black-clad Ṣaqr operatives advanced like cats, each pulling a small canister from his jacket pocket. Frankie and Paz were now at the front of the BMW, and Paz clicked the key to unlock the car. The interior lights went on, the parking lights blinked, and that familiar *beep beep* echoed across the parking lot, which was largely devoid of students. The women were still laughing about something when the two black-clad figures appeared at the back of the car startling them. In an instant, they sprayed something in the faces of the women and pushed black cloths over their noses and mouths. They were immediately unconscious. Zayed and Rasid gently guided them to the ground.

The black van silently glided to a stop behind the BMW. The side door opened, and a fifth member of the team, Sulayman al-Raja, leaped out and helped his colleagues lift the two women into the van. As the doors slid closed behind them, Sulayman yelled out, "Done!" and Hazem drove the Volkswagen slowly out of the parking lot putting on his headlights as darkness enshrouded the area.

Nothing was said as the three men in the back went about securing the women. A hospital mask replaced the black cloths covering the noses and mouths of the unconscious captives. Zayed sprayed each mask with the canister he had used in the parking lot turning his head away and covering his nose with his arm as he did so. A black hood was placed over the head of each woman, and the three men then sat on the floor cradling their knees as the van accelerated toward *Nacional* I, the main highway in the north of the city.

"Both of them, Assad? Both?" asked Zayed softly. He peered at Assad as if to question the wisdom of their actions.

"Both," Assad al-Amin confirmed. "The American is equally—no, maybe *more* valuable than the Spaniard." *It was an unplanned bonus,* he thought, *an excellent achievement despite Ali's faulty intelligence.* "We had luck with us tonight, my friends," Assad said, turning his head and looking at the still bundles on the floor of the van.

Chapter Two

Frankie woke first. She was seated in what felt like an armchair and was immobile except for her hands and head. She saw nothing but blackness due to the hood over her head. She tried twisting her torso but realized her arms and legs were bound to the armchair. And she had a headache—a *buzzing* headache. No, it was more like a muffled buzz and it wasn't in her head; it was all around her. A little bump and a slight tilt of her body led her to believe she was on a plane.

Oh my God, she thought. "What's going on here? Help!" she yelled.

Someone placed a hand gently on her shoulder and pressed a finger against her lips outside the hood.

"Shhh, Miss Fontana. You must be quiet or we will have to put you to sleep again," a man whispered.

Frankie detected an accent that was not Spanish. *What? Arabic? The man's an Arab? Maybe.*

"Will you be quiet?" the man asked.

"Yes, yes, but please, where am I? Where are you taking me? Is Paz all right? Please tell me what's happening!"

"All will be made clear to you shortly, Miss Fontana, but only if you cooperate, behave, and do as you are told. Your friend is right here next to you still sleeping. If you promise to behave, I will remove your hood. Do you promise, Miss Fontana?"

Behave? "Yes, yes," Frankie replied nodding repeatedly.

The hood was removed, and the hospital mask had fallen around her neck. Pale light assaulted her eyes; it took a few seconds for her to bring her surroundings into focus. She was indeed in a plane. A small one. A private jet she surmised. A man was leaning over her. He placed his hands on her shoulders and slowly turned the chair she was strapped into.

"See? There is your friend. Still sleeping as I said."

Frankie looked across an aisle. Paz was slumped in a brown leather armchair, a black hood covering her head.

"She will awaken shortly," said the man.

He had curly black hair with a neat five o'clock shadow. An intentional one. Although the light was dim, she detected a dark complexion. *Definitely Arab.*

"What do you want from us?" She trembled and tried to hold back her tears. "Where are you taking us?"

Again the man placed a finger to her lips. "Shhh. No questions."

He rose and walked toward the back of the aircraft and out of Frankie's view.

Her lip quivered from fear and anxiety, and an ache rose in the pit of her stomach. And she still had a headache.

Fucking bastards! The fucking bastards have kidnapped us! She kept repeating *fucking bastards* to herself with her teeth clenched. Her lip stopped trembling, and the ache in her stomach subsided. *Still have a fucking headache.* She balled her hands into fists and tapped them on the armrest in a constant rhythm to the extent that her bound arms permitted. *Fuck-ing bas-tards* the fists tapped out in sync with her thoughts. *Fuck-ing bas-tards ...*

Chapter Three

Still tapping out her angry chant, Frankie looked at Paz, who was still unconscious with her hooded head slumped to the right. She saw Paz's chest moving as she breathed and the hood fluttering a little when she exhaled. While Frankie couldn't see her face, she knew it was Paz by her caramel-colored leather jacket, blue jeans, and short boots that matched her jacket. Looking at her friend—her best friend—the fear and the ache came back. She gripped the armrests tightly.

Frankie thought of Paz as a sister, and even though she was American and Paz was Spanish, a native *Madrileña,* everyone thought they looked alike enough to be sisters. Their friendship had begun years earlier when Michael, Frankie's father, was managing director of the Spanish subsidiary of an American pharmaceutical company based in New Jersey.

In those days, it was essential that foreign pharmaceutical organizations have Spanish companies as collaborative partners. Spanish companies received priority attention and favor in new product health registration and with the critical pricing process. More important, Spain did not protect foreign patents, so the market was rife with local companies' pirate brands. One way to avoid that consequence was to align with a Spanish partner and co-market your pharmaceuticals with both salesforces under two brands. This partnering kept other Spanish companies out of the market with pirate brands and generally made the best out of an unfortunate situation. Rodrigo de la Cruz was Michael Fontana's Spanish partner for two new prescription drugs, an association created years earlier when the managing director of the American operation was a wily Swiss executive who understood the realities of the Spanish pharmaceuticals market.

Rodrigo de la Cruz, who was always referred to by Fontana as Don Rodrigo, owned de la Cruz Farmaceuticos, SA, a midsized company in the heart of Madrid, manufacturing facilities and all. Don Rodrigo's company had started out the same way most of his Spanish colleagues' companies had—pirating American, British, and German pharmaceuticals—but in the seventies and eighties, he formed legitimate licensing ventures; first with a German company and later with Fontana's predecessor.

Don Rodrigo and Michael Fontana met monthly, generally as part of a three-hour lunch that usually ended after five in the afternoon. Fontana always reminisced on those occasions, that while his colleagues in New Jersey were generally wrapping up their days at that hour, Michael was returning to his office—after lunch. The two men infrequently met socially, the notable exception being once-a-year every spring. At that time, Don Rodrigo and his wife, Remi, hosted Michael and his wife, Sherry, for an incomparable afternoon and evening of Spanish elegance, opulence, and adventure.

The festivities would begin with what was a late lunch served in Don Rodrigo's private dining room at his office. *Lunch* was a totally inadequate word to describe a feast that began with the finest *Iberico* ham from the south of Spain, roasted red peppers with garlic and olive oil, superb *Manchego* cheese, and a wide assortment of other typical Spanish *aperativos*. From magnums of Vega de Sicilia, Ribera del Duero, the finest crystal goblets were filled with red wine, and for most normal people, the meal could have ended there with everyone around the table sated. But no, then came roasted lamb, or superb suckling pig, or the finest steaks two inches thick and grilled to medium-rare perfection. Salads garnished with virgin olive oil and the potent vinegar from Jerez complemented the meats, and desserts, espresso, and Spanish brandy completed an afternoon of olfactory delight.

Then the two couples walked a short distance to Las Ventas, the fabled bull ring in the center of Madrid. Six *corridas* later, with Sherry Fontana always turning away at the moment of truth, they departed the bull ring. End of the evening? Not quite. Don Rodrigo's driver then whisked the couples away to one of a few favored *mariscos*—seafood— restaurants, and the taste and smell orgy began again but at ten-thirty in the evening. Again, Fontana would picture his colleagues in New Jersey, cozy in their pajamas, getting ready to watch the eleven o'clock news while he was sitting down to dinner.

The annual ritual took on a new character after an offhand remark Michael made at one of their monthly lunches. He mentioned that he had taken Francesca, who attended the American School of Madrid, to a bullfight when the family spent a long weekend in Sevilla. While Francesca did not enjoy the gore, she appreciated the pageantry and majesty of the event and the exhilaration of the man-versus-bull confrontation. That following spring, Don Rodrigo's invitation was addressed to "Señor y Señora Fontana y hija"; Frankie was included in the invitation, and the de la Cruzes' brought their daughter, Paz.

The two girls were the same age, the only children of their parents, and were attending high school then. The girls looked alike and had outgoing, confident personalities, and they soon became best friends. When Frankie returned to the US to attend college, the two kept in touch constantly and spent the summers together—one month in the States and another in Spain. They went on to study law, and Princeton approved the Fontanas' request for Frankie to study one year at the

University of Madrid. There was no question that Frankie would stay with the de la Cruz family at their spacious city apartment. The two women commuted the half-hour ride to the blue-collar town of Alcobendes and then to the university's attractive Cantoblanco campus.

Michael and Sherry Fontana had returned to the United States with Michael accepting a senior executive position in the US operation of his company, which generated almost a half of the corporate revenue. His position had greater importance and responsibility than the Spanish operation, but he soon longed for the lifestyle and the more entrepreneurial nature of running the Spanish business. That responsibility was far more rewarding than the bureaucracy-bound home office. Frankie on the other hand worked hard at keeping her connections with Spain and Madrid strong, and Paz was an important part of that world. Frankie emerged from her trance and looked at Paz, who barely moved with her head slumped on her chest. Frankie clenched her fists again and beat out her staccato melody over and over—*Fuck-ing bas-tards* …

Chapter Four

Captain Mercedes Garcia Rico of the Spanish National Police Force—the *Cuerpo Nacional de Policia*—CNP—got a call in her Madrid office that the daughter of Rodrigo de la Cruz, a prominent businessman, had gone missing along with an American woman who was staying with the de la Cruz family; both were students at the University of Madrid. The Madrid Police Force had jurisdiction on the case, but because of the father's position—and connections with all levels of the local and national government—and the fact that an American was involved, the National Police Force was asked to take a role in the investigation. If this was found to be a kidnapping, the case would fall to it anyway.

Not long after the phone call, around midday, two Madrid detectives were sitting in Captain Garcia's office, notepads out, bringing her up-to-date with what was known at that point, about fifteen hours after the women had been reported missing.

"We got a call at eight-thirty last night. The girls had not returned home from the university, and calls to their cell phones went unanswered. The parents feared they may have been in an accident and asked us to investigate," said Detective José Luis Campos. "After checking out the accident reports, we sent a car out to the campus. The de la Cruzes' BMW was still there at ten forty-five p.m. Everything out there had been closed for some time. More important, the keys to the BMW, a 530 M Class, were found on the ground just below the driver's door."."

The captain was in her late thirties, about five-six, with penetrating blue eyes and black hair pulled back and gathered in a braid held tightly against the back of her head. "So what do you think?" she asked. "They were taken? Two girls in plain view?"

"We are only piecing things together now," replied Detective Castilla, Campos's partner. "There wasn't much the unit could do in the middle of the night. We found the keys, which raised our suspicions, and based on names provided by Remi de la Cruz—the mother—we made some phone calls to friends of the girls up until eleven-thirty last night. Got nowhere with that. José Luis and I spent the morning at the university asking around. We still have men out there canvassing everything and meeting with the law students who attend classes at different hours. That's where the girls are studying, the law school. We know the names of all the students who were with the girls at their last class yesterday afternoon, and we're still chasing down a few of them. *Nada*—nothing—so far."

"We know when they left the building presumably to go home," added Campos. "It was around eighteen hundred, just after six p.m. It was starting to get dark, and no one noticed anything. Most of the students were still milling around the classroom, but the de la Cruz girl—Paz—and the American—Francesca Fontana—were in a hurry to leave. Something about the American going to Skype with her parents in America at seven-thirty last night. And that's the other thing. Once the Fontana girl missed her scheduled computer linkup, her mother called from the US, and now, we have the American family completely distraught and probably planning to be here tomorrow."

"And nothing from your interviews this morning?" asked Garcia.

"The only thing a little out of the ordinary was that two students said they had noticed a black van in the back of the parking lot. It stood out because all the other vehicles were cars except for a few SUVs. None of the students drives a van that we have been able to determine so far, but I have someone going through the university's parking permits. We should be able to determine if someone has a van," said Detective Castilla flipping his notepad closed.

"*Jesús,*" said Garcia. "I know about Rodrigo de la Cruz. He owns a pharmaceutical company here in Madrid. And now we have an American missing as well? The you-know-what is going to hit the fan."

"That's why we're bringing you in on this now," said Campos. "This is going to be a big deal with lots of eyes, and our superiors thought it best to give the CNP the reins on this. We can support you in any way you want, but you have to lead. You have better resources than the city does. Our chiefs are probably talking to your chiefs right now to make everything official."

"I think you're right," answered Captain Garcia. "Especially with the American involved, it takes on a broader perspective."

"And just how is it that there's an American involved?" Garcia asked.

"The two girls know each other from when the American girl's father worked in Spain some years ago," replied Campos. "He ran an American pharmaceutical company and had a partnership with Rodrigo de la Cruz, and from that relationship, the girls became friends. Francesca Fontana is spending a year at the University of Madrid and is staying with the de la Cruz family. Both girls are in the same law curriculum. By the way, they look like they could be sisters." He produced photos he had received from Remi de la Cruz the previous night and put them on the captain's desk.

The captain stared at the photos. "Okay, we got it. Give us everything you have by the end of the day—copies of all the interviews including those you got today. Have you done anything out at the crime scene, processed anything at the car?"

The two detectives turned and stared at each other. "No," said Campos.

"Okay, call out to your men at the university and tell them to put crime scene tape around the car, five meters out all around, and secure it until our people get there," Captain Garcia instructed.

Chapter Five

Frankie Fontana noticed a change in the plane's airspeed, a throttling down. At the same time, she noticed Paz starting to move. She jerked her head up, shook it, and tried to move her arms jerking them a few times and then shouting, "*Oyé! Qué pasa?*"

"Paz, it's me, Frankie. We've been kidnapped. They're flying us somewhere."

Assad appeared and squatted in the aisle facing the two women. He again placed a finger to Frankie's lips. "Shhh, Miss Fontana. I asked you not to speak." He removed the black hood from Paz's head. It was morning, and bright sunlight streamed in from the large oval windows. Paz squinted and shook her head as the light pained her eyes.

"*Qué*—" Paz started to say, but Assad put four fingers against her mouth.

"No talking, *señorita,* no talking."

"But—" Paz said, and again the fingers pressed gently against her mouth.

"Shhh," replied Assad. "You have been sleeping for many hours. Unless you would like to be put to sleep again, I ask you to be silent."

Paz looked at Assad pleadingly and then turned to Frankie, her eyes widening, eyebrows raised, as if asking her friend, *What is going on?*

"Now that you are both awake—you are awake, *señorita,* yes?" Assad asked Paz, who nodded. "Good. As you can see, you are in a private plane. You are being taken to a place where your fate will be decided. No one will find you—ever. We have removed the SIM cards and batteries from your cell phones and disposed of them. There will be no trace of you in Madrid, and I am sure your families will forever miss you, but a new life awaits you that may be very pleasant—or not. That will depend on you."

"You bastard," said Frankie, her face tightened into a poisonous stare.

"Now, now, Miss Fontana, you must learn to relax. All this tension will only make things harder." There was another shift in air speed and then the sound of landing gear being lowered. "Ahh," said Assad. "We will soon be at our destination. Fasten your seatbelts," he said with a laugh. "Turn off all electronic devices, ladies, and prepare for landing."

"They're Arabs, Paz. We've been kidnapped by Arabs," Frankie whispered.

"Why?" Paz said quietly. "What do they want with us?"

"I don't know, Paz, but it can't be good. Hang in there. We'll figure something out. We will. We will."

Chapter Six

Eugene—Gino—Cerone walked into the headquarters of the CNP and peeked into Captain Garcia's office. "Mercedes, you want to get some lunch?" He walked to her desk, and the two exchanged a quick kiss.

Gino had gotten to Madrid via a very circuitous route. Three years earlier at about the same time of year, he traveled to Granada, in the south of Spain, to arrange for his sister's body to be transported back to the US for burial. Gina Cerone had been killed in what was thought a roadside accident in the mountains outside Granada. Gino, who headed up the Attack On Principal training unit of the US Secret Service and then-Lieutenant Mercedes Garcia Rico of the National Police Force soon discovered that Gina's car had been sabotaged; she had been murdered. All leads to why and who methodically disappeared with a series of untimely and suspicious deaths of those who might have shed some light on the mystery.

Gino retired from the service, relocated to Granada, and had been allowed to work with Lieutenant Garcia in investigating the conundrum of his sister's death. Ultimately, that investigation led to the discovery of an unfathomable conspiracy that dated back to the time the Moors surrendered their kingdom in Granada to the Spanish monarchs, Ferdinand and Isabella, in 1492. The two were able to uncover the conspiracy involving a prominent Spanish family—whose lineage went back to the last kingdom of the Moors—and ultimately bring it down, solving the mystery of his sister's death in the process.

Lieutenant Garcia was then promoted to captain and assigned to the CNP operations in Madrid. Because of his leadership and tenacity in stopping what amounted to a silent revolution to return Spain to an Islamic monarchy Gino was asked to assist the Spanish government in unraveling the tentacles of the plot that reached far and wide throughout the country. That work was coming to an end. Over the time they had worked so closely together, they had developed more than a professional relationship. Their partnership evolved into a true romance, and they were living together in an apartment in the city.

"God, I wish I had time for lunch," said Mercedes. "We have what looks like a kidnapping of two girls at the University of Madrid last night. One is the daughter of a prominent business leader here in Madrid, and the other is an American who was staying with the Spanish girl while they both attended the university. Here, look. Beautiful girls, no? Paz de la Cruz and Francesca Fontana."

Gino looked at the photos on Mercedes's desk. "Yes, beautiful. Look alike, don't they?"

"Yes they do. I'm going out to the university now. The de la Cruz girl's car is still there. They may have been abducted from that spot. Haven't heard anything from potential kidnappers regarding any ransom, but I have two officers at the de la Cruz apartment in case contact is made. How are things coming with you?"

"Well, as you know, my assignment is almost done. We've arrested scores of people tied to the plot who we believe were part of the conspiracy to take political power. That part of the conspiracy has been destroyed, but bringing charges against those responsible is a challenge. We've been able to get quite a few of them talking, so we're encouraged, but identifying all the conspirators remains a challenge. It's been a nightmare."

Mercedes smiled enigmatically at Gino. "I have my own nightmare right now. An American girl and the daughter of a big-shot Spaniard kidnapped. You know what kind of a spotlight we'll be under. Some of that spotlight will likely be from your colleagues in the States. Likely FBI-types. Just what I need."

"If you need someone to run interference if that happens, let me know. I earned some gold stars back home from our cleaning up of what almost happened here, so I may be able to help, *mi amor*. Go I'll catch up with you tonight."

* * *

Mercedes drove to the university. Paloma Retuerta and José Maria Duarte of the CNP Scientific Unit followed to see what forensics could be ascertained from the assumed crime scene. The Madrid police hadn't secured the area until that morning, but it was unlikely that there was anything of importance to be discovered. Paloma and José Maria had worked with Mercedes in Granada on the case involving Gino's sister, and their work had been instrumental in uncovering evidence that ultimately brought the conspiracy to light.

Orange traffic cones were all around the white BMW when Mercedes arrived; the two forensic investigators were only minutes behind her. As per her instructions, yellow tape was wrapped around each cone making a symmetric rectangle around the car. A uniformed Madrid police officer was standing guard. "*Buenas tardes, Capitán,*" he said as Mercedes approached the taped area.

"*Buenas tardes, Oficial ...* Martinez," she replied, leaning in to read the officer's nametag.

At the same time, Paloma and José Maria were donning plastic booties and gloves preparing to enter the taped-off zone.

"The car keys were found there," offered Martinez pointing to an area below the driver's door. "They were just under the car almost out of sight. That's all we found. Pretty clean parking lot. Not much debris anywhere."

"I'm guessing they were forced into a car or perhaps that black van about here," Mercedes said gesturing to the lane immediately behind the BMW.

"You're sure it was a kidnapping?" asked Paloma from inside the taped-off area.

"No, not sure, but that's the working hypothesis for now. I'd rather work on the worst-case scenario until we know better," Mercedes replied looking up and down the lane and then at the ground adjacent to the taped area. "No tire marks, and you're right, *Oficial* Martinez, no litter anywhere. Clean kids. Paloma, is the car locked?"

Moving to the driver's door, Paloma pulled up on the handle, opening the door. "No. Probably the girl unlocked the car with the remote and then she was attacked or whatever."

"Whatever. Yes, whatever. That is the question," mumbled Mercedes as her eyes kept sweeping the area.

Half an hour later, Paloma and José Maria looked at each other. "Nada," José Maria said rising from his knees. "Let's have the car towed to headquarters. We'll go over everything there including dusting for prints inside and outside, but I think there's little to find."

"Maybe there will be contact with the parents. I'm going to go there now and see if there's anything they can add to this," Mercedes said, walking to her car. "Let me know if you find anything of interest. Ciao. Talk to you later."

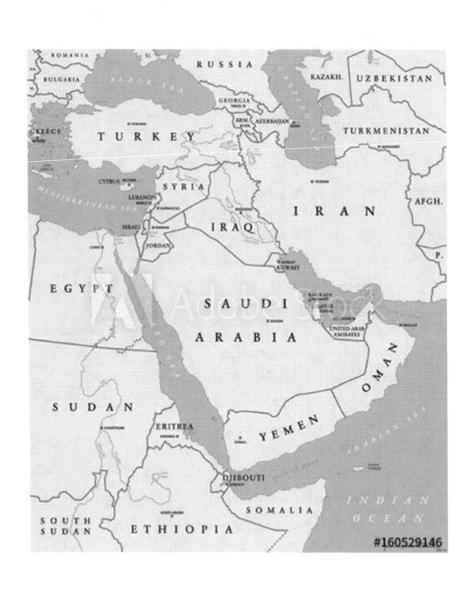

#160529146

Chapter Seven

The Gulfstream 550 was gently descending on its approach path to Dubai International Airport. Assad reflectively gazed out the window not really seeing the shimmering images of downtown Dubai in the distance. With the Spaniard and the American, that would make eight Western women who had been whisked away from their homelands without a trace, he thought. *Eight in almost seven years*. Eight placements weren't nearly enough to change the world—or at least that part of the world—but each abduction had been a very precise and time-consuming process, and while Assad thought about the need to expand the operation, no one had yet discovered that these abductions were linked. *Maybe just keep it as it is—for now.*

The former major of the Omani Security Force laughed to himself thinking about how this had all begun. Pacing outside his monarch's business office, he was convinced that his destiny would be the swordsman's block. At that time, his primary thoughts were whether his eyes would be open when the executioner reached into the basket and pulled out his head by his thick ebony hair. He hoped they would be closed and his brain dead not having registered the horror of the moment.

Assad had been called to the sultan's office. Some years earlier while he was on security duty on the sultan's exquisite yacht, he had saved his monarch's favorite nephew from drowning. With no children of his own, the sultan would often host outings with his brother's children. The family was spending the day in the Gulf of Oman, and nine-year-old Sharad was cavorting on a jet ski making faster and tighter circles with his craft and rollicking with laughter. At one point, his jet ski crossed his own wake and the machine flipped skyward and came down on the boy. Though he was wearing a life vest, Sharad was stunned and wound up floating face-down in the deep blue waters of the gulf. Without hesitation, Lieutenant al-Amin dove into the water, raced to the unmoving boy, inverted him, and brought the royal prince back to the aft platform of the yacht. The boy had a bruise on his forehead but was otherwise fine.

From that day, Assad al-Amin was a favorite of the sultan, and he had quickly advanced with the Royal Security Force. He had it made as they would say in America. A favorite of the royal family, an undemanding, prestigious job for life in a country insulated from the tensions and strife elsewhere in the Middle East. He indeed had it made.

But Assad thought his life was too good and without direction. It caused him to think far beyond his responsibilities. He was a Muslim but not overly devoted to the religion, and he certainly lived a privileged life. He had earned a degree in economics from Cambridge University in England. His father was chief engineer for the Royal Omani PetroGas Corporation and was convinced that for the foreseeable future, the business of the Middle East was oil and war. He wanted his son to be prepared for both and had convinced Assad to spend one year at the London War College before returning home and joining the Royal Omani Armed Forces. In less than a year after returning home, he was training for the Royal Family Security Force, a somewhat more militarized version of the US Secret Service.

During his time in England, Assad was exposed to and thought about sociological issues beyond his tight, little circle of self-interest.

He saw that there was a great influx of Middle Eastern immigrants into the UK mainly from Pakistan but also from a large swath of Africa and the Arab world. Those who did not arrive in their private jets and did not have bespoke suits and shirts made on Saville Row, made it to England in less-auspicious ways and cleaned the streets, collected the garbage, and did every menial job conceivable. They lived in self-contained, ghetto-like districts in drab apartments that the British lower class moved up and out of when they could. To British aristocracy, this was life as it should be, reminiscent of their colonial period in Asia and Africa when colonized people catered to the privileged British military establishment. The immigrant workers were largely invisible to the British, who looked right through them.

However, it did not escape Assad's assessment that the privileged groups in oil-rich countries in the Middle East practiced the same attitudes. They brought in construction workers from the poorer Arab and Asian countries such as Nepal and Indonesia and held them in almost slave-like conditions while they built their cities, hotels, and palaces, and they housed them in far worse conditions than those of the London ghettos. At least in England, Europe, and America, they might be invisible, but they were free. Bound to their circumstances but still free. How affronted could Assad be when his brethren might be the most hypocritical of all? So while the invisibility of this class of people was unfortunate, it was what it was. Life was not always fair to the weak and the poor wherever they were.

But what most impressed Assad while in England and caused him to spend much time pondering, was the role of women in Western society. There was of course the queen and a history of queens leading the British Empire including Queen Elizabeth I and Queen Victoria. A legacy of female monarchs leading to the Iron Lady—Prime Minister Margaret Thatcher. And while there was no question that the UK was still a male-dominated society especially in its government, things were changing. Women entrepreneurs who were sometimes locked out of corporate career advancement built their own business. From what he could glean, that was even more advanced in America, and Germany might have been the most advanced in Europe in this regard. At the university, he saw the strength of character among the type of women he never saw even in advanced and more open societies such as Oman's. Intelligent, strong-willed, confident, articulate women. In more-fundamentalist societies in the Middle East, the gap between male and female was incalculable.

So Assad's formative years were a jumble of conflicts. His years in England were without incident. As a foreigner of privilege, he experienced no discrimination particularly at Cambridge though he was unsure how the friends he made would feel about his dating their sisters. But his time at the university and in England—including some travel on the continent—allowed him to see more of the world beyond his little corner of the Middle East, where Oman was bordered by Saudi Arabia, Yemen, and the United Arab Emirates on the Gulf of Oman and the Arabian Sea. He was never concerned about the Crusades and who had done what to whom in the tenth century. He cared for the plight of the Palestinians, but Oman was unique in supporting the peace treaty between Egypt and Israel, so he had not been brought up with the searing rhetoric about Israel that countries such as Iran spewed.

It was Iran, however, that started a fire throughout the Middle East that pushed the Israel-Palestine dilemma to the back of the line. Fundamentalist ayatollahs created a radical Islamic following with grievances against the US, UK, and all Western nations but also against other religions, free speech, the internet, and most dramatically, keeping women subservient to men. The Iranian revolution was the spark that inspired other madmen under the guise of Islam to introduce to the world suicide bombers, beheadings, seventy virgins in paradise, mass murder—and of whom? Mostly their own men, women, and children. Hate the West but kill your own people—the *Shia, Sunni, Kurds.* Assad wondered how that could have made sense.

Appalled by all the death and destruction, Assad also felt appalled about the fate of women in countries such as Afghanistan, Pakistan, Yemen, Somalia, and Sudan; the radicals in those places purportedly being financed by Saudi Arabia. The white-robed *Wahabi* Saudis, who practiced the strictest and most fundamental form of Islam, drove around in their armor-clad Mercedes' and Rolls Royce's creating a society in which women were relegated to second-class citizenship with a host of restrictions. A rich-beyond-imagination family of men, close ally of the US and UK, who prohibited women from driving and insisted that they encase themselves head to toe in *abayas* and some the more restrictive *burqas,* with only their eyes visible to the world. In the more radical Islamic states, women were even barred from getting educations; they were not much better that the immigrants brought in to build their cities or the slaves who raced the camels of the rich.

The Gulf War was a prelude to yet another fire in the Middle East. Saddam Hussein decided it was an opportune time to invade Kuwait and gain access to even more of the world's oil reserves. The US joined by many Western allies quickly expelled Iraq from Kuwait and order was restored—for a while. The Americans and their coalition forces were fighting Iraqis using weapons supplied to them by the US for use in their ongoing conflicts with Iran. At the same time, a similar coalition of forces would be fighting in Afghanistan against the Taliban, who were using weapons supplied to them by the Americans in the Afghans' fight to drive the Russians out of their country. The good guys and the bad guys kept changing sides.

Then came the inferno that may never be extinguished. The attack of 9/11 followed by invasions of Afghanistan and subsequently Iraq created an era of guerilla warfare, suicide bombers, improvised explosive devices, infidels of all persuasions, and destruction that touched much of the Middle East and North Africa. This was the world Assad lived in, and he still bore strong resentment against Western powers but was not blinded by fanatical, religious rage. He felt they needed to be punished for bringing such disorder, not only to the Middle East, but also by extension to the world. The fanaticism unleashed by the West had touched cities all over the world. There had to be a cost to be paid, Assad thought.

Chapter Eight

The Americans had their shock and awe—devastating, destructive technology without equal. The Middle East had low-tech, persistent terrorist insurgencies that produced their own shock and awe with kidnappings, beheadings, and mass murders—a total disregard for human life. In the background of these travesties stood their uneducated and silent women wrapped in *burqas*. These societies—if one could call this chaos societal—would likely never advance in the league of civilized nations and would relegate women to the Middle Ages forever unless the insanity was stopped. Was there a way to build a targeted albeit long-range, collaborative strategy out of this chaos—recognizing that *long-range, collaborative,* and *strategy* were oxymoronic in his part of the world? Assad didn't know, but more and more, he thought about how to punish those who had created this chaos.

Assad saw that the daughters of Western families were always held as something special, unique treasures to be loved and protected. Daddy's little girl was a concept of great emotional value and pride. In the Middle East, it was always about sons, who would inherit the mantle of leadership from their fathers. Daughters were often considered inconsequential and thus vulnerable.

Assad hoped that one day, his part of the world could beat the West at its own game. Make education a priority for men but also especially women and at all levels of society and not just for the oil-rich, privileged members of royal families. Start to earn all the awards in science and math and technology, something the Chinese and Indians were achieving. Create a hundred-year mission for Middle Eastern countries. If these lands could look back to perceived injustices a thousand years earlier, surely they could look forward fifty to a hundred years. The Arab world needed leaders with the foresight to see this.

Second, three or four generations hence, those in the Arab world could run more of the world's businesses backed by the capital oil brought in but spread deep within society. That could be a new, reformed, and targeted type of terrorism taken to new and sustainable levels where Arab countries could emerge as equals to the Western powers and gain new levels of respect on the world stage, Assad reasoned. *But first, bring them to their knees.*

And so Assad began to create relationships primarily outside Oman. The sultan often traveled in the Middle East with Assad always with him. On those occasions, Assad met many military and security officers and learned about them and the leaders they served. He found many who would like to take action against the West but not with roadside bombs and suicide vests. They talked, corresponded, and discussed potential ways to strike back albeit very theoretically. When he had free time, he visited Saudi Arabia, the emirates, and other countries where like-minded men made plans.

Assad remembered the two large doors to the sultan's office opening noiselessly and the sultan's key vizier, Abdul Azziz al-Sheik—a trusted advisor who served as chief of staff—emerging and beckoning him to enter. As the major, in full military dress, walked into the inner sanctum of the royal palace, the sultan stepped out from behind a massive desk and moved forward to greet his visitor as he would an old friend.

"My dear Assad," the sultan said, embracing the petrified soldier and clapping his hands on the major's upper arms. "I hope you are well, and your parents—both well I trust?"

"Yes, yes, your majesty," replied Assad, moving to a chair in front of the desk as designated by the sultan. "We are all well."

The sultan sat in the adjoining visitor's chair facing the desk and crossed his legs. "Abdul, please have some tea brought in for the major and myself," he asked, and Abdul silently backed out of the room.

"Major, are you sure you are well? You are perspiring in a room that is kept at a constant nineteen degrees Celsius as it is in the reception area. It is hardly warm in here."

"Forgive me, your highness. I am fine," Assad stammered.

"Assad," the sultan replied, again using the major's first name to ease his tension, "you have been in my service for many years now. I regard you as someone more than a trusted member of my security team, but things have come to my attention that cause me some concern."

As Assad swallowed hard to keep the lump in his throat from choking him, the large doors behind the two men opened and a slender woman wheeled in a cart with a beautiful porcelain Omani tea pot and two embossed glasses on an engraved silver and gold tray. She set the glasses on gold saucers and poured tea, first for the sultan and then for his visitor. She left never once looking at the two men sitting before the great desk. The sultan beckoned Assad to drink. The major lifted his glass, took some sips and then some gulps, and set the glass down. The sultan refilled it and then reached for his own glass and sipped the dark amber liquid only once before replacing it on its gold saucer.

"Are you not happy here, Assad? Are you not pleased serving this royal family? Are there things that have driven you to seek friendships with others outside Oman, others that harbor discontent?"

Assad was shocked that the sultan was aware of his activities if not his thoughts. He had heard that the sultan's vizier was all knowing. Now he was sure of it.

"Your highness, believe me when I say that there is no greater honor for me than to serve you and your family. I sometimes curse myself for not accepting and enjoying life as it is and the goodness you have shown me, but there are issues burning in me that I cannot control, and they have bothered me for some time."

He spoke of the injustices he had perceived and how he felt that the West—the US and its allies—must pay for the chaos they had created.

If the sultan was shocked by or lost as to what Assad was talking about, he didn't show it. He sipped his tea and sat in silence waiting for Assad to continue.

"The West," Assad went on, "continues to treasure and open opportunities to its women, and they are beating the men at every turn. More women than men graduate college today. More women than ever are running major corporations. The Israelis showed the world the role and strength of their women in the military and in government, and that is happening more and more all around us, well beyond our desert borders. We need more and better leaders, strong in their knowledge and strength of character, and we must make our women part of that leadership hierarchy, but not before the West is dealt a blow to its self-assured psyche."

The sultan leaned back in his chair pondering the passion of Assad's words. "Take some more tea, Major," he said. "Please help yourself."

Assad's throat had been parched for the last few minutes; he felt as if he were immersed in the dust storms so common in the interior of the country. "Thank you, your highness," replied Assad filling his glass to the brim with tepid tea from the porcelain pot. He drank it down and poured another glass.

"You are quite right about your observations, Major," the sultan commented as Assad composed himself. "But as they say in the West, perhaps you should get to the point. Is this some crusade you wish to lead? Do you want to leave your service here in Oman and join some jihadist group cloaked in dirty black robes and hiding out in the rubble of a once-great city?"

"No, your highness, that is not what I want to do or who I want to be."

Assad told him of his vision that in three or four generations, committed monarchs, presidents, whatever leadership, should be able to transform their nation. That transformation would be achieved by creating strong leadership driven by educational and developmental opportunities for its women and for those at the lower end of society. "We would be respected, your highness."

"So you want a better and broader educational system in the Middle East. That is hardly visionary, Assad."

"I agree, your highness. All the schooling in the world will not build strength of character, cunning, daring, and the intelligence and desire to lead. I see no Saladins, nor Ataturks, or even Janah bin Sa'ids—yourself—on the horizon. And certainly no Margaret Thatchers, Golda Meirs, Joan of Arcs, or Shahrazads—the heroine in *The Tales of the Arabian Nights*—on the horizon either.

"I am honored to be included in your list of heralded leaders, Assad, even if it is somewhat gratuitous as I inherited my throne from my father almost forty years ago."

"Ahh, but your highness was only thirty when you came to the throne. You led Oman from the image of a land of frankincense and myrrh to a modern country that brings more to its people every day. Literacy is nearly eighty percent, suffrage is universal for men and women, more and more foreign workers are being replaced with educated, trained, and well-paid Omanis, and we are part of the World

Trade Organization. Do we get the recognition we should from the global community, the West? No, but that could change. You are a global, visionary leader, and royal succession is both clear and promising. But we are one among many, and the many color the future for all of us and ultimately the fate of the Middle East. I cannot lose sight of the fact that Western cultures really do not want that to happen. Oil and servitude are all they want from us, and for that, they need to be punished deeply and everlastingly."

The two men spoke as equals for an hour, going one by one over the Islamic countries of the Middle East, monarchies as well as important non-monarchies such as Iran, Iraq, Egypt, the forever lost Afghanistan, and Pakistan, the only Islamic country with nuclear weapons—and no righteous leadership in sight.

"But what do you want to do, Major? The leaders in these countries, particularly the oil-rich monarchies, bring in educators from all over the world for their children. They also send them to the finest schools in Europe and America."

"Yes they do, your highness, even if is only for show. They need to keep the oil revenues flowing and protected, and they do, but how many Omanis are there looking to strengthen their people? Not many, maybe not any," replied Assad. "What we need to do is create a catalyst, perhaps an unfair and evil catalyst, which will bind some of these leaders together. If not at the very top, perhaps a few rungs slower. The Saudi royal family has hundreds and hundreds of families tied to the king by direct line and marriage."

"The rich men and boys in their Ferrari convertibles," the sultan said with a laugh.

"Yes, they and the women they have married, who probably yearn for a turn in the Ferrari. We need to light a spark in these women, some of whom are merely part of modern-day harems though you don't hear that word anymore."

"Because our religion allows men to take up to four wives," the sultan interjected.

"Yes, that's part of it, and yet another way we defile and degrade our women even if it is less and less common among the educated and the elite. Jordan has certainly taken such a path."

"So get to your plan, Major, your vision."

"Yes, your highness. The last piece of the puzzle is why I fear the worst for this region. The leaders in the Islamic world who are emerging are the terrorists who have adopted a radical, fundamentalist philosophy that takes us back to the Middle Ages. And they are succeeding. They recruit more and more followers who have nothing to lose. Some are criminals, anarchists, the downtrodden, and the invisible ones who suddenly become somebodies, at least in their own eyes. Most are exploited by using perceived injustices against them or their ancestors to create chaos. It brings respect to some and fear to others, but it ultimately gains power, which I believe is the primary motivation.

"If they succeed, our brothers will eventually fall like dominos, and then we will all become a large Afghanistan as the West broadens its military response to these atrocities. Look at Syria—great cities and historical sites in ruble. These actions and the Western retaliation will take these countries back to donkeys and camels, and their women will be reduced to slaves—illiterate slaves. Countries ruled by fear and terror, the scimitar replaced with AK-47s, RPGs, and suicide bombers. Is that what we have to look forward to?"

"You are depressing me, Major."

Chapter Nine

"What do you propose? What is this unfair and evil catalyst you speak about?"

"Your highness, no matter how closely some of our brethren purport to be allies of the West, we know it is just for expediency's sake. After World War I, Europe carved up our lands and created artificial borders that produced anything but a unified populace. The British and the French not only divided ethnic tribal societies; they also created a never-ending tension in these newly labeled countries by mixing the Sunnis with the Kurds and the Shiites. In places like Iraq, until recently, Sunnis ruled over a largely Shiite population. In Syria, it was the opposite—generations of Alawite Shiites now challenged by Sunni Muslims. The West has created a tension, a systematic chaos that may plague the region forever. So the pretense goes on. The richer nations need customers for their oil, suppliers for their aircraft, and providers of their arms. Others need markets for exports and some a flow of tourists. Mostly Sunni, they also need to be part of a buffer against Shiite Iran and Syria.

"And they would all like for the West to afford us more respect than they do. We have to be more than the people who clean their streets and pick up their garbage. But this becomes even more of a challenge in light of what is going on today. The new leaders in the Islamic world are radical fundamentalists who are creating cities and villages of rubble and destruction with children roaming the streets with no home."

Looking a bit exasperated, the sultan interjected, "Major, you have given me a history lesson combined with the news of the day. I have not heard anything I didn't know or haven't heard before. I must insist you get to the point."

"The point is this, your highness. I propose a two-part plan. First to generate, as they say in the West, buy-in by those with means and influence in the region. We need to entice them with what is first a way to deal a blow to the West but not something as meaningless as indiscriminate bombings. Something much more powerful. And then, the second part of the buy-in is a commitment to the hundred-year plan to transform our countries."

"Oh, that's all?" the sultan replied. "And how do you entice them, Major?"

"We kidnap the best and brightest female leaders from universities throughout Europe."

"Kidnap? Are you mad, Assad?"

"Yes, kidnap. This is the evil catalyst I referred to earlier. As you said, anyone who can brings in educators for their children. Supposedly, the most learned scholars are retained by our brothers in the emirates, Qatar, and elsewhere to teach our children. A modern-day *Anna and the King of Siam* is happening every day. Prestigious branches of American and European universities are established in the region, and like myself, many of our children are also sent abroad to gain the best education possible. But it does nothing to make the changes from within, the changes we must make over generations to save us."

"So you become a new kind of terrorist, Major. A kidnapper and destroyer of families. I don't even know how to respond to this madness."

"It is mad, your highness, mad and terrible, but perhaps just the right kind of catalyst to create a unity of purpose, a collaboration among those who care about our future. I am proposing a terrorist strategy that does not aim to enlist the weakest but instead the strongest. If not the kings, then the princes, the sultans, and the sultanas—especially the sultanas. I spoke with my parents. My father is aware of potential collaborators. Many would like to bring some measure of hurt to the West but not via terrorist bombers in a London subway, or on a Paris street, or in a Boston parade.

"No, we take the best female leaders we can find and bring them to the families of those who become part of our hundred-year plan. Their role will be to educate and build leadership and strength of character in our children, the children of our supporters. From there, we start to build networks of education and development—deep in our societies— led by the women we have brought here and those they have developed."

"And where do keep them, Major? Are they to be chained to walls in cells, let out to teach a class and then returned to their bonds?"

"No, your highness. Obviously, they would be brought here against their wishes and they must be prisoners of sorts, but their role would be that of special educators. Their lifestyles would be privileged, but they would be denied freedom. I said this was evil, but it is for an important, transformative purpose."

"Two questions, Assad. First, what if your collaborators don't want educators? What if all they want is to add a Western face to their harems or worse, simply engage in high-level human trafficking—something not so unusual in this part of the world? And second, what if your victims don't want to do it? You take them away from their families, their worlds, their hopes and ambitions and expect them to comply with your demands?"

"As to your first question, your highness, we cannot control what happens to these women. We hope that our collaborators will have a higher purpose, but the women will be subject to the whims of whoever obtains them. Unavoidable, but the collaborators we enlist subscribe to our vision. As to the women, they comply or they disappear, your highness. Our goals for retribution and transformation are simply too important for us to fail. They will comply,"

The sultan raised his eyebrows and slumped into his chair. "And how and where are these kidnapped women to be placed?"

"The process needs to be something that will capture the interest and imagination of our collaborators, but this is only in the discussion stage, only conceptualizations at this time. It will likely be some kind of auction but high tech, using an advanced telecommunications system. These are details to work out if we ever get that far. First, however, we will need to create a network of students—a network to be constantly updated—in the best universities in Europe designed to identify targets for our purposes. A small team will eventually be dispatched to abduct and transport the women back to our designated base, where the auction and placement will take place."

"May Allah help me, but how do you transport a kidnap victim from, say, Paris, to wherever you hold your auction, Major? Certainly they will not be brought to Oman."

"No, not Oman, but again, these are details to be worked out, your highness. You summoned me here at a still early part of our planning, but many of those we wish to enlist have their own planes and move freely in the West. My goal is to be able to have access to their resources," replied Assad.

Chapter Ten

Another forty-five minutes of discussion ensued, heated at times, with the sultan peppering Assad with challenges to his visions and the execution of his plan. The sultan asked Abdul Azziz al-Sheik to join them and provide his insight into Assad's proposal. The sultan's vizier was shocked at the audacity and danger of this vision for retaliation. Eventually, the sultan had heard enough. Assad would not lose his head that day. Instead, he would be released from his duties and allowed to pursue his quest to organize an elite team of stealth warriors who would operate under the name *Saqr*—falcon.

"Go ahead with your mission, Major, but I will not be one of your collaborators. I too know of people who would like to escape this redundant cycle of suffocating traditions, but I regard your plan as abhorrent. I wish you had simply resigned and I had not heard any of this. This is no small task, and the probability of failure is great. You will be on your own. I will provide you with a stipend, not for your mission but in appreciation for your past services to my family. I want no connection of this monarchy with what you are doing. You understand this, Major?"

"Yes, your highness," replied Assad standing at attention in front of his sovereign. Despite the three tons of imported Trane air conditioning keeping the room quite cool, Assad's tan uniform showed dark stains of perspiration under his arms and down the center of his back. As he saluted and prepared to leave, the sultan again cautioned him.

"Do what you can to shake up these tired old men and their labyrinths of relatives—princes and high-ranking bureaucrats—but know that what you will be doing, despite your lofty goal is treacherous and despicable, a punishing, evil act intended to correct the hypocrisies and distorted traditions of our Islamic brothers. You will be operating on the dark side, Major. Remember also that when you speak of a hundred-year plan, you will not be around to execute it for the next hundred years. You will need a management system in place, one that will succeed you and keep the plan functioning. Without that, your ambitions are worthless."

Assad nodded.

"This is the last we will ever speak of this, Major al-Amin. The risks associated with the Saqr initiative are all yours, and they are formidable. You want to punish the West and transform the Middle East. Ambitious or insane—more likely insane—you will begin by resigning your commission. My family and I will sincerely miss you. I wish you Allah's guidance and protection."

* * *

Assad's reverie was broken as the wheels of the Gulfstream touched down in Dubai, Saqr's base of operation. The United Arab Emirates was a loose association of individual, schizophrenic country states—Abu Dhabi, Ajman, Dubai, Fujairah, Ras al-Khaimah, Sharjah, and Umm al-Quwain—with Abu Dhabi as its capital and Dubai as its business hub and leader in opulence. The emirates and their neighbor Qatar were modern beyond imagination, and despite Sharia law as their main source of legislation, there were many more freedoms in the emirates for its women. On the other hand, there remained a viable slave trade that imported individuals—young boys—to be camel jockeys at their racetracks and household help. Using boys as camel jockeys had eased off somewhat as robot jockeys had become the more acceptable norm. It was a high-tech world everywhere. Gaining some world attention of late, however, had been the fate of the workers they brought in to build their hotels, casinos, shopping malls, and palm islands. Asians and Africans from the poorest countries were contracted to work in the most arduous conditions. Money sent home to their families was earned in a system that would not have been tolerated anywhere in the West.

At the same time, however, many in positions of leadership wanted more for their people and country. The resources they had access to—oil and natural gas—would allow for systematic improvements down to the deepest levels of their society—if they cared to do that. Some wanted to break out of the traditions that had bred this schizophrenia of character and purpose. Deep down, they didn't want to just emulate the West; they felt they could be better than the West, and Assad found his first group of collaborators and sponsors among them.

Chapter Eleven

Captain Garcia drove to the de la Cruz apartment on Paseo de la Castellana overlooking the Retiro, a large park in the center of Madrid similar to New York's Central Park. She was greeted at the door to the penthouse apartment—which occupied the entire expanse of the twentieth floor—by Remi de la Cruz.

"Anything?" she asked after the captain had introduced herself. "Have you found out anything yet?"

"No," Garcia replied. "And I gather no one has been in touch with you."

"Nothing," replied Rodrigo de la Cruz as he entered the foyer and beckoned the captain to join him in the living room.

The apartment was large with many windows but was not opulent in the classical sense. No provincial furniture but a more modern motif in black and white with marble floors, large leather sofas and armchairs positioned around a white marble table on a large oriental rug.

Attractive and comfortable, thought Mercedes, *not a museum setting to be looked at.*

On the walls—also white—were an array of paintings, some Picasso-like, which probably were originals. Others may have been by Miró with bright colors accenting the black and white setting.

"Please sit," he said to Mercedes, "and tell us what you know."

Mercedes went over the police reports and what they had found out after visiting the university. "I'm sorry, but we have little of relevance at this time. Your daughter's car is still at the university, and her keys were found adjacent to it. We are taking the car to Madrid for further forensic examination, but preliminary analyses have told us very little yet. We are treating this as an abduction. I was hoping that someone had been in contact with you by now."

Remi gasped—an abduction had not been considered. The family feared a traffic accident, but that brought new fears, and she began to sob.

The doorbell rang. A maid appeared and went to the door. Two men entered carrying cases of equipment.

"These are our technical people," Mercedes said as the men joined them in the living room. "With your permission, we'd like to set up a monitoring system in case you are contacted by phone. We will also need access to your computers. Does Paz have a computer?"

"Yes," Remi replied. "And Frankie has a laptop in her room. Conchita, please show the gentlemen to where the computers are," Remi said to the maid.

One man followed Conchita down a hall while the other began to hook up recording and tracing equipment to the telephone in the living room.

"If you have cell phones, please give them to the technician so he can include them in our monitoring system," Mercedes said. "And please, if the girls have cell phones, what are their numbers? And what have you told Miss Fontana's parents?"

"Only that they did not come home and we feared for their safety," replied Rodrigo. "They said they would fly to Madrid immediately, and they should be landing any time now," he said looking at his watch.

As if on cue, the telephone rang. The Fontanas had landed, were picked up by Don Rodrigo's driver and were en route to the de la

Cruz apartment. Don Rodrigo gave Michael the news of an apparent abduction of both girls making their transit even more tense and fearful.

"The Fontanas will be staying with us until we can put an end to this madness," Don Rodrigo informed Captain Garcia, who nodded but was not looking forward to discussing this incident with American parents who would be obviously distraught.

Chapter Twelve

The Gulfstream came to a stop at a remote section of Dubai World Central/Al Maktoum International Airport. Along with Dubai International Airport, Dubai was the busiest international passenger hub in the world having overtaken London's Heathrow in 2013. There was however no evidence of such congestion where Assad's plane shut down its powerful engines in front of a small, white building with no signage or markings. Two black Mercedes SUVs were parked adjacent to the building.

"I want you ladies to put these on," Assad said pointing to two black *burqas* Zayed was carrying from the back of the plane. "If you need to use the facilities, do it now and then put on these coverings."

Both women took turns using the restroom, returned, and pulled the *burqas* over their heads. Assed arranged their head coverings so that only their eyes showed.

"I will allow you ladies to deplane with no constraints if you assure me there will be no trouble," Assad said looking first to Frankie and then to Paz. "I want you to leave the plane and enter the back seat of the first SUV. Just get out and walk to where the door will be open for you. Enter, sit, and say absolutely nothing. Clear?"

The women could not disguise the fear in their eyes, which was the only thing showing from their garbs, but they nodded.

"We are going to a place not far from here. You will be able to rest, eat something, and wait. Tonight, we will travel a short distance, where your fate will be made clear. One thing you must know and reconcile yourselves to accept is that you will never go home again. Your new lives will begin after this night, and we expect your full cooperation. Anything less will generate dire consequences. Do you understand?"

The two women looked at each other as the tears rolling from their eyes were absorbed by the black cloth covering their faces. They quietly moved from the plane and descended the steps while holding their robes so as not to trip. They walked to the black SUV.

They traveled in silence for about half an hour on a modern highway and then exited into the city and eventually onto a street lined with small, white houses with terra-cotta roofs. The SUV pulled into a driveway. A garage door opened. The vehicle entered the garage. The door closed behind them.

Chapter Thirteen

Michael and Sherry Fontana arrived at the de la Cruz residence. Conchita led them to the living room, where Remi and Don Rodrigo embraced them and introduced them to Captain Garcia, who went over the information she had previously given the de la Cruzes.

"We've already set up monitoring equipment in anticipation of the kidnappers contacting the de la Cruzes," Garcia said.

"You're sure the girls have been kidnapped?" Michael asked.

"As sure as we can be, *Señor* Fontana," the captain replied. "That is the assumption we are working with as there can be no other reason for their disappearance. All evidence that we have indicates abduction. *Señor* de la Cruz is a prominent businessman in Spain, and you were the head of a large American company here not long ago. That could have made your daughters targets."

"Is this a frequent occurrence in Spain nowadays?" Fontana asked.

"No. It is almost unheard of. But the economy is weak. There is widespread unemployment, and desperate people do desperate things. Thus far, we have so little to go on that we think it prudent to prepare for this possibility," Garcia answered.

The two mothers sat beside each other on a sofa holding hands and sobbing while the fathers stood conversing with the captain.

"I want to return to headquarters. We still have forensics to complete on your daughter's car," Garcia said to Don Rodrigo. "We are not optimistic that there is more to learn, but we need to cover all avenues. I am leaving two detectives here with the technical people in case there is contact and a demand for ransom. If that happens, I want you to keep the caller on the line as long as possible. Ask to speak to your daughters. That is very important. We want to be sure they are safe. If a ransom is demanded, agree to their conditions whatever they are. I will return immediately, and we will develop a plan to get your daughters back unharmed."

"Money is not an issue," Michael stated, and Don Rodrigo nodded.

"I realize that, *Señores*. Getting the girls back is our only priority," Captain Garcia said.

* * *

Gino was still in Mercedes's office when she returned. "Anything new?" he asked.

"Nothing. The American girl's parents are here staying with the de la Cruzes. They are old friends and business partners from the days when Fontana was managing director of his company in Spain. Obviously, there is much apprehension on the part of the parents."

"I can imagine. You know, Mercedes, we have to contact the American Embassy. The kidnaping of a citizen has to be reported to the FBI. They have international units that get involved in situations like this."

"You mean I'm going to have a team of FBI agents to deal with?"

"Very probably. They have an International Operations Division that dispatches agents to work with local law enforcement in such instances. I'll make the call. I still have close ties with the embassy from the work we did here. Maybe I can find out what their plan is. I also have contacts with the bureau, and that will help build a relationship with you."

"Okay, but I don't want them trying to take over. If they want to help, fine, but this has to be our case to manage."

"From what I understand, it will be," answered Gino, "but remember, Michael Fontana is a big-shot American businessman, and he'll likely demand all the help he can get if this drags on."

Chapter Fourteen

Frankie and Paz were taken into a fashionably furnished living room. Directing them to a brightly upholstered sofa, Assad said, "Sit."

Paz pulled the black *burqa* she was wearing over her head and dropped it on the floor.

"What are you doing?" exclaimed Assad. "Put that back on!"

"You put it on," retorted Paz. "It's like wearing a bedspread. And it smells. Don't you ever clean these things?" Her ire was surfacing.

Frankie stood and removed her *burqa* as well.

"I told you there would be consequences if I did not receive your full cooperation! Are you two mad?" Assad asked looking from Paz to Frankie. Neither he nor any members of the Saqr team ever carried weapons of any kind; he thought his stern tone of voice would be enough to quell this little rebellion.

"Hijo de puta!"—Son of a bitch!! Paz spat out. "Of course I'm mad. I'm angry, and if my life as I know it is over, so be it. Let it end, you pigs!"

Assad laughed while the rest of the Saqr team looked on mouths agape. *Well*, he thought, *the Spaniard has certainly lived up to her profile, and this Francesca, she is equally strong and spirited. We will do well.* "Oh just sit down and be quiet. If you behave, maybe you'll get something to eat and drink."

He turned to Hazem. Speaking in Arabic, he said, "Did you get more background on the American while we were in flight? We will need a full profile to send out before the auction."

"I think I have enough," replied Hazem. "Top student at Princeton University, one of the best universities in the United States. She is spending a year in Madrid as an exchange student staying with the Spanish girl. Her parent's friendship with the de la Cruzes goes back many years. From her Facebook page, I found that she is also an equestrian. She has won a few dressage events in New Jersey, where she lives. I'll lay it all out for you, and it will be ready shortly."

"Good, good," replied Assad. He turned to Sulayman. "Please prepare something for our guests. They slept for most of the flight and may require some sustenance." Turning to the girls, he asked in English, "You are hungry, I assume, no?"

"First the bathroom," said Frankie standing. "Then maybe some coffee please."

Assad pointed to the hallway. "Tea. It will have to be tea." As Frankie moved to the hallway, he shook his head. *It will be good to be rid of these spitfires soon.*

* * *

Gino talked to his embassy and reported the abduction of Francesca Fontana and Paz de la Cruz. The FBI would be notified, and as soon as the embassy received details of its response, Gino would be apprised and Captain Garcia officially contacted by the assigned team.

"Gino," said Mercedes, "I have to get back to the de la Cruz apartment and speak with the Fontanas. Come with me. Your presence—a fellow American—will give them degree of comfort."

"Of course. I can understand what's going through their minds. Can you imagine their anxiety over an eight-hour flight with no information whatsoever? Devastating."

"And we still don't have much in the way of information to give them," said Mercedes. "I have a bad feeling about this," she said shaking her head. "A bad feeling."

* * *

At the de la Cruz apartment, the meeting with the Fontanas went as expected—many questions, still no answers, and two very strong and prominent men who wanted action.

"You know there are no limits, no barriers to doing whatever it takes to get our daughters back," said Michael Fontana. "Whatever it costs, whatever is necessary, we do it. You understand that?" Rodrigo de la Cruz nodded in agreement.

"We understand, *Señores,*" replied Mercedes. "I feel your frustration. We hope there will be some contact from those responsible, and we will keep officers here day and night to monitor the phones, but for now, we can only wait."

"And as soon as we have information about FBI involvement," added Gino, "you will be apprised immediately."

"But there will be a ransom demand," Sherry Fontana called out from across the room. "Right?"

"We hope so, *Señora,*" answered Mercedes. "That will be the best-case scenario. It will give us something to respond to and establish communication with the abductors."

"And if there is no ransom demand?" Michael Fontana asked. "Then what?"

"Then we continue to try to find out what is behind this. For what purpose have the girls been taken? Some kind of retaliation against either of you given the nature of your business? I would like to have Officers Castilla and Campos interview each of you to see if something could have triggered this, something in your business dealings that could have driven someone to take such an action. Enemies you might have, something to do with the medicines you market, some side effects that may have created the need for revenge. Think carefully about this possibility. Contact your medical departments, your litigation people. I will assign people to go through newspaper reports that refer to your companies and see if something shows up. Other than that, we wait." Mercedes sighed.

"Waiting is something Rodrigo and I don't do easily, Captain," replied Fontana, "but for now, we have to put our faith in you and the FBI when they get here."

* * *

On the way back to headquarters, Gino asked, "Suppose they just took the girls for some kind of human trafficking thing. Where would they take them? How would they transport them?"

"With Europe's open borders, they can go anywhere. Just get in a car or a van and drive. They could go to a port or a beach, get on a boat, and go," replied Mercedes. "I think I have to bring Interpol in on this just in case, but pray for a ransom demand, Gino. That's the best we can hope for right now."

Chapter Fifteen

Frankie and Paz spent several days at the villa in Dubai sitting in their bedroom or on the sofa watching Arabic shows on a big-screen television. Some of Assad's team came and went, primarily to stock the residence, which was apparently where Hazem lived. They provided the girls with an array of toiletries, which served their needs. Hazem spent most of his time with Assad on a computer in a room adjacent to the living room.

One evening, there was considerable activity among the four men. The girls had eaten earlier and were offered tea. They were anxious and fearful about what was going on. The butterflies in their stomachs had never quite subsided, and that night, the hot tea helped a little. Paz yearned for a glass of red wine and Frankie wanted one of her father's single-malt scotches to steady their nerves, but the tea would have to suffice.

"Time to get dressed, ladies," Assad said. "Time to put on your bedspreads again." He laughed. "We need to take a short ride."

They boarded the SUVs in the garage. The door opened and they silently departed into the night.

Dubai, like most Middle Eastern countries, was replete with souks, bazaars—indoor or covered marketplaces where all manner of goods are bartered for and bought by tourists and locals. They were a tradition dating back centuries. One of the most famous and popular was the

Grand Bazaar in Istanbul, with sixty-one covered streets and more than three thousand shops. Morocco lay claim to some of the finest souks, primarily in Marrakech, the Old Medina Essaoira souk, and the Medina Fez souk, the largest in the Arab world. Also noteworthy were the Muttrah Souk in Muscat, Oman, one of the oldest marketplaces in that part of the world, and the Khan El-Khalili souk in Cairo, which dated to 1382. The gold souk in Dubai was relatively new but world famous with more than three hundred jewelers carrying on their trade.

The cars drove by the gold souk and along the Dubai Creek to the Deira Old Souk, not far from the spice market. The old souk contained a labyrinth of stores and shops selling everything from gold, handbags, and supposed antiques to all modes of Arab dress. The SUVs moved to a secluded area away from the front entrance and parked. All merchants had departed, and the group entered from a back door, Assad punching in numbers on an electronic keypad. Smells from the spice market permeated the air.

The group proceeded for a short distance down a narrow passageway dimly lit with sparsely placed light bulbs. They passed shuttered shops and stopped at a double-wooden door with some Arabic letters across a beam above the doors. Assad opened the door on the right with a key and felt inside for a light switch. Dim lights lit up a small room that had a counter with some artifacts enclosed behind glass. To both sides of the entrance were piles of carpets. "One of our other businesses," said Assad. "We have staff who sell hand-woven carpets and prayer rugs on the weekend."

The group went to the back of the small shop, and Assad unlocked another door and turned on the lights, much brighter fluorescent fixtures that revealed a larger chamber. Frankie and Paz saw a small, round platform to the left and an array of electronic equipment, chairs, and computer consoles to the right. Hazem turned on the equipment, and green and yellow lights began to blink and a series of beeps sounded.

"How long?" asked Assad.

"Ten minutes," replied Hazem. "We have to activate the website and be sure everyone's logged in."

The Saqr team, primarily Hazem, had created an elaborate, sophisticated, and highly secure website for their clandestine operation. As in centuries past, there would be an auction not unlike those in which slaves were sold to the highest bidder. That night, however, potential buyers would log in for an online auction. Flat-screen monitors were arranged on a wall in the chamber on which bidders would be visible and their responses recorded. The bidders were part of a network created by the Saqr group; princes, sultans, members of a royal family, and prominent businessmen in the Arab world who would bid on the women Saqr abducted from across Europe. The best and the brightest women from Germany, Italy, and England were destined to become part of the households of these powerful men, teaching their children and building their leadership skills. That had been going on for almost seven years, and the money that changed hands went to fund the Saqr group and its mission.

"We are ready, Assad. The profiles of the women have been posted," said Hazem.

Assad said, "Miss de la Cruz, please remove your covering."

Paz shrugged out of her garment. "Okay, *Qué mas?* —What more?"

"Over there," Assad said pointing to a platform toward the back of the chamber.

Paz moved to the area indicated, turned, and said, "And …?"

"Just stay there … Stand or sit," Assad said gesturing to a folding chair on the platform.

Paz sat, crossed her legs, and folded her hands on her lap. Assad spoke in Arabic, and the women saw men on the monitors who were talking with him. That went on for quite a while with Assad directing his comments to someone on one screen and then someone on another. At one point, someone must have made a joke as all the men on the screens and in the room laughed.

"Would you please stand, Miss de la Cruz?" Assad asked at one point.

"Screw you," Paz replied and remained seated. The men on in the screens laughed again.

More conversations in Arabic ensued over the next twenty minutes; then Assad said to Paz, "It is done. Business concluded. You now belong to Sheikh Saud bin Nassr al-Sisi, emir of Ras al-Khaimah."

"Belong? Are you kidding me? I belong to no one—*Nadie!*" Paz said. She stood and looked at Assad and then at the monitors, where men in beards, some with head coverings, stared at her.

"Miss de la Cruz, please come back down here and sit," Assad said indicating for Paz to return to the other side of the room, where Frankie was sitting. "Just remain calm and relax."

"Relax? *Mierda del toro!*—Bullshit!" she retorted as she moved across the room and sat beside Frankie. Her mind was racing with fear. *Sold? For what purpose?*

"Your turn, Miss Fontana," Assad said indicating for Frankie to move to the platform.

Understanding that they were being put on some kind of display, Frankie moved to the designated area, turned, and bowed to each of the screens. "You are a very sorry looking group of men," she said and then sat looking only at Paz, who raised her eyebrows, shrugged, and smirked. She heard the men in the screens murmuring to each other.

Assad began speaking in Arabic again occasionally referring to some notes he had in hand. Again, those on the screens talked back in Arabic.

Before long, there was prolonged discussion between Assad and one of the screens, that of Sheikh Saud, the man who had just bought Paz. There seemed to be some discord at having the same bidder acquire both women, but apparently, he had substantially outbid his competition.

Sheikh Saud of Ras al-Khaimah had a small but quality stable of some on the finest horses in the Middle East and had been swayed by Frankie's experience in dressage events. He was very impressed with Paz's credentials and while content after the first round of bidding, adding another woman of strong character plus some equestrian talents drove the sheikh to go for two and break precedent in the process. Quieting the protests from the other men, Assad closed the auction and officially awarded both woman to the sheikh from Ras al-Khaimah, one of the smaller, lesser known emirates in the UAE. All the monitors went black.

Assad turned to Frankie and Paz. "We have never had one member acquire two of our offerings, much less in the same auction and for an extraordinary sum. You will be going to Ras al-Khaimah, not very far from Dubai. I don't know if you will be seeing very much of each other, but you will soon have a new home and new challenges."

"You turd!" Frankie responded. "Selling us like you would cattle? Are you so evil that you would do this to human beings? Are we part of a white slavery ring or some sultan's harem? Kill us now. I'm not going anywhere."

"White slavery? No. We are not the barbarians you imagine. You will have new lives but as teachers and mentors to our young. We want what you have instilled in our children. To grow and develop them into something worthwhile, to be somebody important, not by their birth but by their capabilities. There will be a new and successful Middle East one day, and you will help in that transition," Assad responded with passion.

The women stared at each other. *"Oh Dios mio,"* sighed Paz. *"Dios mio."*

As they turned off the computers, Assad was feeling elated. He was always inspired by this bartering process that went back centuries. Bargaining and bidding for goods as his ancestors had, he felt close to his roots though outside the room was absolutely nothing that resembled his ancestry. Dubai had to be the most modern city state in the world, but in the souk, Assad carried out his business as his forefathers had and thought, *Saqr made close to two million euros today.*

Chapter Sixteen

Days passed in Madrid with no news. Investigations into Michael's and Rodrigo's business dealings had revealed little. They were upstanding pillars of their communities, business leaders of accomplishments and integrity. Dead end.

A team of FBI agents from the International Operations Division—the International Response Team—had arrived and were working closely with Captain Garcia and her investigators. Gino did not know them but had heard of Clark Breslau, the leader of the group—a solid, no-nonsense special agent who had worked all over the world investigating crimes against American citizens. He had been involved in one kidnapping case in Colombia that had been resolved successfully. In that instance, a ransom had been paid and the victim, a businessman, had been returned, but the perpetrators had escaped. Nevertheless, a successful outcome. Gino liaised with the FBI as his responsibilities with the Ministry of Finance had basically been concluded.

Breslau's team went over the same ground the Spanish investigators had—interviews at the university and with friends of the women, sessions with both sets of parents, background checks—with the same results.

"I don't know where to go with this, Gene"—as he was referred to by the US agencies—lamented Breslau. "We talked to the same people at Interpol as Captain Garcia did, and they have loaded this into their system, but the silence is deafening. We've looked at this from all angles, and it appears the girls were just taken, but to where and why, we're at a standstill. We're already stumbling over what Garcia's investigators have done and haven't been able to add a damn thing. Frustrating."

"I know," Gino said. "Mercedes has also been going around in circles. The girls' pictures have been circulated everywhere and as you know have been carried widely in all the Spanish newspapers and on TV. You'd think something would have turned up by now."

"Look, Gene," Breslau said, "we've been here for a week and have come up with nothing. Our resources are stretched, and I hate to do it, but I'm going to have to pull the plug. Usually by this time we would have had some leads, but not in this case."

"You're going to abandon these girls?" asked Gino. "That's not your usual protocol."

"No it isn't, but as I said, our resources are really tight. I have a suggestion, however. We've worked well together this past week, and I'm very familiar with your background and successes. As your work on this revolution thing has concluded, how about staying here as part of the FBI International Response Team? I checked with Quantico, and there are no issues. They'll set up a consulting agreement, and you can continue digging, working with Garcia, Interpol, and whoever else is necessary. I'll have the embassy set up a fund for you to draw on. You can report back to me weekly or more often if necessary. Interested?"

"Sure. I just don't want our government to walk away from these girls, and for sure that will give the Fontanas some comfort knowing an American is still on the case."

"Good. I'll arrange for you to have an ID. You'll be part of the IRT."

* * *

The Fontanas eventually returned to the US as shells of themselves as the fear of never seeing their daughter again grew greater every day. Gino promised to keep in constant communication with them, and they did feel somewhat better that an American investigator remained dedicated to finding the girls.

One day in her office, Mercedes said, "Gino, this morning I was contacted by someone at Interpol. An analyst, Marie St. Laurant, was doing some digging for me. It seems that over a five- or six-year period, a number of women went missing from different universities in Europe. Actually, there have been many reports of missing persons. Some were eventually found. Others were victims of crimes, even murder, but there are several without any resolution. And there's a pattern. Top students, leaders in their class who disappeared without a trace. What do you think?"

"You may be on to something, Mercedes. This is worth a trip to Lyon."

Chapter Seventeen

Interpol—the International Criminal Police Organization—is an organization based in Lyon, France, that facilitates police cooperation throughout the world. Established in 1923, it includes membership of almost two hundred police forces in a hundred member countries that provide for its funding through annual contributions. Its charter calls for it to be politically neutral, and it has no agents who can make arrests. Its strength is in providing data, communications, and investigative assistance to its member law enforcement agencies. Its focus is on cross-border crimes against humanity including child pornography, human trafficking, computer/cybercrime, drug trafficking, terrorism, genocide, and war crimes among other transnational criminal activities.

Invaluable is its internet-based, encrypted communications network that allows its agents and member police forces to contact each other at any time. The organization's 24/7 network offers continuous access to Interpol's databases of criminals including fingerprints, photos, and DNA samples as well as crime trends and alerts. It expanded to critical areas such as airports and border access points, where documentation is recorded.

* * *

The flight from Madrid to Lyon took under two hours. Interpol headquarters, only a short taxi ride from the airport, was in an impressive steel and glass structure on Quay Charles de Gaulle near the Rhône River.

"Have you ever been here before?" Mercedes asked Gino.

"No, first time. This is quite a place."

"They moved here from Paris about twenty-five years ago."

Gino took in the multistoried building surrounded by manicured lawns and landscaping. "Don't think they went with the lowest bidder when building this facility, do you?"

Mercedes laughed. "With a hundred governments paying the bill, probably not."

They went in and asked to see Marie St. Laurant. In short order, she came out to greet them. She was probably in her late twenties, tall, thin, with long, blond hair and wearing a navy-blue knit dress. She had large, round, black-rimmed eyeglasses that slipped down her nose as she strode to greet Mercedes and Gino. Her gait was energetic—long, smooth, athletic—and as she neared, a warm, welcoming smile adorned her attractive face.

"*Bienvenue,*" she said extending her hand to Mercedes and then to Gino. "I am very pleased to meet you," she said in pleasantly accented English. "We all have heard of the magnificent work you did in Spain uncovering that incredible conspiracy. It is a privilege to be able to work with you. I hope my research will help your investigation," she said constantly pushing her glasses up.

She led Gino and Mercedes through a door at the far side of the reception area. Passing many cubicles, she eventually stopped at her station, which was surrounded by partitions on three sides. She maneuvered two chairs closer to her desk, sat, and began typing on her keyboard. Gino and Mercedes sat on either side of her.

"Here, look. Not including your Spanish and American victims, there have been six unexplained disappearances over the last five years all remarkably similar. The best and brightest female students from different universities in different countries missing with absolutely no trace."

Gino and Mercedes pulled their chairs closer and looked intently at the screen.

"I thought about giving you a more formal presentation on what I found, but I t this, here, could serve as a working session that would let us delve into areas of interest easier. And of course if you think this is worthwhile, there will be a full report of all we review here. My superiors also thought this would be the best way to proceed at this stage.

"*Comme vous le voyez*, uh, as you can see, Camille La Monde gone from the Sorbonne University in Paris, December 2012. Gabriella Santini disappeared from the Politecnico di Milano, Italy, in November, 2013. Elizabeth Mills vanished from the International School of Economics in London, May 2014. Jana Weigel went missing from the Heidelberg University, Germany, in May 2015. Claire Windsor, another in England, disappeared from Queens College, Oxford, April 2016, and Greta Mulder gone from the University of Amsterdam, December, 2016. And now, Paz de la Cruz and Francesca Fontana, your girls, abducted from the University of Madrid, November 2017.

"Eight girls, women really, just gone, and no leads whatsoever. No demands for ransom, nothing. No trace. There has to be some connection, don't you think? All were among the very best students, each a leader in some capacity at her school, popular, destined to be a leader in her chosen field of study."

"Are they engaged in similar fields?" asked Gino.

"No. One in England was an economics student, the other pre-med. The German was a computer science major, and the Italian, biomedical engineering. The Dutch girl, econometrics and operations research, and the French girl, education. And of course your girls—law students. All over the place, no pattern at all, except that they were clearly recognized as leaders in their classes, the best of the best."

"If there is a pattern, it might be that all were taken out of the country," said Mercedes. "We've come to believe that's the case with our girls as there would seem to be little reason for them to be taken and remain in Spain. There has to be another purpose, but what we don't know."

"I would have to agree," said St. Laurant. "It would not be very difficult to take them out of the country certainly to some other place or places in Europe, but to take them out of Europe, that would be a little more complicated … but perhaps not that complicated especially if they were taken by boat. There would be a million places for a boat to dock without ever coming in contact with the authorities. A small boat ferrying people to a larger boat, and from there to anywhere. Easier than by plane."

"We thought about that," said Mercedes, "even showed their pictures to all commercial airlines and Immigration"

"It would have to be a private plane," Gino said. "They'd never get them on a commercial airplane—far too many checks—but with a private plane, I'd guess that any number of shortcuts could be arranged, and once in the air, as you said, anywhere."

"But we showed their pictures to the private air terminals as well. Immigration officers there, had no records of the girls. *Mierda!* —Shit! Should have looked into that deeper," said Mercedes. Let's start again in Madrid and see exactly what private planes were there at the time of the abduction, when they departed, and to where. We should do the same with all Spanish airports wherever and whenever private planes were on the ground around the time the girls went missing. Leaving by boat would be virtually impossible to figure out. Planes are something we can dig into further."."

"I can initiate a similar investigation in the other cities," Marie said. "As you saw, some of the abductions go back a few years. Our databases might have something, but if not, we'll work with local authorities and hope their databases go back as far as we need to, especially in France and Italy, the sites of the earliest abductions. This might take a while as we will need to look at multiple cities in each country just in case, but it's a good place to start."

After meeting with Klaus Schickhaus, Interpol's head of the Human Trafficking Unit and bringing him up to date with the work completed with Marie St. Laurant, Gino and Mercedes returned to Madrid. While in the air, they determined that there were two executive aircraft terminals at Barajas International Airport capable of handling up to fifty planes and offering 24/7 maintenance and elaborate VIP lounges. Considering that the university abductions were relatively recent, records regarding incoming and outgoing traffic would be readily available.

Mercedes, as a captain in the National Police Force, handled the initial inquiries notwithstanding a high level of multilingual competencies at both facilities; she asked for records for a week before and after the disappearances. There had been 260 private planes that had departed during that time—110 from the Gestair terminal and 150 from Multiservicios Aeropuertarios. Gino collected data from Gestair and Mercedes worked with the Multiservicios staff. They stayed at the airport for over two hours going over dozens of flights including charters, corporate planes—many oil and technology companies—and planes belonging to celebrities and rich vacationers.

They camped out in an office in a customers' lounge and compared notes. On the day of the abductions, eighteen private planes departed from Madrid. A number of mining company corporate jets, several oil company planes, a Hollywood movie star's plane, and a plane registered to the Saudi Arabian Ministry of Commerce and Prince Azam Azziz bin Turki. The prince's plane, a Gulfstream 550, had been on the ground for five days before the kidnapping and had left the evening of the abductions with a flight plan to Dubai. Five passengers not including the two-man crew went through departing immigration all with Bosnia-Herzegovina passports citing addresses in Sarajevo.

With that information, Mercedes sought out those who had handled the immigration process. One of the officers in the Guardia Civil, who ·manage entry and departure processes, remembered the men primarily because the Gulfstream 550 was one of the most expensive private jets there was. It had Saudi registration, but the responsible party, the prince, had not been on board. Not a uniquely unusual situation as private planes were often leased or loaned to other parties.

Only one passenger other than the crew arrived on that jet in Madrid, a Mazar Hussain. The officer remembered that the man had mentioned he was in the oriental rug business. One arrived and five departed, but that also was not unusual. All the passengers were relatively young, and their passport photos showed three with neatly trimmed beards and two clean shaven. On departure, another officer of the Guardia recalled that they loaded two large, rolled-up rugs onto the aircraft.

"Two large rugs rolled up and taken on the plane. What do you think, Gino?"

"Wow," he sighed. "What if …? Well, it's the best lead we've had. It's the only lead we have. But for good order's sake, you'll have to assign investigators to analyze what transpired at private plane facilities in other cities, and that will take a while, but let's see what we can find out about Prince Azam Azziz bin Turki. Have the Guardia check the legitimacy of those passports with Interpol. That whole area is a bit complicated spanning a number of new countries following the collapse of Yugoslavia. Bosnia-Herzegovina is a mishmash of ethnicities—Bosnians, Croats, Serbs—and it came into existence only about twenty-five years ago. I know there is a large Muslim population, so being in the rug business fits, but we have to corroborate their documents including their Sarajevo residences."

"I'll also let Schickhaus know what we've found and see if anything like this turns up at those other cities. We may be on a wild goose chase with this Saudi prince, and I don't want to put all our eggs in one basket, but while we're checking out the other airports in Spain, Interpol can mine their databases, which includes airport entries and departures. We now have some names and faces," Mercedes added. "Marie St. Laurant will love digging into this."

For the first time in weeks, the investigation took on an air of anticipation; Gino thought it important to bring Clark Breslau up to date as soon as they returned to Madrid. He also planned to ask Clark whether the FBI would likely need some US State Department assistance or even guidance if this Saudi connection remained promising. Being a prince, he was somehow connected to the Saudi royal family, and that could prove to be touchy.

Chapter Eighteen

Working through the US State Department and Interpol, Gino and Mercedes ascertained that Prince Azam Azziz was one of thousands of princes in the Saudi royal family. The current king had more than fifty sons not to mention dozens of daughters, and the sons had begat hundreds more sons and daughters. Hence, the royal lineage grew exponentially. And the king's brothers and sisters grew their own lines of royal family members. In essence, Saudi Arabia was a monstrous welfare state providing annual stipends from nearly $500,000 monthly to those closer in lineage to the king to several thousands of dollars monthly to the more remote members of the royal family. But the system included all kinds of money-making opportunities through schemes, loopholes, and notorious means of skimming from budgeted government programs. And additional stipends were granted for each child providing incentives to procreate.

As Saudi Arabia was a polygamist society with the men having up to four wives under Sharia law, the kingdom's untold riches were spread across a family tree that would make Ancestry.com's analytical processes implode. *Imagine trying to marry someone whom you were not related to in one way or another*, thought Gino as he read through the report. *Impossible.*

Prince Azam Azziz was in the grand-nephews' line of the royal family, not in the more lucrative line of the family of Saud but high up enough to have some significant responsibilities and benefits. Fortunately but also unfortunately, the prince had diplomatic status. The fortunate part was that the State Department had a profile and some background information on him. His status, unfortunately, might make him somewhat untouchable should something nefarious come to light.

Azam Azziz was one of a number of directors in the Ministry of Commerce with imports and exports as his primary area of responsibility. He was married with three wives and eight children; he lived in Riyadh and traveled quite a bit, primarily throughout Europe and the Middle East. The State Department believed he was among the more moderate members of the royal family and aligned himself with the current crown prince, who was destined to succeed the current king.

The State Department said that Saudi Arabia had long been among the more conservative Islamic monarchies tied to the rigid Wasabi sect of Islam, but there seemed to be some trends to loosen that hold and bring the kingdom into a more modern image and more closely aligned with Western values—slowly. Prince Azam was not someone you would think would be involved in a human trafficking scheme, but the Middle East—Saudi Arabia included— had always been an enigma—part of the Stone Age in terms of human rights and misogyny but an ally and important trading partner with the West. An endless supply of oil drove that relationship, but with oil prices at an all-time low and alternative sources of energy growing by leaps and bounds, Saudi Arabia had to think hard about its future. Its lifelong opposition to Iran—the Sunni versus Shia forms of Islam—aligned them with most of the West and most important with the US. Schizophrenic might be the best way to describe what Saudi Arabia was and what it wanted to be. Prince Azam seemed to be on the side of bringing Saudi Arabia into the twenty-first century.

* * *

Interpol discovered that the other four passengers departing on the Gulfstream—Azhar Sheed, Walid Shaloub, Junaid Ismail, and Yasar Ali—had entered Madrid on the same day Mazar Hussain arrived; they had come from Marseilles, Marrakech, and Lisbon—two from Lisbon but on different flights. More important, the names used in entering and departing Spain were false. There were no immigration records of them in Bosnia-Herzegovina, and the addresses in Sarajevo also appeared to be falsified. With Bosnia-Herzegovina being members of Interpol, cooperation with authorities proceeded smoothly.

"I think we have our abductors," exclaimed Mercedes on receiving the information from Klaus Schickhaus, the primary liaison with Madrid and the FBI international team. "Schickhaus was very pleased that they had uncovered this information so quickly, and he gave Marie St. Laurant all the credit for tracking this down."

"Yes, she has proven to be quite a gem," replied Gino. "We now have leads on those responsible and a possible connection to a Saudi prince except that only the prince is real and the Bosnians—if that's what they are—are really just shadows. But we do have their photos, and that's critically important. Interpol has confirmed that the flight plan was legit with the plane landing in Dubai and later returning to Riyadh, Saudi Arabia, but there's no record of any passengers on either flight, no record of anyone going through immigration in Dubai or Riyadh, so now where do we go? They can't still be up in the air."

Chapter Nineteen

Assad and his team brought Paz and Frankie back to the villa. Arrangements had to be made to transport them to the palace of Prince Saud bin Nassr in Ras al-Khaimah. The sheikh had spent €1.9 million—€800,000 for Paz and €1.1 million for Frankie, well over two million US dollars.

The bidding system devised by Assad with the help of Hazem—the computer genius of the team—was twofold. Using their encrypted and secure website, notices were sent to over sixty members of the Saqr network with profiles and photos of the abducted women. Minimum bids started at €250,000, and twenty-four hours before the auction, the five highest bidders were permitted to participate in the live, online auction. That was the only way Assad deemed the process to be fair and manageable, and it seemed to be working. Over the years, the number of affluent businessmen and members of royal families throughout the Middle East who were part of the Saqr network had grown from ten founding members to more than sixty, and Saqr was being pressed for greater productivity.

The profiling and selection process was arduous and time consuming, and it included an onsite network of collaborating students and university staff, who were the first line of the identification process. The planning and execution of the kidnappings were the responsibility of Assad and his small Saqr team, and kidnappings took months and months of preparation. That was why over five-plus years, only six women had been taken and placed—now eight with the two from Madrid.

Sheikh Saud bin Nassr al-Sisi's €1.9 million was confirmed to have been received by Habduja Bank, AG, in Geneva, Switzerland, where Saqr kept the income from their operation in a secure numbered bank account. Habduja had a branch in Dubai where Assad transferred funds from time to time to manage operating costs including stipends and housing for the team. It was a costly enterprise, but Saqr was fortunate to be able to use Prince Azam Azziz's Gulfstream for extractions. That was totally financed by the prince, who occasionally skimmed money from the Ministry of Commerce's sizeable budget. The prince had been the first in the network to acquire one of these treasures, the girl from the Sorbonne in Paris.

The Saqr operation was turnkey. Sulayman and Rasid of the Saqr team worked with the successful bidder and his staff. They profiled the household, the number of wives and children, their ages and areas of aptitude, and special educational interests. Curricula for study were acquired for each child and were generally based on the British or American educational system. Processes for accreditation were established and ultimately ascertained, and all would be transferred to the designated computer information system in each household. The women—the would-be teachers—would have a full and complete educational system established for them to implement for each child. The women would be assigned assistants chosen by the head of the household, members of his staff, or sometimes the wives depending on how much they chose to be involved in the process. As many as fourteen students in one instance across a wide-ranging age group would be an almost impossible task for one person, and the teachers' assistants would be critical to achieving success. But the abducted women would be the masters of education at each location and responsible for the development of their charges.

* * *

Paz and Frankie were delighted to have been kept together, though what and where Ras al-Khaimah was remained a mystery to them.

"Can you believe this shit?" exclaimed Frankie. "Sold at a slave auction like in the Middle Ages."

"And we're supposed to be teachers and mentors? That's what I gathered. These people could probably hire anyone they liked from all over the world to teach their kids and they kidnap us? This cannot be real," said Paz.

"Well, we're here, and it's real, that's for sure. Fucking unbelievable."

The women tried to sleep that night, but emotions clouded their thoughts. They weren't being sold into a prostitution ring or some kind of white slavery operation, but it was slavery nevertheless. How they longed to see or even just talk to their parents. Occasionally, sobs could be heard from outside their room.

* * *

After a few days to set up the curricula for the children, Assad gathered everyone in the living room of the villa. "Tea and toast, ladies," he called out, "and then into your *burqas*. You are about to begin your final journey. It will not be the hardship you were anticipating. In time, you will accept and embrace the role you will be playing. You will be historic figures in the transformation of this region doing something important and worthwhile. You don't see it now, but you will. Now eat your breakfast and prepare yourselves for a new life."

"It would be nice to have some coffee," said Frankie. "Aren't Arabs supposed to be famous for their coffee?"

"I think that's the Turks," said Paz. "Turkish coffee—mud in little cups, right?"

"Maybe your new home will have coffee," replied Assad. "Here we have tea. Enjoy it or don't. Your choice, but we leave in thirty minutes."

After breakfast, the girls freshened up, put on their garments, and went to the garage and the waiting SUVs. They traveled out of the city to a small airport with a white stucco building with many antennas. Alongside the building was a sleek, silver aircraft not very different from the one that had brought them to Dubai. There was an emblem on the tail that they speculated was the UAE emblem, but it may have been something associated with Ras al-Khaimah. They did not recall any markings on the plane that had brought them there, but they had never really looked.

They left their wooly, black *burqas* in the SUV. Frankie called out to Assad as they moved toward the aircraft's access stairs, "Send those damn things to the laundry, will you? They definitely need freshening up."

Assad laughed. He told Rasid, "On the way back, stop at the cleaners." He was pleased but also a little sad to be rid of these women. *I think they will test the patience of Sheikh Saud bin Nassr,* he thought and then recalled an American expression he had heard before: *Tough cookies.*

Chapter Twenty

Klaus Schickhaus organized a video conference that included Mercedes Garcia representing the National Police Force in Spain and Clark Breslau of the FBI International Operations Unit along with Gino Cerone, a hybrid involved with both agencies. Members of agencies representing the other countries and cities where abductions had taken place were also included, but in most cases, the local police agencies had been replaced by national criminal investigation units as they no longer looked like one-off local crimes.

The agencies represented and their responsible investigators were Maria Marzano, Guardia di Finanza, Milan; Carl Mittermaier, Bunderskriminalamt—BKA, the Federal Criminal Investigation Office, Wiesbaden, Germany; Arnold Beishar, Dutch National Police—Korps Nationale Politie, The Hague, Netherlands; Clive Kavanaugh, Thames Valley Police, the county responsible for Oxfordshire; Theresa Sommersfield, Scotland Yard, London; and Claudine Montand, Police Nationale—formerly the Surete, Paris.

Schickaus, a former high-ranking officer in the German Bundespolizei, the uniformed federal police force, was a man of medium build whose long, chestnut-brown hair was slightly graying at the temples. His nicely shaped hair gave him the appearance of an orchestra conductor, which on that day was not far from his role in the conference. He had moved to his position at Interpol five years earlier around the time of the first abduction. He spoke in English but was proficient in French, Spanish, and Italian as well as German and had a smattering of Arabic.

"Officers, detectives, and special agents, over the past few weeks, my office has discussed with each of you or your associates what we now believe to be coordinated series of abductions of unique women from your universities. In setting up this teleconference, I have advised each of you who is the responsible Interpol investigator in each of the cities where the abduction occurred, and I thank you for having them with you today.

"Special Agents Breslau and Cerone have responsibility for the American girl, Francesca Fontana, and Captain Mercedes Garcia of the National Police Force in Spain has responsibility for Paz de la Cruz. Each of you has been apprised of the kidnap victims of the other cities in Europe, eight women as of now."

Schickhaus went over the profiles of each of the women, outstanding students and leaders in their universities.

"We have set up a special website for each of you to access that will update your local investigative information as well as receive updates from Interpol and from each of your colleagues in this video conference. Communication is one of Interpol's primary responsibilities— communication and coordination—and this secure and encrypted website, code name Missing, is designed to keep you up to date on the developments in each of your—and our—investigations.

"As you have been informed albeit somewhat briefly, we believe that the abducted women departed from your countries in a private aircraft belonging to or at least used by Prince Azam Azziz bin Turki, a director in the Saudi Arabian Ministry of Commerce. His plane was on the ground in or nearby the cities where the abductions took place. In the case of the Madrid abductions, we believe that five operatives—for want of a better description—entered Madrid by various routes except for one who arrived on the suspect aircraft. Spanish immigration has identified that the other four came to the city via Marseilles, Marrakech, and Lisbon. We were able to backtrack their routes to Madrid based on the passport information registered when they departed the country. Their documentation proved to be false, but their facial images and passport photos have been recorded.

"The Saudi prince was not on the plane neither at arrival nor departure. Our investigation has identified that this is their usual modus operandi—arrive at the city of the abduction via independent routes, which could be by commercial air or via land routes—and leave always as a team, all five, on the Saudi's Gulfstream. We still have some pieces to fill in as they were using false passports, apparently very good ones, but for those departure sites with facial recognition software, we can make identifications providing they are not using disguises. That analysis is ongoing, and we're working with each of your customs and immigration authorities. One caution however is that you take absolutely no action regarding the Saudi prince. Please leave that to us. We cannot alert anyone to this if we hope to eventually track down and locate the women.

"One issue we ask you to delve into, however, is how such an operation was organized. The abductors do not just fly into a city, go to a prominent university, and kidnap the best female student there. They have to have a system set up, and we need for each of you to go back to your original investigations and see what you can uncover. Now along those lines, I ask Captain Marzano to relate to the group her experience in Milan. Captain?"

"*Grazi,* Colonel Schickhaus," the investigator from Italy said. "After the abduction of Gabriella Santini, the Milan police interviewed students, professors, and administrators at the university and even janitorial staff. Those who interviewed Lorenzo Raimondi, a professor of chemistry, noted that he rarely made eye contact with them. He was always tinkering with something, picking up a flask, moving a beaker, but never looking at the detectives. Even in his office, he moved papers, pens, books, but his eyes never met theirs. That made the investigators suspicious, and they noted that in their interview transcripts. He was a naturalized Italian citizen of Italian parents born in Tunisia and lived for a time in Abu Dhabi. Not the usual background for a professor at Politecnico di Milano. The investigator's notes had a few apostrophes and underlines in this section of the transcript.

"Undisputed, however, was that Raimondi was a highly qualified instructor. In the past, he worked as a research chemist at Diatech Pharmacogentics in Jesi, Italy, and for a time at the medical school in Bologna. He published a number of research papers in his field. He moved to Milan about seven years ago and has had no issues with students or faculty over that time. He was not married and led what was believed to be a quiet, academic life except for traveling at least once a year, sometimes to Abu Dhabi and a few trips to Cairo. Nothing out of the ordinary.

"But there was something, so we pressed. We showed up without appointments sometimes at the laboratory, other times at his office, and a few times at his home. We discovered nothing, had no basis for a warrant, but the detectives were always around. We honestly had nowhere else to go, as each of you know so well, but the detectives associated with the case just didn't want to let it go.

"Then one day, the carabinieri reported a dead body in a car on a side street off Via Giuseppe Verdi not far from the Teatro La Scala. It was Lorenzo Raimondi. He had a gunshot wound to the head, and a small-caliber Beretta was found beside him on the front seat of his Fiat 500. It looked like a suicide. It was then that the local police brought this to our attention, and together, we looked into this further. A warrant was authorized, and what did we find? Nothing. No laptop, no computer, no cell phone. His apartment was in pristine condition with no signs of any search—except for those missing devices—and we found little information. At the university, however, there was evidence of a break-in at his office. His computer hard drive had been removed, and in his student records, there was no file for Gabriella Santini.

"The carabinieri had officially ruled this a suicide. The Berretta was not registered to the professor, and we have not been able to trace it to anyone. With what looked like a systematic cleansing of all records from his home and university office, we have kept this investigation open, and the suicide ruling was deemed suspect. The Guardia took responsibility, and we have linked it to the Santini abduction, but it has not progressed further in the ensuing years. Not until now."

"You said there was no cell phone, Captain Marzano," asked Mercedes, "but you have his cell number from telephone company records. Have you checked into his contacts?"

"Yes of course, Captain Garcia," replied Marzano. "We found only the normal contacts you would imagine for the most part, but there were a number of incoming and outgoing calls to untraceable cell numbers in the months prior to the abduction and several after—all outgoing. But we have not been able to do anything with this information except to raise our suspicions."

"So you see," added Schickhaus, "a possible connection as to how the abducted girl may have been identified, but this is pure speculation. Is this a network or only an individual connected to this abduction? Or does this have absolutely nothing to do with the disappearance of Gabriella Santini? We don't know. But it is something, and however remotely, it's possibly tied to a Middle East connection. We need you to go back again and with your local police forces and revisit that ground. For older crimes, students have undoubtedly moved on, but faculty and staff who knew those who had been abducted might still be there.

Tear it up," Schickhaus said, "but again, no further investigation on the Saudi unless under Interpol's direction."

After a few more questions and comments from the group, they said their goodbyes and the screens went dark. Gino asked for his connection to Breslau to remain open.

"Cristo"—Christ, said Mercedes. "Now what do we do? Look for more Arabs? I thought we were done with them after what we had to deal with in Spain."

Gino laughed. "In the States, that would be very politically incorrect. Some group would likely get a judge to issue a cease and desist order, isn't that right, Clark?"

"Probably. I don't think you'll encounter the same civil sensitivities in Spain, but keep it under the radar. Do full background checks on students and faculty, and as Captain Marzano did, all janitorial and maintenance staff. The Madrid case is still very fresh, so get your detectives back in there—a full-court press. Uh, that's a basketball term, Captain. It means—"

"I know what it means, *Señor* Breslau," Mercedes interrupted. "Basketball is very popular in Spain. But this is starting to look like a very sophisticated and organized operation. And we still have our Saudi prince and his infamous plane. Let's call Schickhaus back. He said to stay away from the Saudi, but we need to understand how that end of the investigation is going to proceed and how Interpol intends to take the lead on this. Very touchy issue I imagine."

Chapter Twenty-One

Sheikh Saud bin Nassr al-Sisi's Cessna Citation touched down at a private airstrip not far from the Ras al-Khaimah International Airport. Ras al-Khaimah was both the name of the state and its principal city. All around was bleak, caramel-colored sand, but buildings could be seen in the distance softened by the sun and morning haze. A modern, antenna-bedecked, tile-covered building was at the end of the runway with two white Mercedes SUVs parked outside and a military-like vehicle off to the side. As the Citation taxied close, the women saw a few robed and headdress- attired individuals standing in front of the SUVs. On the short flight, other than the pilots, they had been attended to by an attractive stewardess dressed in a beige uniform with magenta accents and an unusual hat, almost a derby but with a short, thick brim all around tied down with a beige and magenta scarf that wrapped around her neck. They were offered tea, but almost as soon as they departed from Dubai, they began their descent to Ras al-Khaimah. While in the air, the stewardess sat in a leather armchair facing the girls. The plane's interior was very similar to the plane they had been on from Madrid to Dubai.

"We are here," she said in lightly accented English. She stood as the plane came to a stop. "Time to go."

Deplaning into the bright desert sun caused Frankie and Paz to shield their eyes to get their bearings. As they descended the stairway, which opened out from the side of the plane just behind the cockpit, they moved haltingly toward the gleaming white SUVs and the robed individuals. A handsome, middle-aged man probably in his forties moved from the group toward them. He was dressed in a white, full-length tunic and red-checkered headscarf that came just below his shoulders; it was ringed with a thick black cord just above his forehead. As was Assad's, his beard was black and neatly trimmed. His complexion was a dark tan highlighted by his white garb.

"Greetings, ladies. Welcome to Ras al-Khaimah. I am Sheikh Saud bin Nassr al-Sisi," he said in flawless English. "This is my emirate, part of the United Arab Emirates, and you will soon be joining my household. There is much to go over, much to learn and understand, but first, we will get you organized and settled into your quarters at the royal palace. Arrangements have been made for your clothing and personal necessities." Gesturing to two people at his left and right, he said, "This is Majid Khan, my most trusted aide, my chief of staff, and this is his sister, Samira. They will see to your needs, and Samira will be your primary contact and liaison to my wives. You know, in Islam, men are permitted up to four wives, but I am one of the more modern Muslims." He laughed. "I have only three. My eight children are six to fourteen. Samira will fill you in on them. In the meantime, please," he said gesturing to the SUVs, "let us go home."

The SUV had heavily tinted windows, but the glare from the desert sun was still strong. Paz whispered to Frankie, "The first thing I need is sunglasses."

"Me too." Frankie laughed though trepidation gripped her body. "Strange," she said quietly to Paz, "he speaks English almost like an American. Assad had a British accent."

"Maybe he went to school in the States. Who knows?"

The two women viewed an endless expanse of desert and thought about three wives and eight children.

Soon, they saw something in the distance—a bright glare on the horizon. Sunlight bouncing off an edifice blurred the image; it was only when they got closer that they made out an enormous structure with a large center dome and two smaller ones on either side. A multileveled palace lay before them surrounded by what looked to be frosted, glass-paneled walls. Scores of tall palm and date nut trees ringed the walls accented by green shrubs with tiny red blossoms.

There was a large, un-gated opening in the walls with two small cupola-topped, round buildings at each side of the entrance. *Guardhouses probably*, the women thought. An enormous courtyard lay within, and beyond, a wide, tapered, stone staircase. More palm trees and shrubs brightened the earthen courtyard offering a beautiful contrast to the sand. Several autos, most of them white, were randomly parked to the side. The women spotted at least two Bentleys or maybe Rolls Royces, some BMW sedans, and several tan, camouflaged Land Rovers. Several military personnel stood at attention as the vehicles entered.

"Welcome to the oasis," Frankie said. "Isn't there a song like that?"

"Midnight at the Oasis," replied Paz.

"Well this is Midday at the Oasis, Paz. Have you ever seen anything like this?"

The SUVs pulled up at the base of the stairs, and the women saw at least four stories to the tan marble- or granite-covered edifice and two large wings, perhaps two stories tall were on each side of the staircase at ground level. The ornate decorations framing the windows looked as if they were made of gold by the way they glowed in the desert sun. A mixture of brightly colored and muted mosaic patterns festooned the buildings, and red and pink bougainvillea clung to the lower walls of the two wings.

The women were drawn to a fountain near the base of the stairway. In the center of it was a statue of a black horse on its hind legs. It stood about ten feet tall with water arching from four sides onto the stallion making it forever shiny and gleaming. Frankie and Paz slowly took in the scene before them, mouths agape as they looked left and right, up and down. Almost simultaneously, they moved to the fountain and the majestic creature rising above it.

"That is Midnight," Samira said in a lilting Arabic accent as she joined the women. "He is our most successful racehorse, a purebred Arabian stallion that has won many races in Europe. He is retired now living a life of luxury at the emir's equestrian compound not far from the palace. You will see it soon, and you will see much of it, Miss Fontana."

"Well, Paz, you had it right—Midnight at the Oasis," commented Frankie.

Chapter Twenty-Two

FBI Director Shane Guiness and Special Agent Breslau sat in the office of Undersecretary of State for Middle Eastern Affairs, Matthew Luxmore. It was late at night, and they had the ambassador to Saudi Arabia, Richard Durand, on a secure telephone line from Riyadh, the capital.

"Dick, you know the story—a Saudi prince's aircraft present at all the sites of the mysterious abductions of female students from the best universities in Europe. And now an American added to the list of victims," Guiness said. "And the guy has diplomatic status no less."

"I started to dig into this after Matthew alerted me to the situation," replied Ambassador Durand. "I can't imagine how to start such a conversation with the prince except to say that whatever we do has to be done very carefully."

"Based on customs and immigration records in each of the countries, it seems that the prince was never a passenger on any of those flights coming or going on those dates," Breslau said. "That's strange because there were many instances when his business activities took him all over Europe and beyond with him traveling on that plane. Immigration records have documented this. So how and why are these flights without him? It doesn't seem possible that his plane travels to various cities in Europe and he doesn't know about it."

"No, it certainly doesn't, but there were passengers on that plane, and we know that at least in Madrid, false documents were used. We have to come up with some kind of credible bullshit for me to at least open a conversation with him," the ambassador said. "The guy is not way, way up on the totem pole over here, but he *is* on the totem pole. His import/export office is vitally important to the kingdom, and he has been tapped as one of the guys we want to stay close to. He seems to be one of the more modern members of the royal family, not entrenched in the Middle Ages, somewhat in the mold—either formally or informally—of Crown Prince Mohammed bin Hasan, who's in line to be the next king. The crown price appears to be intent on bringing Saudi Arabia out of its archaic Islamic quicksand and into a more modern political and social culture. We pray this new group of leaders makes it—notwithstanding the history and tradition of this kingdom—and you want to link him to kidnappers, some kind of human trafficking conspiracy? Hardly a way to make friends and influence people."

"Shit, Dick, we know that. And we don't want to link anything to the next king. We don't want to go anywhere near there. That's why we need your insight on this," said Undersecretary Luxmore. "This is a big deal. Some kind of human trafficking network but for what purpose we cannot imagine. And for this to involve a member of the royal family, no matter how far removed, is mind-blowing. Our relationship with the Saudis has never been better, and we can't risk offending them in an irresponsible way. Check that. Responsibly or irresponsibly, we just can't offend them."

"Do you think we might be able to come up with some kind of drug trafficking story, one that has a measure of credibility and involves the use of private aircraft without the owner's knowledge? A conspiracy involving rogue pilots of private aircraft building an international network to smuggle drugs into Europe?" Breslau asked.

"We can bring in the CIA and Interpol to research the use of all private aircraft, how often they are used, how long they just sit around, and how often they are recorded as flying without their owners. This could include prominent businessmen, suspected criminals, and royalties from anywhere, entertainers, particularly those with planes entering and departing European cities, without the presence of their registered owners on board. Customs and Immigration along with the FAA and European Air Authority should be able to give us some insight on this."

"Maybe," said Guiness. "In all likelihood, many planes could be airborne without their owners on board but almost assuredly not without their knowledge. Allowing their plane to be used for friends and family, shopping sprees, whatever. Probably happens all the time, but for the purpose of this story, we have to make a case for their being unaware. We just need a handful of incidents to make this scenario believable, and the more I think about it, that actually could be happening."

"Good," said Undersecretary Luxmore. "I'll talk to the CIA, and Breslau, you get the Interpol people working on it as well. Doesn't hurt to research this from two perspectives. Let's give it a week and see what we have. If we can develop a credible story, we should try to get a news story placed somewhere, even in an American newspaper. We have some journalists we can work with on this. Then if it looks good, we'll have Ambassador Durand set up an approach to Prince—what the hell is it? Ah yes, Azam Azziz."

* * *

Mercedes and Gino went over the plan with the Madrid investigation team to interview and re-interview a wide band of individuals at the university. Their goal was to get full background information on students, professors, administrators, and all university employees. Warrants were approved to review files and university records.

Despite its seven hundred years of Arab occupation through the fifteenth century and its possessions on the coast of North Africa—Melilla and Ceuta—Spain probably had the smallest Muslim population of all countries in Europe. Despite the terrorist attack on Madrid commuter trains in 2003 by Moroccan terrorists and the backlash that brought, conditions had been softening somewhat in recent years. That was until Gino and Mercedes uncovered the conspiracy to bring Spain back to an Islamic monarchy. But the Spanish were a tolerant people, and with a socialist government in power, a more liberal attitude prevailed. So it was not surprising to find a handful of students with Muslim backgrounds with student visas studying at the University of Madrid. Several university employees were also from Middle Eastern countries including a law professor—Nabil Mousa—originally from Damascus, and several janitorial staff whose lineage traced back to Morocco. Among students, six had Middle Eastern backgrounds ranging from Iran and Turkey to Qatar and Oman. The student from Qatar was studying law and in the same curriculum level as Frankie and Paz. That student, Ali Abdul Aziz Ali, known simply as Ali at the university, had however dropped out of school in the weeks following the abductions. He had lived in the university dormitory at the Alcobendas campus and had roomed with Devon Akmon, a pre-med student from Muscat, Oman.

Akmon told investigators, "Ali said that he had gotten a call from his family and had to return to Qatar. That's all I know," said Akmon.

Immigration had determined that Ali Abdul Aziz Ali had left Madrid on a Sunday morning and had flown direct to Doha, Qatar, on Qatar Airways flight 149, an almost eight-hour flight, and had arrived at three local time that afternoon.

"Ali had matriculated at the university for two years," one of the investigators reported to Captain Garcia. "He was a good student, not top of the class, but performing adequately in all his classes. He was also popular, and he participated in a number of student associations. Wouldn't have given him a second thought except that now we're looking at Middle Eastern connections and of course, he's gone home. Suspicious, no?"

"Suspicious yes," replied Mercedes. "Gino, let's have a chat with Professor Mousa."

Nabil Mousa was an unremarkable man. Short of stature, shiny black hair and a full beard—not unlike many Spaniards—starting to show flecks of gray. In his fifties, he has been at the university for ten years and was also a partner in a Spanish law firm, Duarte y Associados, specializing in immigration.

"Yes, I am very familiar with Azziz Ali," Professor Mousa said to Mercedes and Gino. "I was first approached by his family in Qatar a few years ago to help secure his student visa. The family could have gone through the standard immigration and visa protocols but came to our law firm to complete all documentation and expedite the process, which we did. He seemed like a fine young man. I had him in two of my classes, Administrative Law and Evidence, and he was a good student. He intended to focus on corporate law and return to Qatar and participate in that country's booming economy driven by oil and natural gas exports. He never said so, but I suspect his family may have been connected to the al-Ta'anari royal family in one way or another. While he never flaunted it, I believe there was some affluence in his background. I also remember that he was very anxious to participate in many student activities. He seemed intent to mix with the Spanish students and make friends. I thought that was very admirable," Mousa related.

"Did he advise you that he was leaving the country?" asked Mercedes.

"No. That was surprising. While we were not close, I felt I was somewhat of a mentor to him considering our Middle Eastern backgrounds. I was very much surprised when I got word from the administration that he had left the university."

"Something or nothing," Gino lamented to Mercedes as they drove back to Madrid. "Why don't you meet with the de la Cruz parents and bring them up to date? Carefully though. I'll call Breslau and the Fontanas back in the States and do likewise. We need to inform Interpol and update the Missing website. It may help in the follow-up investigations in the other cities."

"And Nabil Mousa?" asked Mercedes.

"My gut is that there's nothing there. We haven't uncovered anything nefarious in his background, but let's keep tabs on him anyway," replied Gino.

* * *

Ali Abdul Aziz Ali returned to Doha and enrolled in Qatar University assimilating seamlessly into the pre-law curriculum. Qatar actually had an outstanding educational system. The Rand Corporation had been contacted in the 1970s to develop its k-12 system, which was still in place. Branches of Cornell Medical College, Carnegie Mellon School of Computer Science, Georgetown University of Foreign Service, Northwestern School of Journalism, and Texas A&M School of Engineering all had presences in the capital city.

Ali felt quite content to continue his corporate law studies there after completing his mission in Madrid. It had been his responsibility— under direction of his father—to identify the best and brightest female students at the university and report on them to his father via secure email communications. Ammar Abdul bin Ali has been part of the Saqr network since its inception, and despite Qatar being ruled by Sharia law and somewhat shunned by its UAE neighbors over human rights and terrorism issues, it was slowly moving toward modernity. Having achieved the rights to the FIFA World Cup in 2022—perhaps under suspicious means—the kingdom was intent on breaking out of its authoritarian—however justified—image and present a more tolerant face to the Western world.

In addition, Qatar was an important ally of the United States and Europe serving as headquarters for the US Central Command for the Gulf War and the invasion of Iraq in 2003. The USA had a major military base in Qatar, another example of the schizophrenic policies in that part of the world. The ruling royal family walked a thin line between its repressive past—perhaps not so far in the past—and accelerating Qatar's westernization and acceptance by the world community. Ammar Abdul bin Ali wanted to be part of that transformation albeit via very dark methods—employing the services of his son, Ali.

Chapter Twenty-Three

Paz and Frankie settled into their quarters. They were in different areas of the palace—but relatively close to each other—, which had separate sections for each of Sheikh Saud's wives and children. *Harem quarters,* Frankie thought. Samira arranged for each of the women to have a full wardrobe of Western clothing and a bathroom stocked with toiletries. A seamstress made any adjustments necessary to the clothing, and Samira asked them to provide her with a list of anything else they required.

Samira met with the two masters of education—*should be mistresses of education,* thought Frankie, but she chose not to press it—to set up the teaching plan. Two classrooms had been set up—they were meeting in one of them—midway between the family wings, and they were equipped with laptops, telecommunications and audiovisual equipment, whiteboards, and a library in English. Each student had the most up-to-date iPads as would Frankie and Paz. Student desks were not the typical classroom variety. They were more like work stations, the kind you'd find in Silicon Valley enterprises.

"The children, you should know, have had a number of tutors over the years—British for the most part—so they were being educated," Samira told them. "You will see that they are quite bright. Their records and progress are available in our IT systems. But there were always issues, sometimes conflicts with the mothers and sometimes just not connecting with the children. Curricula and teaching plans have been established for each child and have been recently updated based on the Massachusetts Public School System, the finest educational system in the United States rivaling and even surpassing many well-regarded private school systems. Using these curricula, you will have a road map, so to speak, for each child. You each will be assigned two aides, locally educated women with education degrees as we realize your days will be quite busy. I will go over the individual teaching plans for each child with you and your aides. We will start later today."

"You know," said Frankie to Samira, "we're not teachers. We were students just like these children. We've never taught anybody."

"Ahh, but you are smart," countered Samira. "This is why we brought you here. We want you to teach our children in accordance with their curricula, but as important—if not more important—is for you to build their confidence and leadership skills, especially the girls'. We want them to eventually take back seats to no one and whether in government or in business to someday become new leaders in Ras al-Khaimah, or anywhere else for that matter. Not because of their family name but because of their competency. They will need to learn how to assimilate and deal with Western societies, governments, and businesses.

"In the emirates and countries including Qatar, Bahrain, Oman, and now Saudi Arabia, there is a small but growing cadre of leaders, many of who are tied to royal families that rule the country—all of them men—but most of the countries are run by foreigners. Sometimes, that is because the elite do not want to get their hands dirty actually running things. Sometimes, it is because they do not have the necessary competencies to do it. So they bring in others who can, and that goes from street cleaners, construction workers, and shopkeepers all the way up to executives in banking, energy, engineering, and all else. Seventy to eighty percent of the population of these countries are expatriates.

That has worked for a while as we have developed, but it has to change if we are to become respected throughout the world. Our money has to be aligned with our competency and leadership skills.

"In addition, there needs to be a greater emphasis on information technology. Google, Amazon, and Microsoft are powers greater than most governments, and your classrooms will be equipped with sophisticated computer systems. You'll have traditional papers and pencils around, but the children will be working with these new technologies daily.

"Your aides will have special skills in this area, and when needed, we can bring in the necessary—how do you call them?—computer nerds to assist and keep the children at the forefront of this new enlightenment. The palace is very technologically advanced, something the sheikh is passionate about based on his time at Cal Tech."

"The sheikh studied at the Cal Tech?" asked a stunned Frankie.

"Yes, and his brother at Northwestern University," replied Samira. "And our head of IT studied at MIT, so you will have all the necessary resources to draw from. You will have access to high-speed computers. You will be locked out of any email communications and social media, but your computers will meet your information needs. Any issues, come to me and you will have all the technical support you need immediately.

"You said you were not teachers, but you will be, and as you can see, you will have all the support you need to succeed. Also and very important is the fact that you have been brought here against your will. I am sorry about that, but as you say in the West, it is what it is. It may not be forever, but it is here where you will be for the foreseeable future. None of this, however, is to be revealed to the children. We want—we demand—a cordial, pleasant environment for these children to develop. No lamenting, no tears. Do that in your quarters. In front of the children, all is well. Is that clear, ladies?" Samira asked.

Frankie took a deep breath, held back a sob, and nodded. Paz looked at Frankie and then Samira and also nodded.

"And Miss Fontana," added Samira, "you will have additional responsibilities at our equestrian center. We'll discuss that later. Good. Much to be done, but first, you must meet your children, your students. They are fluent in English, and that will be the language in the classroom. And Miss de la Cruz, you will add Spanish to the teaching plan as well, okay?"

Samira rose and left the room. Frankie and Paz looked at each other silently contemplating the daunting task before them. "Christ. Are we fucked!" said Frankie.

"You should never use the words *Christ* and *fuck* in the same sentence, Frankie. Bad things can happen to you if you do."

"Yeah, like getting kidnapped and taken to the middle of the Arabian Desert."

"You're right. Since bad things have already happened, I give you permission to use Christ and fuck in the same sentence."

"*Gracias, amiga.*"

* * *

Samira shortly returned shepherding six children into the classroom followed by three women—their mothers. The children stood in a line dressed in Western clothes with their mothers behind them.

"This is Sheikha Aisha," began Samira acknowledging the woman at the left of the group, "and her children, Mariam and Omar. Mariam is fourteen and Omar thirteen. Both are quite advanced academically and are nearing their high school years, a very critical stage of their learning.

"And this is Sheikha Yasmina," Samira said, gesturing to the woman in the center, "and her daughters Khadijah, age twelve, and Inaya, ten.

Sheikha Yasmina was the second of Sheikh Saud's wives, and you will find Khadijah and Inaya very eager and capable students.

"Last we have Sheikha Angela with her daughter, Hamdah, who is nine, and the youngest of the sheikh's children, his son, Ahmad, who is six. All the children are royalty, but for your purposes, using their first names is totally acceptable."

Looking at the women and then sweeping her eyes across the children, Samira said, "Your highnesses, please meet Miss Francesca Fontana and Miss Paz de la Cruz. Miss Fontana is from the United States, and Miss de la Cruz is from Spain."

Two of the mothers, Yasmina and Angela, were dressed in Western garb, blue and green dresses respectively. Yasmina wore a necklace of silver with blue stones. Angela's necklace was gold with what appeared to be a cluster of emeralds at its center. Both wore moderately high-heeled shoes. Aisha, clearly the eldest of the women, was dressed in a lightweight, white, full-length *abaya* trimmed with gold embroidery, a simple, loosely draped headscarf, and no facial veil. All the women looked serious—no smiles—and each gave a short nod when introduced. The children were more expressive. The two boys did a kind of bow, and the girls curtseyed and smiled broadly all except Mariam, who looked contemplative.

"And Miss Fontana," said Samira, "Mariam is quite the equestrian." She turned to Mariam and said, "Miss Fontana is an excellent horsewoman who has competed in dressage events in her native New Jersey, and we expect you will spending some time together at the equestrian center." Mariam's eyebrows rose slightly at hearing that. Samira addressed Frankie. "Her brother, Omar, is not as interested in our horses but is becoming quite good with his computer skills and the use of his iPad. He often helps his siblings in this area." That made Omar smile and glance at the other children. "But he also gets distracted with sports," which now made Omar bow his head and look at the floor,

"Now I suggest we let these ladies get to work organizing your lesson plans and schedules. In three days—is that okay, ladies?—we will post a weekly schedule for each of you," she said looking at the children. "Then it is back to school."

Frankie and Paz looked at each other and then at Samira with unenthusiastic acknowledgement. "And your highnesses," Samira said directing her comments to the mothers as the entourage was leaving, "feel free to set up meetings with each of our instructors as you deem necessary. While Miss de la Cruz and Miss Fontana were carefully selected by the sheikh, they also are working for each of you."

The women nodded to Samira and moved out the door with their children behind them.

"The individual curriculum of each child is in you computers," said Samira. Handing them each a piece of paper, she said, "Here are the names of the children, their ages, and a summary of their schooling up to now as well as any idiosyncrasies, likes, or dislikes. This too is in the computer. Log on with your name, password Emirates 7, enter 'curriculum,' the name of the child, and it will bring up all information you need. It will also provide instructions on how to update progress, grades, comments, whatever, within each subject and lesson plan. Your aides can help you learn to navigate, which reminds me, you need to meet them."

Samira then rushed out the door and in a few minutes returned with four young women.

"Miss de la Cruz, this is Fatima and Latifa. They will be your aides for whatever you deem necessary including teaching some classes. Miss Fontana, Jumilah and Farah will work for you."

The women, all in their twenties, about the same age as Frankie and

Paz, moved forward and bowed their heads with the introductions. "I think it best that we leave you two alone for a while to sort things out. Someone will be by when it is time for lunch, which might be nice to have with your aides so you can get to know one another."

"Sure," said Frankie.

"*Bueno*," added Paz as Samira and the four aides departed the classroom.

"Shit," said Frankie. "Now I know we're fucked."

Paz laughed. "You're getting to like that word, but we might as well get started at trying to figure this out. We'll have to decide which of us will be responsible for each subject. We'll both work with each child but divvy up who does what, okay?"

"Sure," said Frankie. "We'll lay out the lesson plan for each, probably using Excel Worksheet, then familiarize ourselves with each subject, the instructional guidelines set up for each, and then identify our resource material and the kids' resource materials. Not sure if we use books or if everything is online. God, this is scary. I hope we'll be able to really teach this stuff. Some subjects we probably know shit about, and we start in three days. You're better in math that I am, so you take that. I'll do the sciences. We'll figure out the rest. Need to find out our aides' skills as well."

Paz was silent for a moment. "So we're just gonna do this? Become instructors to this guy's kids and that's that? That's who we'll be?"

Frankie looked at Paz. "That's who we'll be to them. That's not who we are. Samira said we were smart, so one way or another, we'll figure a way out of here. We're somewhere in the middle of the desert, but not forever Paz, not forever."

Chapter Twenty-Four

Most of the oil and gas revenues of the United Arab Emirates came from Abu Dhabi, the capital of the UAE, which shared a part of its earnings with the other emirates, each ruled by a royal family. Dubai on the other hand had diminishing oil reserves and set its future on real estate—the bread and butter of its economy—which had fallen severely. In recent years, however, conditions had improved and a building boom was on again. At times, it appeared that there were as many towering construction cranes in the city as there were skyscrapers.

Ras al-Khaimah was one of the more anonymous emirates along with Fujairah, Ajman, Sharjah, and Umm al-Quwain, all seven countries of the UAE occupying a pointed peninsula between the Persian Gulf and the Gulf of Oman and bordering Saudi Arabia and Oman. Its population was nearly three hundred thousand, and it had been regarded by some as the sleepy sheikhdom, but it was successfully focusing on tourism and trade thanks to a long shoreline of beaches and ports on the Persian Gulf.

Sheikh Saud bin Nassr al-Sisi had been named the supreme ruler of Ras al-Khaimah in 2010 following the death of his father, Sheikh Nassr bin Mohammed, who had ruled for more than sixty years. Originally, succession was to pass to Crown Prince Qasim, another of his seven sons, but in an unprecedented move, the Supreme Council switched the crown prince title to Saud. Qasim was a more confrontational and controversial leader who was opposed to the invasion of Iraq and was seen to be anti-US. The UAE leadership was a close military ally of the US, and the al-Dhafa air base—about an hour from Abu Dhabi—was host to a US Air Command of fighter jets and drone operations, and US Navy ships used port facilities along the coast including ports in Ras al-Khaimah. The country needed a leader to support UAE alliance strategies.

Sheikh Saud was US-educated as was his younger brother, Mohammed, who was named crown prince following his return from university studies at Northwestern. Both had strong backgrounds in technology and business. Economic conditions had greatly improved under this leadership in an atmosphere of political stability and a strong relationship with the US. The brothers, who had been part of Assad al-Amin's Saqr network since 2012, longed for the day when the shackles of perceptions of the Arabian Peninsula were broken.

Images of unorganized, corrupt, untrustworthy, and uneducated tribes, camel herders, and horsemen living in tents and wandering the desert as portrayed in *Lawrence of Arabia* still colored the minds of the West. In contrast to this were the images conjured from the oil riches discovered beneath the undulating sands and the opulence beyond imagination generated among those very few royal families. The first image dated back thousands of years; the second was only half a century old. And then images of the burning Twin Towers in New York, carnage on London subways, massacres in Paris, suicide bombers, improvised explosive devices—chaos. Al Qaeda, ISIS, Hezbollah, and on and on. Terrorism often with support from these same royal families—directly or indirectly.

No, the emirates had to break those shackles. No antiquated dress codes, education for men and women equally with women given opportunities to govern, lead businesses, and compete in the world on an equal footing with Western nations. The brothers believed that day would come, notwithstanding the dark and unorthodox methodologies required to get there.

Chapter Twenty-Five

Assad al-Amin's legal residence was in a high-rise condominium tower in Abu Dhabi. The other members of Saqr lived spread apart in the southern end of the Arabian Peninsula. Sulayman al-Raja lived in Assad's home city of Muscat, Oman; Rasid bin Seray in Doha, Qatar; Hazem al-Sawai in Dubai in the villa where Frankie and Paz had been taken after the flight from Madrid; and Zayed Falaj in Dubai as well. The villa was on Jumeirah Road near the Hudhelba district and not far from the tourist beaches. It was in a row of attached townhouses with two-car garages or carports at street level. As Hazem was the IT expert for Saqr, the villa on Jumeirah Road was well wired to manage all aspects of the operation including the network of Saqr operatives in European cities as well as the member portal. Assad managed all finances using the secure system Hazem had set up. It was a very tight and technologically sophisticated operation.

Assad was opening the Saqr network for an online conference with the others in the unit to discuss the next operation. Planning generally took months. The strategy was never to go back to a university where they had completed an extraction regardless of its prestige or the caliber of its students. Going back to the same country, however, as they had done in England, was considered a possibility; it depended on the input from field operatives there and the logistics.

"We have strong input from Rome, but our last incursion in Italy went badly," Assad said.

"But we had no problem getting the Santini girl out," Zayed, the principal field operative, said.

"True, but having to go back and deal with Raimondi should be considered a setback. I don't want to have to resort to such measures again. It adds to our footprint," Assad said.

"I prefer using student rather than faculty contacts," Rasid said. "We can easily get them out as we just did with Ali in Madrid."

"Yes, but we risk establishing a pattern if we continue with that tactic. We have done that twice, three times now, but classmates of the abductees disappearing a short time after extraction could raise red flags. Ali decided to leave on his own, probably encouraged by his father, but it creates suspicions. No, next time, I want to manage it differently."

"Well, Akram Zaatari at the University of Rome is a senior," Hazem said. "If we go after his target there, he can simply remain in school, get his degree, and return home ..." He stopped to look at some papers, "... back to Kuwait."

"We'll think about it, but I want to review all targets currently identified and our operatives in each location. We must make sure each target is very proficient in English. You remember that the German girl, Jana Weigel, was barely satisfactory in that respect. What do you have, Hazem?"

"On your screens," said Hazem, "click the scimitar icon and a chart will open up." He waited as the others went through the process. "As we discussed, Akram Zaatari is a pre-med student at the university in Rome. His target, Sophia Randazzo, also pre-med, is president of the senior class. On the next line is Khalid bin Mohammed, an engineering student who works part time in the admissions office and has been at the University of Vienna for three years. We found him through his cousin, an Iraqi who left Baghdad at the time of the American invasion and is currently an economics professor at the American University in Cairo. Target, Claudia Schiff, foreign relations student but also a world-class concert pianist."

"The music angle should entice some of our members," added Assad.

"Yes, I think so," replied Hazem. "And last, Omar al-Baluchi, engineering student at the University of Utrecht, Netherlands. He is a junior there, and his target, Gertrudes Muldur, is majoring in advanced math. We have other possibilities, but two are in London again and the other is from the University of Edinburgh. We should put London aside for now. The potential target in Scotland bears watching but needs more time to develop."

"I like Rome primarily because it will be a little easier to enter and depart considering the congestion and confusion all around the city, but the Schiff girl intrigues me. Her music capabilities could create aggressive bidding. I vote for Vienna," said Assad, "but logistics have to be letter- perfect." The others agreed. "So Vienna it is. Hazem, please send us a detailed profile of Claudia Schiff as well as a full background on Khalid bin Mohammed. Zayed, put together all details and options regarding entry and exit points for the operation. It may be best to not use Vienna. Let's look at alternatives nearby. And Rasid, see if we have residence information on the target—where she lives, dormitory or residence, and look at all maps of the area. I want to know the terrain. Okay, Hazem will set up follow-up one week from today. Then we will start to think about a more earnest conversation with Khalid and assess local logistics. *Ma'a as-salaama*"—Goodbye.

Chapter Twenty-Six

An approach to the Saudi prince was being created. The investigation revealed that it was not unusual for a private aircraft to be used without the presence of its owner, which in many instances was a corporation. Businessmen and women were the most frequent passengers having access to corporate jets usually governed by an executive hierarchy. Those who wanted to use an aircraft for business or at times recreational purposes contacted a coordinator, and if no one higher up had reserved a plane's use, it was theirs. Depending on the management level, there was little if any accountability; an executive who wanted to take two board members on a golf outing simply had his or her administrative assistant make the arrangements.

In other scenarios, the very privileged allowed others to use their planes for family shopping trips, ski trips, and vacations without going themselves. This included many members of Middle Eastern royalty across half a dozen countries as was the case of Prince Azam Azziz.

Richard Durand, the US ambassador to Saudi Arabia, requested a meeting with the prince at his Riyadh office. Owing to his role governing imports and exports and with the US being a prominent trading partner, the meeting would not have been considered out of the ordinary, though the two had not met before.

Durand and the prince exchanged the normal pleasantries along with the traditional serving of tea accompanied by a small plate of dates. While the prince was not at the highest level of his ministry, he was high enough to command a large office, which was decorated with typical Saudi artifacts and framed photos of the prince with foreign dignitaries and upper-echelon members of the house of Saud. Brightly upholstered sofa and armchairs were in the middle of the office on what Durand thought was a vintage, traditional Saudi hand-woven carpet, not Persian, considering the Sunni-Shia tensions between Saudi Arabia and Iran. Smaller woven tribal wall coverings adorned other parts of the office. Behind a desk in the rear of the spacious room were floor-to-ceiling windows overlooking the city, which was bathed in bright, midmorning sunlight.

The prince was of medium stature, slim with a nutmeg complexion and a neatly trimmed beard and moustache. Were it not for his hawk-like nose, he would have been considered very handsome. He wore the typical, white *thobe* tunic and a white *ghutra* head scarf banded with a thin red and white cord. The prince beckoned the ambassador to sit and partake of the tea.

"Mr. Ambassador," began the prince, "it is a pleasure to meet you. You have been here in my country for what is it, two years now?"

"Yes, your highness, two years in January," responded Durand.

"And how can I be of assistance to you and the United States?"

"I am here today on a somewhat delicate mission primarily to alert you to some circumstances that could unwittingly affect you and the ministry.

"It has come to the attention of US and European law enforcement agencies that private aircraft are being used without their owners' knowledge in some illicit activities. Many times, aircraft—corporate and personal—can sit on the ground for weeks at a time. In some cases, pilots of these aircraft have been contacted and recruited by drug cartels for quick, in-and-out flights without the knowledge of their owners.

Interpol has been tracing flight patterns, and immigration and customs authorities have noted that the private owners or responsible parties were not on the aircraft cleared by local authorities. In most instances, nothing nefarious was evident, but in some cases, questions arose about the legitimacy of such travel."

Durand noted that the prince's facial expression did not change; he continued to listen attentively with hands folded on his lap and smiling.

"It has been noted that your Gulfstream has been recently used without your being among the passengers in a flight to and from Madrid and last year to Amsterdam. Interpol has raised questions, and I just want to alert you to the situation and make sure that the use of your plane was with your knowledge. I am sure your pilots and flight crew are above reproach, but I feel compelled to advise you to possibly ward off any embarrassing consequences for you, your ministry, and Saudi Arabia itself. I am sorry to bring this up, but considering the relationship between our countries, we do not want any rogue associates to put you in a difficult situation. When this was brought to my attention, I insisted that I bring this situation to your attention rather than Interpol agents."

"Ambassador, I cannot thank you enough for your concern. I appreciate the awkwardness you feel in alerting me to this. However, I can assure you that the use of the ministry's aircraft has always been associated with ministry business or in some instances where I have authorized its use by associates, friends, and family. My plane carries the palm and crossed scimitars emblem on its tail fin. It is the emblem of my country and represents the integrity of this regime, the royal family itself, and as such is beyond reproach. I take that seriously, and any passengers on that aircraft are colleagues I have been associated with for many years on Saudi business, sometimes new and developing lines of business, which is exciting. No." He laughed. "My flight crew members are not part of any drug trafficking network. Never, I can assure you."

"Your highness, that is totally as I expected, but I felt compelled to alert you. Better safe than sorry as they say in my country," said the ambassador, whose face showed relief as he sat back in this armchair and drank some more tea.

The two men then chatted about dates as a plate of them was on the table. Saudi Arabia was among the foremost exporters of dates throughout the world, and they talked about the wide variety of dates produced in the country and their favorite varieties. Then the prince rose again thanking the ambassador for his concern and inviting him to visit more frequently. As Durand exited the prince's office, his administrative assistant, a young man, presented the ambassador with a package. Turning back to the prince, the prince laughed and said, "Dates of course!"

* * *

Azam Azziz returned to his desk and withdrew a cell phone from a drawer. He pressed a single number; Assad al-Amin answered, and Azziz recounted to him the substance of Ambassador Durand's visit.

"My friend," the prince concluded, "we must make some changes in our operations. In hindsight, it may have been a mistake to have my plane so close to your operation. We should even consider not having the whole Saqr team depart the target city together. I understand they came to Madrid via different routes, but if it is manageable, maybe they should depart the same way."

"You may be right, Azam. That was my overconfidence. I also concur that we should make another alteration in our planning and have the aircraft enter and depart from a location farther from where the operation will take place. Our stealth activities and meticulous planning will allow us to transport the individual by car or van anywhere in Europe using remote locations to exit the country. We may need to change vehicles, but that is doable.

"We must also assess the feasibility of paying on-ground authorities to alter arrival and departure details and particularly passenger details. That is more risky, and we have to really think it through, but by recording no passengers on the plane, we will mitigate further suspicion. I think it will also be useful for you to take a few trips to Europe now, maybe to Paris and Amsterdam. We are not close to our next mission, and having you documented as being on board will be useful."

"That's a good idea, Assad. I remain committed to the cause and would hate to have to withdraw your use of the Gulfstream, but I need your assurances there will be no further instances of overconfidence jeopardizing the mission."

"You have my assurance, Azam," replied Assad.

* * *

Back at the embassy, Durand organized a conference call with Undersecretary of State Luxmore, FBI Director Guiness, and Colonel Klaus Schickhaus of Interpol in which he related his conversation with Prince Azam Azziz.

"Well," started Guiness, "with the prince stating that the use of his aircraft was with his authority, we now have a can of worms."

"Yes," replied Luxmore. "As his plane carried five individuals traveling with false passports, it does implicate him, doesn't it?"

"It does," said Durand, "but there is no way I was going to bring that up. We would have gotten nowhere by making such an accusation. It could have created a major diplomatic rift."

"It could have," added Schickhaus, "but the key players in the Saudi administration may be totally unaware of this rogue operation.

This guy's actions would be very detrimental to the king and crown prince and the new image they're trying to create, so at one point, they would want to shut this down. Silently of course. But for now, it gives us something going forward. We can track the movement of that plane and monitor everywhere it goes and who the passengers are. I will set that up immediately. One last point. Considering the delicate nature of this situation, I won't update the Missing website with this information. We'd risk leaks from local police departments."

"Agreed," said Guiness. "I will however update Breslau from the IRT and his agent in Madrid, Gene Cerone. He's the FBI's liaison with Interpol, and I want him on top of where we are. For now, we continue the investigation path we're on, particularly in confirming the presence of that Gulfstream at all the other abduction sites and it's passengers, and going forward, we red-flag wherever it goes."

Chapter Twenty-Seven

Paz and Frankie began their teaching schedule in accordance with the curriculum for each of the children using separate classroom facilities. It was awkward at first—six students of different ages though the twelve-, thirteen-, and fourteen-year-olds were less complicated. Their lesson plans were somewhat similar, differing primarily in the level of instruction. The same could be said for the nine- and ten-year-olds, but the six-year-old boy brought unique learning challenges; he was almost a blank slate.

"Back to basics with Ahmad," commented Frankie one morning. "Reading, writing, and 'rithmatic. Thank God he has a good foundation in English."

"Thank *Allah*, girl. Remember where we are."

They laughed heartily.

"I couldn't help recalling the movie *The King and I*," Paz said. "Anna was brought in by the king to teach his brood, I don't remember how many, but it had to be more than a dozen, *una docena,* no?"

"Maybe more, Paz, but that was a story, and Anna was not a prisoner. Now it's Frankie and Paz and the sheikh of Ras al-Khaimah. Not a story but the real thing."

* * *

One afternoon, Samira came into Frankie's classroom where Khadijah, Omar, and Mariam were working with science programs. Omar and Khadijah were in different biology curricula, and Mariam was in an elementary chemistry program. All three used their iPads extensively to support the lesson plans. Addressing Frankie and Mariam, the fourteen-year-old, she said, "A little break for you ladies. We are going to the equestrian center to introduce Miss Fontana to our wonderful stable of horses."

Frankie and Mariam left the building and were led to a white Mercedes SUV. They sat in back while Samira sat in the front passenger seat. Frankie recognized the driver as the one who had transported her and Paz from the airstrip to the palace. They drove for about fifteen minutes east, Frankie thought, gauging by the sun. She and Mariam had developed a cordial relationship, but the teenager was generally serious; their conversation never strayed beyond the lesson plan. It was the first time the two of them were together outside the classroom, and Frankie thought she'd open some conversation.

"I understand, Mariam, that you are quite an equestrian."

"I like to ride," replied the girl, "and I love horses, but I'm not sure I'd call myself an equestrian. That assumes some level of expertise, which I'm not sure I have."

"But you like to ride, and you love horses. That's a fine beginning. I feel the same way. I miss my horses in New Jersey. They are very dear to me."

"Do you have many horses?" asked Miriam.

"Only two. Wicked, a chestnut mare, and Sultan, my favorite, a gray Andalusian stallion." Mariam and Samira exchanged looks at the mention of Sultan. "My father brought him from Jerez, Spain, after we returned home from that country. I actually won a couple of dressage events with Sultan." She paused for a few seconds and added, "I miss Sultan and Wicked very much."

"But who cares for them now while you are here?" asked Mariam.

"My mother rides as well, and during the time I was studying in Spain, she tended to Wicked and Sultan. I miss her and my father very much as well."

Samira quickly turned from the front seat staring sternly at Frankie. "Ladies, we are here. Miss Fontana, behold the equestrian oasis."

The Fontanas kept Wicked and Sultan at a facility in Bedminster, New Jersey. Twenty-four horses were stabled and cared for there, owned by nine or ten families or legal entities of some sort. It had training facilities that included two dressage performance rings and a groomed horse path through the surrounding woods. The administration building was a log cabin-type construction; long horizontal pine logs with wide motar joints, and a gray slate roof. The stables were untrimmed vertical pine boards, giving them a complimentary rustic look, also with slate roofing. Landscaping was totally evergreen; the facility blending beautifully with the pine forest around it.

The oasis before Frankie, however, took her breath away. Curved stucco walls perhaps ten feet high and the color of a Tuscany sunset circled the facility, softened by palm and date trees around the structure. She made out vertical rows of ceramic tiles inlaid in the stucco every twenty feet or so between the palm trees. She couldn't make out what they depicted, but they added an artistic touch. The entrance, an arched portico, bore an image of Pegasus, the winged stallion from Greek mythology high at its center in ceramic tile with Arabic lettering below. Terra-cotta tiles formed the upper border of the arch as well as caps for the walls. The two sand-colored military vehicles, just inside, on each side of the entrance, did not detract from the oasis image.

Directly opposite the entrance and across a packed sand courtyard was a single-story rectangular building in the same style as the outer walls with that Tuscany sunset coloring and a terra-cotta roof. Halfway toward the building was a fountain, another Midnight fountain, an exact replica of the one at the palace, but smaller. Off to the left and right were other white SUVs each with the Pegasus logo on their front doors. Two additional military vehicles were parked in front of the building. The courtyard itself boasted an assortment of palm and date trees all around the perimeter accented with low bougainvillea shrubs with tiny red flowers.

The SUV with the women parked directly in front of the building, and Frankie noted extensive mosaic tiling surrounding the windows and double wooden doors, studded with what looked like miniature shields each about six inches in diameter with gold points protruding from their centers. The door handles were also of ornate, heavy metal design.

"This is the administrative office of the center," said Samira as they alighted from the SUV and walked toward the building. Inside was an open area with several desks each with flat-screen monitors. The back wall was all windows framed with the same heavy, dark timber as on the outside, with another set of double doors at its center, much like those at the entrance, but without the metal shields. Cabinets, shelving, and a pair of single doors were on each side of the building's interior.

Two young men in traditional tunics rose from their desks to greet Samira and Mariam. They spoke in Arabic, and then Samira introduced them to Frankie. As all was in Arabic, Frankie just nodded and smiled. Neither man extended his hand in greeting—just a simple nod—and they sat. A woman in a white *abaya* with no head covering remained at her desk busily typing away at her computer. Samira led Mariam and Frankie through the door in the back, and Frankie immediately felt the impact of leaving the heavily air-conditioned office and going into the desert heat.

A training ring with white wooden railings was off to the left. To the right was a large, domed circular structure perhaps twenty feet high with low horizontal windows near the top. "This is where we do our dressage training," said Samira. "The enclosed structure is identical in size to the open ring but air conditioned and with a small viewing area. It is not feasible to train outdoors in the summer, so work continues inside that building."

The palm trees surrounding both structures presented an image of a lush oasis in the middle of the desert. An elaborate irrigation system, either from deep wells or via an underground pipeline from a desalination plant at the coast, obviously nurtured these botanical gardens.

Beyond the training areas was a large rectangular building in the same style as the administrative building but taller. "The stables," said Samira addressing Frankie, "but that is hardly an appropriate name. As you can imagine, everything is air conditioned, kept at a constant twenty degrees Celsius. We have facilities for nineteen horses though we have only ten with us right now. The sheikh has additional stables in the United States—Louisville, Kentucky, of course—and another in Italy."

They entered the stable through tall wooden doors that opened automatically after Samira input a code on a keypad. A wide pathway ran down the middle of the building with large stalls on either side. Frankie guessed that the stalls were fifteen feet wide. They had split doors that allowed the animals to protrude their heads. Above each door was a ceramic plaque with the horse's name in English and Arabic. As they walked into the stables, heads appeared from most of the half-doors.

"This, the Pegasus Equestrian Center, is the sheik's pride and joy, home to the finest horses in the Middle East. His Emirati brothers in Dubai and Abu Dhabi might argue that point, but it is true. This is a small stable by some standards, but the sheikh wants a quality training and breeding center, not just a horse ranch. Midnight, the star of our center, is in there," Samira said pointing to a much larger stall on the right side of the building.

Midnight's stall is twice the size of the others. It is almost as big as my quarters in the palace, Frankie thought.

"Come, let's meet Midnight," Samira said leading Frankie and Mariam in that direction.

Midnight bobbed his head and snorted as they drew closer. Mariam stroked his forehead, and nuzzled his muzzle. The horse responded by licking her face and hands obviously delighted to see her.

"I don't ride Midnight," said Mariam, "but I often help clean his stall and brush him. He knows me."

"Midnight is a champion," said Samira. "A purebred Arabian stallion, a rare horse like no other. Black Arabian stallions are not very common, and purebred Arabians are not usually successful in racing. Mixed Arabian breeds with traditional racing thoroughbreds are generally the breeds that succeed, but Midnight has won several European races including the Copa del Rey in Spain, and he has sired a number of champions racing in America. One horse Midnight sired won the Kentucky Derby a few years ago. Yes, he is unique."

The girls spent some time stroking and petting Midnight, and Frankie was thrilled at how he responded to her.

"The other horses we have here are Arabians, Andalusians, and Lipizzaners, which are highly regarded in the world of dressage competition," Samira said. "Let's meet them."

Frankie was very familiar with the Lipizzaner and Andalusian breeds related to the Barb breed, the horse of the Berbers. When her father surprised her with Sultan, she did some research on the Andalusian and visited their training center in Jerez. She was aware that crossbreeding

Arabian and Berber breeds produced the strong and powerful stallions that dominated dressage in Europe.

There were two beautiful, white Lipizzaner stallions. "These horses are actually born a dark color," Samira said, "lightening to shades of gray over their first six to ten years. Then they turn white, but their skin below the white hair is actually black. The black skin is protection against the African and desert sun, where they originated. Today, there are none of them wild in the African nor Arabian deserts—some donkeys however." She laughed. "This is Blizzard and Snowstorm," she waved at them in turn. "Not very Arabian names but befitting their beauty."

They moved to stalls housing four other horses all shades of mottled gray. "These are our Andalusian and Arabian breeds—Silver, Zanzibar, Saladin, and Maestro."

Mariam went to Saladin and began caressing him as she had Midnight. Turning to Frankie, Samira said, "Mariam has started working with Saladin."

Moving to the other side of the stable, Samira pointed to two almost black stallions. "These are our youngest horses, Aladdin and Sindbad, and that mare is Shahrazad, the gray one near the end. Next to her, the Palomino, Sunset, came from California. Sheikh Saud rides Sunset from time to time, sometimes with Mariam on Shahrazad. Just riding, no training."

Mariam had moved from Saladin to Shahrazad, going through her ritual of petting and stroking again.

Moving back to Aladdin and Sindbad, Samira said, "We'd like you, Miss Fontana, to participate in the training of these animals. You might find it a pleasant challenge."

"I'd like nothing better," Frankie said; she thought she saw a smile form on Mariam's face.

Samira then beckoned Frankie toward the back of the stable where there was another pair of tall doors that she opened after punching in a code. Frankie saw a racetrack in the distance; her eyes opened wider. "Yes, a racetrack, Miss Fontana. We aren't working with any potential racehorses right now, but we will."

Frankie took in the racetrack surrounded by white fencing with a viewing stand on one side. In the center of the track was another oasis of palm and date trees, bougainvillea shrubs, and other greenery. *Wow,* she thought. She saw two rectangular buildings on each side of the stable toward the rear of the compound. "That building on the right houses our full-time trainers," said Samira. "We have a head trainer, from Portugal, and two assistants. You'll meet them next time. This is their residence with all the comforts. Over to the left is our supply building. Everything from feed, medicine, and vitamins to all types of equipment—it is all there. A veterinarian visits once a week. He has an office in the administrative building. Now it is time to return to the palace. I think you still have a class to teach, Miss Fontana."

Chapter Twenty-Eight

Guiness updated Gino on the outcome of Ambassador Durand's meeting with Azam Azziz. "We now know he's involved, Gino. Plus, Schickhaus has determined that the prince's plane was present at private air facilities outside Milan, Oxford, and Paris at the time of those abductions. I don't believe in coincidences."

"Neither do I, but I assume there's no way we can confront him on any of this. He's flagged, which will be useful in the future, but as for the past, little can be done for now. I'm sure Schickhaus won't update the Missing website with any of this."

"No. This has to remain confidential. We cannot afford to have any of the related police agencies take independent action. That includes your Captain Garcia."

"Of course, but he always has that plane land in Dubai, so that has to be the center of their operations. What happens in Dubai is a mystery, but we have to find a way to go from there."

* * *

Gino filled Mercedes in on the developments from Saudi Arabia and Interpol including the Dubai connection, stressing that the information had to remain between them for the time being.

"I wonder what level of Dubai's leaders might be a part of this as well," she said. "A prince in Saudi Arabia? Perhaps a sheikh in the emirates? *Mierda.* What a nightmare."

"We thought we had challenges with the Zahori conspiracy, but this has touched six European countries and the US, and now we're up to our ears in the heart of the Arabian Peninsula and maybe their royal families as well. Yes, it's a nightmare. We have our work cut out for us."

"Don't discount the progress we've made," said the always optimistic Mercedes Garcia. "We've tied a Saudi prince to the abductions and pinpointed Dubai as perhaps the center of the whole abduction conspiracy." She laughed. "Why is it that since I met you, we've been going from one unfathomable Arab conspiracy to another? Is there something in your Sicilian background that keeps generating these dilemmas?"

Gino smiled. "I thought that protecting presidents and training Secret Service agents was the ultimate challenge. Now we have eight women to find; God only knows where, but probably somewhere in the Middle East. I think we have to start digging in Dubai—its rulers, culture, politics, economy, whatever. If this is where the investigation is taking us, let's get into it."

* * *

In Abu Dhabi, Assad went over the information provided by Khalid bin Mohammed, the student who had targeted Claudia Schiff for the Saqr network. Originally an engineering student, Khalid had elected for a secondary area of study in foreign relations, not unusual for a student with a foreign—Iraqi—background, and he also worked part time in the administration office.

"This Khalid is a junior and Claudia Schiff a senior," noted Assad in a teleconference call with the Saqr team, "but he has had several classes with her and is very knowledgeable of her stature at the university.

Working in the office, he has an excellent opportunity to access all student information. He knows nothing of our mission, but he has been very active in providing a detailed profile of the woman—where she lives, her schedule, friends, and what they do."

"She's very active with her music and is also a fitness devotee," added Hazem. "She runs almost every day, weather permitting, and regularly uses her apartment complex's gym. Her athleticism is something for us to consider when executing the abduction. The report from Khalid says she runs in the park between the university and her residence. Same park, same route every morning."

Looking at his split-screen monitor, Assad said, "I think you need to travel to Vienna, Zayed, and check out that location. We can't leave such a detail to Khalid."

"I'll leave immediately, Assad. What passport would you have me use?"

"Use the UAE one with the Sharjah residence to avoid the visa requirement, and find a few oriental rug dealers in Vienna. This will be a legitimate business trip. Find a hotel near her university, and use the same park for jogging."

"So I have to pack some jogging clothes and shoes? I may be out of practice," replied Zayed.

"The weather there will be much better suited for running than it is in Dubai, Zayed. And nothing loud or fancy. I don't want you standing out."

"Okay, Assad. I'll leave my orange Pumas at home."

* * *

Two days later, traveling as Muhammed Ussman, a dealer in fine oriental carpets living in Sharjah, UAE, Zayed Falaj took off for Vienna. The rug dealership was legitimate. Saqr owned a small retail business in one of the upscale Dubai malls selling carpets from all over the Middle East and Asia including the course Uzbekistan weaves, Turkish selections, fine new and vintage Persian carpets from Iran, and tribal designs from North Africa and Saudi Arabia. The operation was run by a Turk recruited from Kusadasi, and it did a modest but profitable business. The Saqr operatives always carried brochures and samples of the business to help establish credibility.

* * *

In Lyon, Marie St. Laurant received an alert from Austrian immigration in Vienna—a Muhammed Ussman had entered the country at the Vienna International Airport. Facial recognition systems had identified him as Walid Shaloub, who had entered Madrid three months earlier with a Bosnia-Herzegovina passport. Shaloub, a.k.a. Ussman, was traveling with a UAE passport. When he had entered Madrid, he had a Sarajevo residence listed in his documentation. After checking that out, it was found that the address was a building under construction.

All European airport and immigration points had photos of the Madrid passengers in their systems with a Do Not Detain order. Interpol was to receive the alert, and tracking and surveillance was to be initiated by local undercover authorities. No other action was to be taken. The Interpol plan was to identify the individual, assess travel documentation, garner all information regarding the purpose of entry, and then track the individual's movements while in the country—where he was staying, whom he met with, and all activities he engaged in.

Zayed's time with the immigration officer took longer than it did with other non-European Union visitors, and he began to feel uneasy as the officer kept typing on his computer and reviewing his documents with great care. He frequently lifted his eyes to look at Zayed and then returned to his typing. After what seemed like an interminable period, the officer stamped the Ussman passport and cleared the Emirati without comment. As he had only carry-on luggage, Zayed exited the airport and hailed a taxi for the Hotel Royal, a small, family-run hotel in a quiet area of Vienna next to St. Stephen's Cathedral.

More gears began to turn after Vienna alerted Interpol. Liaising with local UAE Interpol agents, the Sharjah residence listed on Ussman's passport proved to be false also—another building under construction with no residents. But again, there was a UAE connection, and he was traveling from Dubai.

A black Mercedes sedan with two plainclothes officers followed the taxi bearing Muhammed Ussman to his hotel. The delay orchestrated at immigration had allowed Vienna police to organize their surveillance. In Lyon, Schickhaus contacted the Interpol branch in Vienna and arranged for two agents to liaise with the Vienna PD for around-the-clock monitoring of Ussman.

Gino was brought up to date on all, and he immediately apprised Guiness in the States. "This is a watch-and-report operation, Shane. There have been no reports of the other four from Madrid entering Austria or anywhere else in Europe for that matter, at least not yet."

"But that doesn't mean a different set of operatives we're not aware of haven't entered somewhere," replied Guiness.

"Right, but this guy entered via a commercial flight. No record of the Saudi's plane anywhere, so maybe it's a one-off thing. That's why the surveillance is so critical. This is a real break. I hope it'll lead us somewhere important. I'll keep you informed, Shane."

Gino then had a thought. He called Schickhaus. "Klaus, can you find out the rest of this Ussman's flight itinerary? When is he scheduled to leave Vienna, to where, and by which airlines? The return flight is vital. When and to where? We'll need to set something up at that other end."

"He came in on an Emirates Air flight from Dubai arriving at one this afternoon. My guess is that if he's returning to Dubai, it'll also be on Emirates Air. I'll get right on it."

Chapter Twenty-Nine

Muhammed Ussman paid visits to two oriental rug establishments in Vienna, and the local investigators later determined that there were discussions about Uzbekistan carpets, a rougher, thicker, and more durable weave typical of some of the nomadic tribes in Asia. That was a variety they did not carry and had told the salesman—Ussman—that they would think about it.

The Viennese investigators also determined that the man in question spent considerable time wandering about several of the university campuses—they were spread throughout the city—and a park near one of the buildings. He jogged there in the morning, stopping to take pictures. When not jogging, he strolled with a camera always around his neck. The attention he was paying the university and some nearby student dorms was a big red flag.

Zayed made no physical contact with Khalid, but he sent him cryptic texts more frequently than he had, and he had several explicit telephone conversations with him. Khalid was unaware of Zayed's presence in the city. Reporting to Assad, Zayed apprised him of the logistical issues they would deal with and the feedback he had received from Khalid.

"This Khalid is quite an eager young man," Zayed said. "He of course has no idea of our intentions but is always asking what more he can do, though I told him he was doing all we required of him. I told him that our contacts would be less frequent and that he should no longer initiate any contact with me unless he detected any change in the Schiff girl's activities. I also advised him to get a new cell phone and to destroy the one he has been communicating with. I'll have two thousand euros delivered to him before I leave, which should make him very happy."

"Okay," Assad replied, "but are you sure you have enough to lay out the extraction plan?"

"Almost. Once back home, with the photos I've taken, I'll draw explicit diagrams and maps covering all logistics and determine when another visit will be necessary."

"Good. As usual, Rasid will find us a van and I'll work with Prince Azam to determine when the plane will be available and where our exit point will be. I do not want it to be in the Vienna vicinity, so we'll likely have a bit of a distance to travel. Azam's pilot will be doing some research on this as I will, and we should have a good idea of exit point options in a week."

"Is this something we would want Khalid to check out? Have input from someone on the ground?" asked Rasid.

"No, absolutely not," replied Assad firmly. "He knows nothing of our operation, and I want to keep it that way. Our dealings with Khalid have ended unless he has to contact Zayed for some reason."

* * *

"Muhammed Ussman has a reservation on Emirates Air 126 to return to Dubai in four days. His flight leaves at ten forty-five p.m. and arrives in Dubai at six twenty the following morning," Schickhaus told Gino. "I have two agents in Dubai who can track him once he lands."

"You'll need more than two agents, Klaus. I've worked surveillance of this type when I was with the service. We'll need around-the-clock tracking with a full team of agents. Let me check with the bureau to see if they have any assets in place there. I'm sure the CIA does, but using multiple agencies will only complicate things. Let me see what Guiness has to offer. In the meantime, get in touch with your guys and have them prepare. I'll get back to you."

Gino called Guiness about this development. "I can get an IRT team to Dubai by tomorrow," Guiness said, "but this is touchy. Our team typically liaises with local authorities, and as no crime has been committed in Dubai yet, I hesitate to bring them in—officially—on this."

"We definitely can't make the Dubai authorities aware of our activities, Shane. We already know that the Saudi connection with Prince Azam makes a government connection suspect, regarding if and to what degree they're involved in this. As all law enforcement down there is government managed and directed, we can't take any chances. They could be involved or simply could be looking the other way. Could-haves aren't an indictment, but this has to be a totally stealth operation. We can always apologize later."

"Okay, no IRT involvement. You said Schickhaus can give us two agents. I do have a couple of people there, stringers of sorts. I imagine that Interpol has agents there owing to issues of human rights and human trafficking. While the Dubai government may not be totally complicit, it does own everything. All those palm islands they've been building have been built by foreign workers, and there's a history of keeping those workers in undesirable conditions. It may not be human bondage as we think of it, but it's close. It wasn't too long ago that there was considerable trafficking in camel jockeys, children really. Now, they use little robots as jockeys and the races are managed with computers and iPads. Despite their clean, super-modern outward image, there is some darkness there. The two stringers I have there can be added to the Interpol team, Gino."

"And Mercedes and I can complete the rest of the team. With six of us, we can do a good job finding out where this Ussman or Shaloub goes after arriving in Dubai. If you're okay with it, I'll assume command. You can advise Schickhaus of the plan and then get me contact information on your two guys."

Guiness paused a few seconds before responding. "Okay, Gino, it's your game. There might be some blowback from the other police agencies that they aren't more involved as the Spaniard is. I'll let Schickhaus manage that if it gets out, but it shouldn't. As you said, this must be a stealth operation, and for now, it's largely an Interpol operation aided by agents with police authority, you and Captain Garcia. And a point of clarification here. My two guys are actually a married couple who run a travel agency there. The guy is American, ex-FBI who retired to Dubai, and his wife is an Italian who worked with IBM down there. No taxes made Dubai a desirable place to set up home and a business. IBM had some issues in Dubai and asked the FBI to get involved, and that's how the two met. We have used them from time to time, and since they have their own business with a competent staff, they have some freedom to assist the bureau. His name is Fred Leamington, and his wife is Gisella. I'll give them a heads-up and send you their contact information."

"Done," replied Gino, "and have Schickhaus send me contact information on his guys, assuming they're guys."

Gino walked to Mercedes's office. "My dear, pack a bag for a week. We're going to Dubai."

Chapter Thirty

Paz's and Frankie's teaching responsibilities were becoming more manageable—more comfortable really. They had decided when they had come to the palace to comply with the mission that had been set out for them. The relief that they weren't being sold into some prostitution ring or other bondage scheme made them decide to go with the flow as Frankie had put it—work with their captors until they could figure a way out of there. Plus, the kids were innocent about what was going on, and they seemed decent enough, so they resigned themselves to let's be teachers.

Frankie and Mariam were getting along especially well. Their schedule allowed them to be at the equestrian center three times a week—every Wednesday, Saturday, and Sunday. The head trainer there was Portuguese, João Carvalho, who had studied under Nuno Oliviera, the great master of Lusitano stallions— a breed similar to the great Andalusians—at the Portuguese School of Dressage. His assistants, three of them, were Indian, from Goa, a former colony of Portugal, where the Portuguese influence was still going strong. As was Carvalho, they were fluent in English.

Carvalho—whose Portuguese name oddly enough, meant hors— worked with Mariam and Saladin on her visits to the equestrian center. Frankie and one of Carvalho's assistants, Fabian, worked with the younger stallions, Frankie with Aladdin and Fabian with Sindbad.

Carvalho had set up a very basic program to begin with; he and Frankie each worked to build a relationship with their animal and gain its trust. That meant grooming and walking them and making them familiar with the riding equipment. The animals would be walked for many days dressed with bridle/drop-nose bands, saddles, side reins, and long lines, with the trainer holding and touching the horse with the lunge whip. Only later, would the rider mount the stallion and with the assistance of the other handler holding the reins, get the horse to be comfortable with the rider's weight. Once the rider was astride, balance and rhythm were most important and then setting a cadence and proper length of stride, all the while developing clear communications with each other. Mounting and dismounting were repeated, keeping the horse calm and trusting.

Sindbad was a bit friskier than Aladdin was, and Frankie was pleased she had the easier one to work with. Despite her enjoying the visits to the center and working with these wonderful animals, Frankie felt challenged by her teaching responsibilities. She wanted to be good at this, but that was something she found hard to embrace given her circumstances. She wanted to tell her captures to go to hell and suffer the consequences, but the kids were innocent of the sins of their father—and probably mothers—but she hardly saw the women and had no idea of their roles—if any—in this nightmare.

Paz felt the same, and one night over dinner, she told Frankie about a project she was working on. "I've introduced Spanish into the program for all the children. Just basic stuff, key words, conversational phrases, no complex grammar, just something to keep them comfortable."

"I gathered that," said Frankie. "I meant to talk to you about it. I saw some words and phrases on the walls in your room, and the other day, Mariam greeted me with '*Buenas tardes, Señorita* Fontana,' and I knew that was your doing."

"Right," said Paz, "but I'd like to build a little more fun into it. The kids are generally serious and committed to learning, but there aren't a lot of smiles. They pay attention and do the homework religiously with no goofing around like we saw in our classrooms from time to time, but a little laughter wouldn't hurt."

"I have an idea, Paz. When I was in the sixth grade, when I began to learn Spanish, I had a teacher, Mrs. King, who really made the learning process fun. We had cooking lessons, like making paella and learning all the ingredients in Spanish. And once, we put on a fashion show, runway and all. We dressed up in outfits of our choice and then paraded down the center of the classroom describing the clothes we were wearing—colors, fabric, style, whatever. And of course we paraded like fashion models, the girls and the boys. She showed us a video of a real fashion show, and we took it from there. Learned a lot too. I wore a communion dress and made believe it was a gown. Walked, stopped, turned, smiled, and told them what I was wearing. I said it was from the House of Sherry—my mother. *La Casa de Sherry.* I remember it well."

"That's a great idea. Certainly the older kids, especially the girls, are familiar with fashion considering they go shopping to Dubai with their mothers regularly. And have you noticed that they all wear designer clothes, top brands like the clothes Samira got for us to wear?"

"Okay, we have a project, and we can work on it together since I'm fluent in Spanish. Two questions. Do they have enough Spanish to carry it off? And do they just wear their regular clothes or get something special?" asked Frankie.

"We have to think this through. I can start by posting fashion and clothing words all over the room along with colors and clothing terminology such as cotton, wool, silk, long, and short."

"I'm in," said Frankie. "Think Samira will give us a hard time with this, or maybe Mariam's and Omar's mother, Aisha, who wears the traditional *abaya?*"

"I don't know, but if we include an *abaya* in the fashion show, that should make everything cool."

"Mrs. King should know we're going to make her famous in the middle of the Arabian Desert," added Frankie.

Chapter Thirty-One

As his alter ego, Muhammed Ussman, Zayed Falaj wandered the university buildings and jogged and strolled in and around Meip Geis Park, which was near the Kabelwerk housing complex where Claudia Schiff resided. The university did not maintain student dormitories, but students had a wide variety of private apartment buildings to choose from, and one of the green and yellow Kabelwerk buildings on Gertrude-Wondrack Paltz was where the Schiff girl had lived for several years. There was also a cemetery and wooded area near AmKabelwerk that afforded the Saqr operative a number of possibilities for abduction and escape.

In between his reconnoitering, he made repeat calls to the oriental rug stores he had visited; the Austrian officers shadowing him being directed not to make any inquiries there—at least for the time being—for fear of alerting Ussman to their surveillance. They did know that one of the dealers was Iranian and the other a Turk, both longtime legal residents of the city with no untoward suspicions in police files.

After a week, Ussman checked out of his hotel late one afternoon and took a taxi to Vienna International Airport. Emirates Air 126 was not scheduled to depart to Dubai until 10:45 that night, so Ussman had a leisurely dinner and browsed airport shops. During his week in Vienna, his Saqr colleagues as well as Prince Azam Azziz's pilots, analyzed a number of airport facilities outside the city. Ultimately, the

Innsbruck Kranebitten Airport was identified as a suitable site for the team's departure from Austria. The airport was 475 kilometers from Vienna, about a four-hour car ride, in the Tyrol's most popular ski area. That location would not allow for a quick exit from the country following the abduction of the Schiff girl owing to the drive, but it was deemed to be the safest in light of the American ambassador's visit to the prince. There was far less airport security, and it was accustomed to hosting affluent ski enthusiasts coming and going with all sorts of luggage in tow, none of it small. The exit plan was taking shape.

* * *

Gino and Mercedes had taken up residence at the Sheraton Jumeirah Beach Hotel in Dubai, selected for no other reason than the reasonable $163 per night rate. They had read about Dubai's seven-star, sail-shaped *Burj al-Arab* hotel that had become the iconic symbol of this emirate city- state but chose something that would not cripple the FBI's budget. Once settled, they planned to meet with the Interpol agents, Raymond Kapur and Rajesh Mitra, both British of Indian descent, who would easily blend in with the Dubai citizenry. They maintained a small office in one of the scores of office high-rise buildings in the city. Interpol had established an open presence there as part of an ongoing human trafficking surveillance operation. All the construction going on in the city often led to workforce abuses, and Interpol was always monitoring and at times challenging practices. The FBI assets, Fred Leamington and Gisella Guigno, joined them for breakfast the day after their arrival.

"We obviously cannot set up a surveillance plan until we know where this Ussman or Shaloub guy is going and leads us there," said Gino. "We know his flight itinerary, but we'll wait for confirmation that it hasn't changed." Looking toward Mitra and Kapur, Gino added, "Your boss, Klaus Schickhaus, will call as soon as he knows. I hope he'll lead us to somewhere in the city. Otherwise, it could be a problem to keep tabs on him. But assuming he stays here and we don't have any logistical complications, the six of us can set up two-man teams … Sorry, ladies, two-person teams, with four-hour shifts. That way, no one will always be stuck with the night surveillance, which will help keep us alert."

"Of course it depends on where he goes and what the logistics look like," Leamington said.

"I know," replied Gino. "I don't want to get too ahead of ourselves here, but it doesn't hurt to map out some of the basics and alter them when we need to. For now, we wait for Klaus's call. We know that flights from Vienna leave in the evening and get here in the morning, assuming he stays with that schedule. Klaus will confirm he gets on that flight."

"Let me suggest that Rajesh and I stake out the airport and we track him from there," Kapur said. "We know the airport and the city, and it won't be difficult for us to set up a tail, me on the inside and Rajesh outside in a car. It's the busiest airport in the world, but we have some credentials that would allow a standby vehicle outside the arrivals area."

"Why don't Gisella and I keep circling the airport in another car, just in case," Leamington said. "A backup."

"Great," said Kapur. "It's a really early flight, so the airport will not be at its usual congestion, but I welcome your help."

"Let's program our cell phone numbers into our phones," Mercedes said.

Gino was writing in his notebook with two different colored pens, and they all looked at him. "What?" he said looking around the table. "My checklist. I like using different colors."

Mercedes smiled and rolled her eyes. She'd seen Gino's penchant for Technicolor planning.

Putting his pens away, Gino said, "Mercedes and I talked about doing some touring while we wait. We probably have a couple of days, and we'd like to get more familiar with the city. We have maps, so we'll be tourists for a while and try to get the lay of the land. It looks like quite a large city, in fact, considering the number of clusters of high rises we saw from the plane, it almost looks like several cities all bunched together."

"Remember that Dubai is a city and a state. It would be as if New York City was a state of its own," Leamington said. "It's unusual in many ways including the fact that about eighty percent of the population are foreigners with one kind of work visa or another. Lots of Indians especially in the service and retail industries. But in construction, which is everywhere as you can see, it runs the gamut from Bangladeshis, Indonesians, Filipinos, Thais, and Malaysians and more and more Chinese popping up everywhere."

"That's where Dubai started to run into trouble," Mitra said. "Those palm islands you hear so much about were built by foreign workers sometimes in almost slave-like conditions. That's when Interpol got involved. There has been some improvement, now that they know they're under scrutiny, but there's always slippage."

"Are you guys known by the authorities?" asked Mercedes.

"Yes, but only in certain ministries and obviously with the construction firms," replied Kapur. "For the purposes of this operation, I foresee no problem."

"*Bueno,*" said Mercedes.

The members of the group felt there was no need for another meeting at least until they were alerted about Ussman's travel.

Gisella said, "Let us set up some sightseeing for you and Gino. We run a travel agency. Instead of your wandering around with a map, let us handle all that for you."

"That's great," replied Gino. "We were going to ask the concierge, but I forgot—this is your business. When can we do this?"

"We have some standard city tours with all the top attractions. Maybe I'll tweak one a bit. I'll have a car pick you up at the hotel, let's say at one o'clock. There will be a driver and a tour guide. Then tomorrow morning you can start at nine, okay?"

"Absolutely. We'll be outside the lobby at one."

Chapter Thirty-Two

A black Mercedes SUV pulled up in front of the Sheraton at one sharp. A slim gentleman in black slacks and a crisp, white, short-sleeved shirt exited the passenger side of the vehicle and approached Mercedes and Gino "*Señor* Cerone and *Señorita* Garcia I presume? Mr. Leamington described you to me. I am Alex."

"Nice to meet you, Alex," replied Gino. He and Mercedes shook hands with him, a man of medium height with a tanned or natural complexion and short, black, and receding hair. He opened the SUV's door for them and introduced them to Salem, their driver.

"Mr. Leamington has planned this afternoon and all day tomorrow to acquaint you to Dubai," Alex said. "If time permits—and I do understand that business could take you away at any time—we can continue your orientation beyond that if you desire."

"Sounds good," Gino replied. "We can play it by ear."

"Your English is excellent," added Mercedes. "Are you from Dubai?"

Alex laughed. "No one is from Dubai, *Señorita*. We all come from somewhere else. That is the nature of Dubai and its residents. I am originally from Beirut, but I have been living and working in Dubai for …, for almost fifteen years now. But Salem," he said nodding at his driver, "is somewhat of a rarity."

Salem smiled at his passengers. He was a dark-skinned man with a red and white checked head covering wrapped in the form of a small turban; he appeared to be wearing a white tunic. "Salem is an Arab but not an Emirati. He is from Kuwait. Most of the other residents and workers are foreign nationalities, with few Arabs."

"I have been told of this phenomenon," Mercedes said. "An expatriate community taken to the nth degree."

"It's a good place to live with more and more people retiring here. It's the most modern of cities. There are no taxes, and you can buy absolutely anything you want. In fact, I have heard some foreigners say that they should change the spelling of Dubai to Do Buy," Alex said laughing. "Further, no alcohol restrictions and no dress codes. It's certainly an Islamic nation, but they don't crush you under its weight. All those buildings you see—those completed and those under construction—are condominium towers, some filled, some only partially occupied. Other condos are purchased for speculation or future use. It's a boomtown again after the recession of the last few years." He waved his arm, and Mercedes and Gino took in the forest of building cranes throughout the city as they pulled into traffic.

"I know Dubai is one of the richest places in the world, but most of the cars I have seen are Toyotas, Kias, Hyundais, cars of little distinction except for the Mercedes taxi cabs," Gino remarked.

"Ahh," replied Alex, "that is because you are seeing the automobiles of the workers—our workforce. You need to wait for the evening when the workers are at home and the Emiratis come out to play. Then the Lamborghinis, Porsches, BMWs, and Ferraris take to the streets. They visit the finest restaurants, fill up the discos, and generally rule the evening. Members of the royal family, the businessmen, bankers—the affluent—come out to play."

Gino and Mercedes looked at each other with raised eyebrows and smiles.

"This afternoon," Alex said, "we'll begin with a visit to the *Burj al-Arab*—the Arab Tower— the sail-shaped, seven-star hotel not far from here. In a disc-like structure protruding almost from its pinnacle, tennis greats Andre Agassi and Steffi Graf held a tennis exhibition and Tiger Woods drove a golf ball into the sea. The building has become the symbol of Dubai. They're also known to have the best high tea, but perhaps we'll save that for another time as we have a lot to cover."

Following a quick visit to the *Burj al-Arab* and a walk around the lobby and shopping areas, the group drove to the *Burj al-Khalifa*, reportedly the tallest building in the world. From the 124th floor observation deck, they we treated to breathtaking views of the city and shoreline.

"Look toward the sea," Alex said. "From here, you have an incredible view of the famous Palm Islands. Landfill brought from the ocean floor was shaped like a giant palm tree. The trunk and palm fronds are filled with elegant structures and marinas. Condominium towers, restaurants, and hotels dot the newly created land, and astronauts have reported that the Palm Islands are visible from outer space. We'll get a closer look at the Palm Islands later in the tour, but their beauty and the marvel of this engineering feat can be appreciated only from a great height. The most coveted hotel rooms offer a view of the Palm Islands."

As they drove, Mercedes and Gino saw mall after mall filled with shops of the finest designer labels. "Each neighborhood with its tall residential and office buildings seems to have its own super mall though some are more distinctive than others," Alex pointed out.

They drove to the Mall of the Emirates, which had a tall, curved structure protruding from one end of the building.

"What's that?" asked Mercedes.

"Why don't we wait until we get inside?" Alex asked, as Salem slid into a parking space in the underground garage. Alex guided them to a glass-enclosed section of the mall that looked like an Alpine village complete with snow. "This is a twenty-two-thousand square meter ski resort," said Alex sweeping his arm toward the glass enclosure. "It's cold in there as you can see from the clothes the visitors are wearing. Artificial snow keeps the village inside perpetually snow-covered. Ski lifts take the adventurous to the top of the mountain for a half-kilometer run down the slope, that gray protrusion you asked about earlier, *Señorita* Garcia."

"I've heard that you can ski down sand dunes in Namibia, right on the sand, but snow skiing in the Arabian Desert is a new one."

"I know what you mean by Do Buy," Gino said. "With money, it seems you can do anything around here."

Visits to the Jumeirah Mosque and the Sheikh Mohammed Cultural Center, typical tourist destinations, made up the rest of the afternoon after which Alex instructed Salem to return to the hotel. "We can continue perhaps with a Dubai by night tour later if you wish," offered Alex.

"No, no," replied Gino. "We're worn out. Let's pick this up in the morning."

They said their goodbyes and agreed to a nine o'clock pickup time the next morning. A shower, some cocktails at the hotel bar, dinner, and sleep completed their evening—no mingling with the Emiratis at discos.

* * *

Alex and Salem were at the Sheraton promptly at nine the following morning. "Today, we start with the Jumeirah area of Dubai, an affluent residential and commercial area," Alex said. "We'll walk along the Jumeirah Beach Promenade. At this hour, it's still pleasant to walk, and after being in and out of this automobile all yesterday afternoon, a little exercise would be good, no?"

"Fine," replied Gino. "We'll follow your lead."

Salem remained with the SUV as they reached the promenade area. "He'll pick us up at the other end," Alex said.

The promenade walk was delightful; Gino and Mercedes walked hand in hand getting a good look at the neighborhood, the residences, malls, and numerous coffee shops and on the other side, the crystal-blue waters of the Persian Gulf dotted with beaches and marinas. They encountered all levels of people on the promenade from joggers to couples strolling and parents pushing babies in strollers. The mode of dress ranged from light and casual, as Gino and Mercedes were dressed, to women in jeans and *hijab* head coverings and others in full *abayas* and *burqas* with only their eyes showing. The promenade was pristine. Gino thought that he had not seen a piece of litter anywhere.

The walk eventually to them to a dock. "We will now take a short boat ride in and about Dubai Creek, which meanders throughout the city, and then into the Palm Lagoon and out to Atlantis and the Palm Jumeirah we saw from the *Burj al-Khalifa* yesterday," said Alex.

The Dubai Creek was anything but a creek, as you would find in mountains or forests. Calm and blue, it was surrounded by high-rise buildings and hotels along with marinas full of gleaming white yachts and sailboats. Returning from their inland tour, they boarded a sleek yacht and entered the Palm Lagoon for a close-up view of the Palm Islands.

"These islands are one of—if not *the*—most luxurious residences in all Dubai," Alex said. "Besides sand from ocean dredging, stones and boulders form the base of the landfill brought from mountains as far away as Oman and Jordan and were finished with earth to form the land to build on. We're in the lagoon system, but the palm islands extend into the Persian Gulf. You can imagine what it took to build this foundation on which these buildings were constructed."

From the boat, really a small yacht, Gino and Mercedes saw

numerous docks and marinas adjacent to the residential towers. Close up, they saw streets and automobiles, and were it not for their view of this wonder of the modern world from the *Burj al-Khalifa*, they could never have imagined the shape and scope of the land created from sand, stone, and dirt. It looked like a normal, luxurious shoreline, if what they were seeing could be called normal. Luxurious was a poor adjective for the Atlantis Palm Island Hotel, which was identical to the iconic hotel in Nassau, Bahamas. The Atlantis was a tourist destination unto itself.

After the boat ride around the lagoon, Alex asked if they were ready for lunch.

"Yes," replied Mercedes, "but something light and fast."

"Not a problem. You can find anything and everything in Dubai."

Salem was there as they alighted from their pleasure craft, and he drove them to one of the malls where they found an elegant sandwich and salad restaurant, where they had a delightful lunch followed by excellent espresso.

"Now we'll visit a few of the famous souks," Alex said, "some elegant and modern and a few more-traditional, older souks, sometimes called bazaars. Perfumes, spices, jewelry, clothing, handicrafts—everything is available in the many souks here."

The Meena Bazaar was a tale of two cities. The modern Dubai outside contrasted with the narrow streets and lanes in it where vendors sold everything imaginable, from elegant jewelry to souvenirs of all kinds. The covered, wide streets and walkways of the gold souk included two levels of stores selling only gold jewelry, from simple to filigreed pieces of all sizes and designs. Pendants, bracelets, chains—shop after shop—all seemingly managed and operated by Indians. "The Indians," said Alex, "are the foremost gold merchants in all the world, and Dubai is probably the world's most important gold retailer, as is this souk."

Mercedes tempered her personal interest in many of the items with the knowledge that women's lives were at stake—their mission here in Dubai—but Gino encouraged her to buy something. After venturing in and out of many establishments and fending off eager Indian salesmen in and outside of each, Mercedes eyed a gold pendant in the shape of a traditional Arab pitcher. "You must bargain," advised Alex, and after some satisfactory haggling, which she was very good at, Mercedes came away with her piece and a gold chain packaged in an elegant, embossed, red pouch.

"*Estás feliz?*" asked Gino. "You happy?"

"*Muy,*"—Very, replied Mercedes, trying to subdue her smile and kissing Gino's cheek. "*Gracias, mi amor.*"

Alex directed Salem to drive to the Alras area of the city, to the Deira Old Souk on Dubai Creek near to the Dubai spice souk, where Mercedes and Gino smelled many aromas.

"I don't think you are in need of any spices, but this souk is frequented by locals. The many ethnicities residing here can find absolutely anything they need to prepare dishes of their homeland. These spices are also important in Arabian dishes as well, but why don't we take a quick look at the Old Souk over there," Alex said gesturing to a building not far away.

Entering the souk, they were greeted by a labyrinth of stores and shops, some merely alcoves, selling everything from gold jewelry, antiques—or newly created antiques—pitchers, curved knives, silvered chests, candle holders, and all things silver. Other shops featured bags, scarves, typical Arab dress items including tunics or *thobes* for men, women's *abayas,* dressier *kaftans,* and *kettnyeh/ghutra* headwear in various colors and patterns. The paths of the souk were hard-earthen, narrow, and dimly lit at times, with simple light bulbs hanging from cables. Gino mused that if they had been there without Alex, they'd need a map to find their way out. It was a world far removed from the bright, white, and modern environment outside.

They called it a day just after five. On the way back to the hotel, Alex said, "We'll be here again tomorrow at nine unless you advise me to the contrary."

"*Bueno,*" remarked a tired Mercedes as they bid goodbye to their guides.

Chapter Thirty-Three

Ussman boarded Emirates Air flight 126 flight at 9:55 p.m. on February 6 as per his itinerary, exactly six days after his arrival in Vienna; it was scheduled to land at 6:35 the following morning. Gino got a text from Schickhaus alerting him of the flight.

He then got a call from Ray Kapur giving him the same information. "It's on us," Kapur said. "We have plenty of time to rest up tonight before he arrives bright and early in the morning." Borrowing a phrase from Sherlock Holmes, he added, "The game is afoot."

Gino called Leamington and asked him to tell Alex they wouldn't be touring the next day.

Kapur had studied Ussman's Vienna entry passport photo very carefully. As it had been recorded by Austrian immigration the previous week, it was clear that their target had shaved his beard since his Madrid entry making him less identifiable for surveillance, but it was the same man.

In the morning, Kapur was in the terminal with a clear view of arriving passengers. The flight board showed that Ussman's flight had arrived on schedule. Kapur was apprised by the Austrian authorities that Ussman had only carry-on baggage. He also knew that Ussman's seat on the flight was 27A, so it would be a few minutes before he emerged.

And soon, there he was—a slim man with black hair, a little long at the back, carrying a brown leather jacket. Vienna was a lot colder than Dubai at that time of year—or at any time of year for that matter. Ray texted Rajesh, who was positioned outside, and slowly followed Ussman out of the terminal. He also alerted Fred and Gisella, who were driving around the airport as backup for the Interpol agents. Their target hailed one of many taxis. Even at six-thirty in the morning, the airport was busy, but nothing like the congestion that would be there later in the day.

Ussman's taxi drove toward the Jumeirah area, exiting at the beach neighborhood with luxury condo towers and private residences. The taxi slowed as it passed villas and townhouses, most attached and a few semi-attached. Rajesh stayed well behind; he was sure that neither the driver nor Ussman suspected they were being followed. Brake lights went on about halfway down the block on Jumeirah Road. The taxi stopped. Ussman got out and quickly walked to a villa. As the taxi drove off, Rajesh proceeded up the block and noted the location of the villa, a white, multilevel building. The front door was up about seven or eight steps. Most other villas they had passed had covered carports, but this one was one of very few with a garage.

With the location noted—there were no house numbers in Dubai—Rajesh and Ray made note of the adjacent buildings and then drove around the neighborhood block by block looking for areas to set up surveillance with their car, which looked like it would not be easy. Ray called advising Fred to lay back as they had the area well covered. He took many photos of the neighborhood with his phone and returned to take a few more of the Ussman/Shaloub residence.

Ray called Leamington again. "Fred, we're leaving the area. It's clear that surveillance from cars is not practical. There's nowhere to seclude ourselves around here. I need you to do some research. Go on the internet and check for villa rentals on Jumeirah Road. That's our best option. As you know, Dubai is starting to use GPS coordinates for house numbers, but without that data, we can't pinpoint a location. When we speak with a realtor, we should be able to tighten up locations as we will need to rent something on the other side of the street from the Ussman villa. We can set up there if we can get something."

With all the speculative investment in Dubai real estate, condo and villa rentals were abundant.

Ray and Rajesh assessed their situation. "We can keep driving around here hoping to see if the guy leaves and what kind of car he drives, but that could make someone suspicious," Rajesh said.

"I know. Plus, we'll have to start pulling strings to find out who owns or rents that villa. It's a long shot, but I'll see if Schickhaus's computer people can find out anything. Our data in Dubai doesn't include private residences unless they're part of a trafficking investigation. I'll send him some of the photos we took. Our hacking team can be quite resourceful, so it's worth a shot. Even Google Earth might help, but renting a villa on that street will be our best option."

Ray texted the rest of the team bringing everyone up to date and waited at the end of the block for Leamington to get back to them on the villa rental search. They decided to ride around for a while and soon found a beach parking area a block away but with no view of the target villa. There they waited for about fifteen minutes before they got a call from Leamington.

"Tons of villas in the neighborhood available for rental, Ray," Leamington exclaimed with some enthusiasm. "It looks like one company, Jumeirah Rentals and Luxury Suites, manages most of them. Costs are all over the place depending on size and length of stay. We'll need to sit down with someone there and work it out. You buying?" he asked.

"Interpol will probably be on the hook, but first let's figure how to go about this," Ray replied. "I'll leave Rajesh here so he can cruise the area every so often just in case, and I'll take a taxi to the Sheraton. I'll call Gino and Mercedes. Let's plan to meet there in twenty minutes. Besides, I need some breakfast. I was lucky to get just coffee at the airport."

Chapter Thirty-Four

Fred arrived at the hotel armed with the villa rental options he had printed out from various web sites. Aziz, Emaar, and Ammac were the top property management agents in Dubai, but Jumeirah looked the most promising. He also conceived a plan for setting up a surveillance operation. Over breakfast with Ray Kapur, enjoying almost everything on the menu, he went over his idea.

"Gino and Mercedes have come to Dubai for an extended vacation and are looking to rent a villa in the Jumeirah area, maybe even make an investment in something long term," Fred said. "We'll make an appointment with someone at that agency. A few have the ten-digit GPS smart codes listed. I'll accompany them, being the travel agent who arranged their visit. We'll focus on those near the Ussman villa. We'll shoot for a one-month lease. I'm sure that won't be a problem. We'll include language dealing with options for extending, purchase, whatever. Good?"

"Very good," Mercedes answered as Gino nodded. "From what Ray and Rajesh said, there's no other way to maintain surveillance on Ussman. What about garages?"

"They said that Ussman had a closed garage but that most of the other properties around there had only carports. We'll take what we can get that offers the best view of the Ussman villa. But if you guys think you'll need a car, we'll have to rent a BMW or something that fits in. If any of us visits the place we rent—and we'll have to—maybe it shouldn't be in the weathered Toyota we tailed him in."

"Fred and I drive an Audi," said Gisella, "so no problem there."

"Good," Gino said, "but a key question is do we use our actual passports for this transaction? They'll require ID. Do you think there'll be any financial checks to secure the rental?"

"Shit, maybe," replied Leamington. "If we include language in the lease covering options to buy or extend the rental, they'll likely want to know where the money's coming from."

"I can get Interpol to transfer up to a hundred thousand euros to Gino's bank account in Madrid," said Kapur. "This is an important operation for us. We'll use Gino—it's Eugene, right?—as this will be more acceptable here. Men continue to rule the roost in this society. Sorry, Mercedes."

"Not a problem. No egos. We need to get this done and fast, so whatever works."

"Okay," said Ray. "I'll need your bank information, *Eugene,* and I'll contact Schickhaus to see how fast that can be arranged. We'll need the full range of costs for these rental options, security deposits, fees, taxes, whatever to determine how much we need to transfer, but a hundred thousand euros will probably be plenty if anyone checks on that. Gino would be expected to have other investments, so his net worth won't be gauged by just what's in his checking and savings accounts. I'll get on the phone now. We might be able to have a transfer made by midday."

"And background checks?" asked Gisella.

"I don't think it'll go that far," said Kapur. "We'll use your actual passports for ID. Gino is a retired American businessman living in Madrid. If pressed, he'll say he was in the security business, and we leave it at that. The agency wants the business. There are just too many properties readily available, and if the money's there, they'll be happy.

There isn't enough time to set up new IDs and background histories for the two of you. You're retired, made your money running a business and investing in the stock market, and you and your fiancée are living the good life in Madrid. You're looking at Dubai for a possible second residence, maybe something even more permanent, considering the tax benefits this country has to offer."

"We have a plan," said Gino. "Once the transfer has been made, we meet with the Jumeirah rental agency. Maybe from there we can find out more about our neighbors."

"One more positive," Leamington said. "Their systems are in English, so once we get a GPS location code, we may even be able to access that and find more about who's living in that villa."

"Let's be diligent with expense records. Interpol has a competent accounting department that will want to know what's happening with their money," Kapur said.

Mercedes and Gino looked at each other. "But of course," they replied, smiling.

Chapter Thirty-Five

Paz's plans for the fashion show—*De Moda* she called it—were coalescing nicely. Joining Frankie and Paz one morning, Samira said she had no objections to the fashion show nor had any of the mothers, each planning on taking an active role in the project, and all intended to be there.

The children were given the assignment of selecting outfits—anything in their closets or acquired from anywhere in the palace, or get their mothers to buy new clothes for them. As promised, Paz made the case that at least one of the outfits should be traditional Muslim dress. Most of the children nixed that idea; they wanted to find something more creative. "I tried," lamented Paz, but then Mariam said she would do it. Paz exhaled a sigh of relief.

All the children would be models and their own catwalk narrators about the style and items of clothing and any accessories. Their narrations would describe their ensembles with a variety of adjectives that described color, design, shape, length and material.

The older kids—Mariam, Omar, and Khadijah—would have an advantage with the language, but Paz and Frankie put key words all around the classroom in Spanish and English and built such references into their iPads. They gave the children some phrases they could memorize or read from cards. They would work with Paz and Frankie to polish their descriptions, learn how to walk, point to the items they were wearing, and smile at the audience. As an example, Paz narrated what Frankie was wearing, as Frankie pointed to what Paz was describing. Because of Ahmad's age, Paz and Frankie decided that Frankie would be his catwalk narrator.

Most of the children were indecisive about what they would wear, but Omar, age thirteen, was very clear. He chose to be Real Madrid's soccer star Cristiano Ronaldo, with the Fly Emirates logo emblazoned across the front his uniform. Mariam would wear a *kaftan*, a dressier *abaya* with complementing *niqab* headscarf.

Inaya finally decided she'd like to be Princess Yasmin from the story Aladdin and the Magic Lamp. Frankie turned to Samira with a surprised look on her face that asked, *Where did that come from?*

Samira laughed. "Before you came here, the children had an English tutor, Katherine Maye. She made use of well-known children's fairy tales to help them learn English. The story of Aladdin and the Magic Lamp was taken from One Thousand and One Nights—Tales of the Arabian Nights as you might call it. These tales are well known and one of the oldest pieces of literature from the Middle East dating to the thirteenth or fourteenth century."

"I'm familiar with those tales," said Frankie. "In fact, half the horses in the equestrian center have names from those stories, and by coincidence, the horse I'm working with is named Aladdin."

"Yes of course," Samira said smiling. "The tales are a favorite of the sheikh. For the children, however, Miss Maye used modern adaptations of the classic tales including picture books. The children read about Aladdin and his adventures—genies and magic carpets and all—and his quest for the hand of Princess Yasmin. The children also read about Sindbad the Sailor and Ali Baba and the Forty Thieves, modern versions written as children's tales without the more sultry texts of the original stories. She also used fairy tales from Hans Christian Andersen, the

Brothers Grimm, and others, again lighter versions without the dark segments of the original tales. The children loved the stories as children probably do worldwide, and the illustrated books allowed them to picture the wonders they were reading about—and above all learn English."

"Princess Yasmin, that's a good idea," said Frankie to Inaya. "Quite appropriate," she whispered to Paz, "considering where we are."

When the others heard of ten-year-old Inaya's idea, they started mumbling among themselves and questioning their original thoughts about the fashion show. "Can we use fairy tales for our costumes too?" asked Khadija.

"Sure," said Paz. "Whatever and whomever you like."

"Then I want to be Beauty," said Khadija.

"Beauty?" queried Paz.

"Yes, from Beauty and the Beast."

"Beast? Yes! Can I be the Beast?" six-year-old Ahmad blurted out. "Can I? Can I?"

Paz and Frankie laughed along with Samira. "I guess so," replied Frankie, "but you all better check with your mothers. If it's okay with them, no problem."

"I want to be Gerda from the Snow Queen," nine-year-old Hamdah called out.

Frankie remembered the Hans Christian Andersen story, having read it when she was young. She also remembered it as kind of scary as the Snow Queen was quite evil. "Have you ever been to a place as cold as where the Snow Queen lived?" she asked.

"Oh no," said Hamdah, "but it would be fun to dress as someone from that frozen place."

The next day, the children arrived at class beaming. "Our mothers said we could dress up like our fairy-tale characters," Khadija said to Frankie and Paz.

Frankie thought that a family outing to one of Dubai's many malls would likely get the children everything they needed for the fashion show. *If not,* thought Frankie, *the sheikh and his wives undoubtedly have access to the finest tailors and seamstresses in the world.*

* * *

The day of the fashion show arrived. An audience section was set up in the classroom. To their surprise, besides Samira and the mothers, Majid Khan as well as Sheikh Saud bin Nassr were seated. *Shit,* thought Frankie. *This better be good.*

The children had rehearsed mostly on their own but at times had asked Frankie and Paz for some help especially with the words for some accessories they were to wear. They rehearsed the whole catwalk procession and commentaries. Paz had thought about having the spectators judge the fashion show and select a winner, but she discarded that thought; she didn't want any losers, especially considering the way the kids had enthusiastically embraced the project and the laughter she had heard when they rehearsed. She and Frankie decided that this would be a fashion show by the fictitious Emirati designer Ali Baba, and programs were printed up with that heading and the list of models and the characters they chose to emulate.

After a brief description of the event in English and Spanish, Paz moved off to the side and pushed a button on the audio equipment. They heard Enrique Iglesias, one of the most popular singers in Spain and throughout Latin America—and son of the world-famous Julio Iglesias—singing *"Bailamos,"*—We Dance—an upbeat song that would give the models a spirited cadence to their promenades, not too fast or too slow; and soft enough to not overpower the narrations.

The children picked numbers to decide on the sequence of the catwalk models—the catwalk being a red carpet running twenty feet, just the right length to allow the models to walk down, pause, turn, stop, and return, turning and stopping one more time before they ended their processions. Frankie and Paz had shown the children tapes of male and female models in fashion shows, to give then an idea on how it was done. Paz and Frankie wanted Ahmad to close the event expecting the six-year-old to steal the show.

Mariam was to be the first down the catwalk wearing a traditional *abaya*. Those in the audience almost lost their breath when Mariam stepped out onto the red carpet and said, *"Yo soy Shahrazad,"* the heroine of the One Thousand and One Nights fables. She was wearing a full length, white ensemble with gold and black trim on the hem, cuffs—which flared out at the wrists—and belted in the same design at the waist. At the left shoulder was an embroidered, gold appliqué embellished with beads of white and red. It was stunning, and she suddenly looked much older than fourteen. Her *hijab* was of the same chiffon and crepe material as the *abaya* but worn tight to the head and perfectly framing her face. Gold thread and small white beads were woven into the garment, around the head just at the forehead and vertically from the center of her forehead, up and then down the back of the turban-like headpiece. At the center of her forehead hung a red stone trimmed in gold and dangling loosely from the gold embroidered thread. On her feet were white and gold slippers with the traditional pointed and curved tips at the toes. Her walk was slow but rhythmic and in time with the music. Stopping at the end of the runway, turning and looking at the gathered audience, she described her *vestido*—dress—as *blanco con adornos de oro y seda negra*—white trimmed in gold and black silk. The material was de *chifón y crepé*. Pointing at the applique on her shoulder, she described it as *un bordado de oro con perlas y cuentas rojas*—embroidery with pearls and red beads. Lifting the hem of her *abaya,* she pointed to her shoes of *seda blanca y de oro,* and then she touched the stone at her forehead and said, "*Y un rubí, un regalo de mi madre,*"—And a ruby, a gift from my mother. Aisha beamed as Mariam turned and retreated up the runway, stopping, turning again, and then quickly exiting from the red carpet.

Everyone applauded as Mariam went into the adjacent room, where the other models waited. Frankie and Paz were stunned and her presentation but more so at how she looked. They hadn't seen the outfit, Mariam having preferred to keep it a secret from them, but they wondered where and when such an elegant dress—*abaya* or *kaftan*—would be used. Undoubtedly at something very formal. *And God, did she look beautiful,* they thought.

Omar followed and was great as the Real Madrid football star gently kicking a soccer ball, a *pelota de fútbol*—his accessory—down the runway perfectly describing his white uniform and his *blanco y rojo*—white and red—athletic shoes. He paused and seemed to take great pleasure at pointing out with a broad smile the Fly Emirates logo across his chest—the Emirates Airline being a major sponsor of the football club. "*El mejor aerolínia del mundo,*"—The best airline in the world,— he added as he turned and pushed the ball back up the red carpet and then lofted a kick toward the open door in the back of the room yelling, "*Gol!*" as it soared through. Almost in unison, the sheikh and Madjid stood, raised their arms, and yelled, "Gooaall!" laughing.

Hamdah, Angela's nine-year-old, followed as Gerda, the heroine from the Snow Queen who saved her friend Kai from the evil queen of the frozen north. In Dubai, Hamdah's mother had found a red velvet cloak just as Gerda had worn in the story, perfect for her walk down the runway. Hamdah wore her dark hair in a braided pigtail that hung halfway down her back, and she took joy in swinging it as she strolled to the music of Iglesias. Spinning at the end of the runway so her cloak would flare out, she described the cape as *terciopelo rojo*— red velvet, *cubrido con estrellas blancas*—covered with white, star-like embroideries—representing snowflakes—*copos de nieve*. She pointed to her red fur boots—*botas de piel roja*—and stood on her toes as she swirled again. Last, she pointed to her head, where a white fur hat— *sombrero del pelo blanco*—adorned her black hair. She swirled again, retuned up the runway, stopped and turned again, and curtseyed before she turned and left looking every bit the heroine of the frozen north.

Angela led the cheers standing while the audience applauded.

"Not bad," whispered Frankie to Paz, who nodded in agreement with a broad smile.

Ten-year-old Inaya emerged as Princess Yasmin, the heroine from *Aladdin,* carrying a magic lamp and standing on what was assumed to be her magic carpet, placed midway down the runway before her entrance. Her outfit was turquoise silk, *"Seda de turquesa,"* she explained, also with a glittering organza overlay. She wore ballooned pants snug at the ankle, and she pointed out the curved, pointed slippers also turquoise on her tiny feet. The outfit was beautiful. What normally would have been a bare midriff was covered with the same turquoise silk. However, everyone was mesmerized by the perfectly coiffed, shiny black wig she wore, full and flowing long below her bottom. Standing on her magic carpet of typical oriental design with long fringe on either end, she held her *lámpara mágica*—magic lamp—to her chest rubbing it until a stream of white smoke emerged from its tip.

Everyone gasped. Frankie turned to Paz. "How the hell did she do that?"

"How the hell do I know? Probably dropped something into water that was in the lamp. Undoubtedly had some help from the palace staff." She laughed. "Talk about creative."

Inaya turned, the audience still in shock, bent down to roll up and pick up her carpet, and went back up the runway turning just her head as she smiled at the audience, who were cheering.

A tough act to follow, but twelve-year-old Khadijah, as Beauty, then stepped to the head of the runway, and everything quieted down. She was resplendent in a gold, ballroom gown, "Hecho de raso de ora,"—Gold satin— she pointed out running her hands along the bodice and then to the billowing folds of the dress. Blue ribbons of silk—*cintas de seda*—hung loosely from the waist and flared out as she swirled rather than just walked down the runway. She wore a full wig, brown with golden highlights, with soft, smoothly flowing curls down to her waist. She stroked the gold gloves on each arm, *"Guantes de oro,"* she pointed out running from above her elbow and covering each tiny finger. At the end of the runway, she swirled and swirled to the beat of *"Bailamos,"* the blue ribbons extending horizontally until she stopped. Then she lifted the hem of her gown to reveal her Cinderella-like shoes of glass—*"Vidrio, realmente plástico,"*—Glass, but really plastic—she whispered. They were amber colored with tiny wedge heels. Khadijah turned and continued swirling to the music until she reached the end of the runway. Like Hamdah, she curtseyed holding out her gown widely as she bent and bowed. *Elegant* was the word that came to the minds of the spectators.

Frankie picked up a microphone and announced, *"Y ahora, el Bestia,"*—And now, the Beast. Six-year-old Ahmad, barely more than a meter high, strolled out to the top of the runway wearing a black cutaway tuxedo with tails, trimmed with gold on the wide cuffs on the sleeves and down the edges of the tuxedo tails. As Frankie would be doing the narration for Ahmad, the trick would be for him to recognize what she was saying and then point to what she was describing. The plan was to keep it simple for Ahmad, but the audience was intrigued because the boy was wearing a full mask, truly becoming the Beast. Frankie described the "*Smoking de negro, hecho de raso,*"—tuxedo of black satin, "*bien adornado con seda de oro,*"—trimmed with gold silk."

Ahmad successfully pointed to the tuxedo and then the gold trimming the cuffs on his sleeves and the full gold lapels. He strolled to the music a little more bouncy than the girls had been and stopped at the end of the runway. He turned to his audience, whom he could barely see through the eyeholes in his mask. It even had little horns above the ears and a mane of hair hanging to his little shoulders. Pinned to his white, ruffled, silk shirt was a large blue stone Frankie described as a *zafir auténtico,*—an authentic sapphire—and Ahmad dutifully pointed it out. His boots—*botas*—were black and shiny with brass buckles, and Ahmad lifted each leg to show them off.

When Frankie paused in her commentary, Ahmad turned and strode back up the runway ignoring the music and walking like a six-year-old. At the end of the runway, he turned, crouched, and roared like a beast. The audience convulsed in laughter and applause and all rose to their feet.

Paz turned off the music, took the microphone from Frankie, and moved to the middle of the runway. She beckoned for all the models of the Ali Baba Fashion Show to come out to the runway and take a bow. Ahmad removed his mask and revealed his giddy smile. Paz thanked the audience and the models and asked each to take another bow as she called out their real names and then the characters they had portrayed. Applause continued for several minutes; the children were smiling at each other and their parents. They turned and were gone.

Frankie and Paz breathed a sigh of relief. "We pulled it off!" whispered Frankie to Paz. "Mrs. King would be proud of us."

Surprisingly, the sheikh approached the ladies, shook their hands, and thanked them for a fine show. "Truly spectacular, ladies," he said, very proud of his children. "What a way to teach a language." He turned, his white robe swirling as he and his entourage exited the classroom. "Brilliant, simply brilliant," Frankie and Paz heard him say.

It's gonna be hard to top this, Frankie thought. *It would be nice if he sent us home.*

Chapter Thirty-Six

Fred Leamington had made an appointment with Victoria Westbury, an agent at the Jumeirah Villa Agency, and later that afternoon, he, Gino, and Mercedes arrived at her office, which was in one of the many modern commercial towers dotting the city that featured restaurants and offices on the lower floors and luxury residences on the upper floors.

Westbury, a slim, middle-aged blonde with a strong British accent, was fully prepared with a listing of available rentals. She offered them tea or coffee, which they declined, and they sat in comfortable leather chairs in front of her desk. She explained that there were many more possibilities for apartment rentals given the number of condominium towers in the Jumeirah area, but she was able to find a number of villas she was prepared to review with them. She turned her computer screen to the visitors and started to go through the available properties.

"We do have a few properties on Jumeirah Road, but not a large inventory there. As I mentioned to Mr. Leamington, we have many more apartments available for short-term rentals close to or on Jumeirah Road and at very favorable prices, but I understand that you are interested only in villas and specifically furnished residences."

"That's right," replied Mercedes. "We like the privacy that a villa provides, and we're very interested in that area. We'd like to move in as soon as possible, so furnished is our best option."

Ray had taken photos of the Ussman/Shaloub residence as they had driven around the neighborhood, so they knew where it was and wanted something on the other side of the street.

Westbury took them through what she had found; Gino and Mercedes took their time and asked all the appropriate questions. Westbury told them that until very recently, Dubai did not number houses, so mail could only go to PO boxes. Sparked by the advent of Uber, they had to devise an electronic map system to identify where Uber drivers could pick up fares. More important was for the need for ambulances and police to get to a location in need. A smartphone system named *Makani*, "my location" in Arabic, was created whereby GPS coordinates of specific residences were identified and a ten-digit location code was established. Many hotels, condos, and office buildings had posted their official Makani numbers though they were not always visible from street level, but private residences lagged behind largely because many of their owners were not living in them. The agency was in the process of establishing Makani codes for all properties they managed. Without knowing where the properties Ms. Westbury identified on Jumeirah Road were in relation to the Ussman villa, Fred showed her a photo Ray had taken. "This is a villa that could be of interest to my clients. I took it because it had an enclosed garage. That might be more desirable. Can you tell by the photo if that property is available?"

"That looks like one of the properties we rented. If it is, it's unavailable, but let me check that out." Westbury scanned the picture Fred had given her and quickly came up with the appropriate Makani code for it. "As I thought, that villa is a long-term rental, but most of the villas in that vicinity do not have enclosed garages, but they are very nice." She pulled up a series of pictures on her computer. "This unit across the street from the villa you identified is a twelve-hundred-square-meter property with carport space for two cars. This other one is a little farther down the street on the same side. It's a little smaller but also very nice."

"Yes, those two look interesting," said Gino after reviewing interior and exterior photos on the screen. "Are they available for viewing?"

"Available right now if you'd like," replied Westbury. "My car is in the car park below."

Gino, Mercedes, and Fred stood almost in unison as Westbury grabbed her handbag; she led them out of her office and to the garage and her white, Mercedes S-Class sedan. *The real estate business in Dubai must be good*, thought Gino.

Fifteen minutes later, they pulled into the covered carport at Makani code ending in 9528.

"As I mentioned, there are a few other villas in the neighborhood, but as you require a furnished property, we are down to only the two I reviewed with you," said Westbury.

"Are there many full-time residents here?" asked Mercedes. "As other properties are unfurnished, I wonder if we would be the only ones living here."

"Your observation is correct. There are many speculative property investments in this area, but on this particular street, there are quite a few leased properties with full-time residents," she replied as she pointed to villas on the other side of the street, where the trio saw the Ussman villa. Gino and Mercedes looked up and down the street and then observed that the parking area, while not enclosed, was well recessed below the villa providing some privacy.

Inside, everything was white marble; while the agent went on about appliances, the number of flat-screen TVs, furniture, and the like, Gino and Mercedes gravitated to the view from the living room, which looked out on Jumeirah Road at the house across the street at a slight angle to the left. *This is almost perfect for surveillance purposes*, thought Mercedes looking at Gino, who knew what she was thinking. They took their time strolling through the property, checking out bedrooms—there were four—bathrooms, the kitchen, and the view out the back. Gino had cautioned Mercedes, "No smiling," and she walked through the rooms with a noncommittal look on her face. "And the other property?" Mercedes asked not wanting to express interest yet.

Westbury took them to the other villa, which was about a thousand square meters and a little less expensive but equally elegant. But it had no clear view of the Ussman villa, and the carport was a little more exposed. They nevertheless took the full tour of the three-bedroom unit asking questions and appearing to seriously consider the villa.

"As I mentioned at the office, we have other villas across the street—all unfortunately unfurnished—where the afternoon sun bathes the front of the house. On this side of the street, the afternoon sun is perfect for sunbathing and using the pool, but ocean view is a bit blocked."

"Yes," said Mercedes. "I like this side of the street better, but I expect everyone tries to avoid the afternoon sun in the summer. It gets quite hot, doesn't it?"

Victoria Westbury smiled and nodded.

"What do you think, Gino?" Mercedes asked.

"Both villas are nice. Why don't we return to your office and see if we can come to an equitable agreement on leasing cost and when we could move in. Oh, and you said this villa's Makani code ended in … 9528. Just curious. The numbers are so hard to see. What's the code for the villa across the street?"

"I have it right here," Westbury said accessing her iPad. "It ends in …9523."

Back at Westbury's office, Mercedes asked about the neighbors. As they would be considering an option to buy, she explained, Mercedes and Gino wanted more insight about the neighborhood and its residents.

Westbury went to her computer and began to pull up information from their files. She explained that next door to 9528 on the right was a German couple—the Kohls—part-time residents in Dubai mostly in the winter—Munich's winter—but they were not there at this time. "The property at 9526 is unoccupied … The property at 9524 is currently occupied by an elderly couple from Oman. They spend most of the year here, and I believe they are in residence now. Modern people, Muslim, but not very traditional. I think the husband was educated in England."

"And across the street?" asked Gino. "It would be nice to know whom the rest of our neighbors might be."

"Ahh, the picture you showed me. A bachelor, a relatively young man, resides at 9523, but the villa is leased by a company," she replied as she scrolled through her computer files, "Saqr, or something like that. Give me a moment. Yes, Saqr is the name, s-a-q-r. He's a businessman. I understand that he travels a lot but is very quiet."

"I noted a few antennas and satellite dishes on that house," Leamington said.

"Yes, I think his business is computer technology, and while I haven't been inside since leasing, I imagine that has something to do with his work. He has a long-term lease and has resided there for a few years."

"Interesting," remarked Gino. "What's his name?"

"I have it here someplace," said Westbury. "Ahh, al-Sawai, Hazem al-Sawai, an Emirati."

Fred discretely texted Gisella, "Check out a company, Saqr, and the name, Hazam al-Sawai."

They got down to money. The villa at 9528 was listed at AED 57,000 per month, about €13,000. The house at 9536 would run €11,000. Gino and Mercedes confirmed interest in the 9528 property and ultimately negotiated an AED 50,000 price, €12,000, and the euro price was used for the contract. One month in advance, one month security deposit, and a discounted option for extended lease terms and to purchase included. Details regarding money transfers were laid out. Immediately after receipt, Westbury would give them the keys and they could move in.

* * *

Leamington called Ray Kapur; they all agreed to have dinner that night at one of the Sheraton restaurants.

Gisella advised the group that Saqr is listed as an oriental rug retailer, selling quality carpets from throughout Asia and the Middle East. "They have a store in one of the malls here in the city. Nothing on the name Hazam al-Sawai; quite a few al-Sawai's but no Hazam amongst them. Maybe he needs all those antennas for that business, but I think not."

"Thanks Gisella, good to know, but now we need to think of surveillance. We need to set up some cameras and sound-detection equipment," said Gino. "Have you used that kind of equipment before?" asked Kapur.

"Camera surveillance, yes, including night-vision equipment," Gino replied, "but not long-distance voice and sound-detection stuff. Some of our guys in the Service did, but not me personally."

"Ray, why don't you and Rajesh look into this," Mercedes asked. "You probably have the contacts to bring in some technical help. And bring Schickhaus up to date."

"I'll get on it first thing in the morning."

"Think about recording equipment also," added Leamington.

"And I'll call Guiness," Gino added. "The time difference is in our favor. I'll call him after dinner. For now, Mercedes, why don't you pick out a good wine?"

Chapter Thirty-Seven

Zayed took a few hours to get organized for his conference call with the Saqr team that Hazem was setting up after his return from Vienna. He had gotten some sleep on the flight, but he brewed strong tea to help his brain cells awaken.

"All is in order," he reported. "There seems to be a satisfactory place for taking the girl. She jogs early each morning near a wooded park. I will have to return to Vienna and lay out all logistics more precisely and develop an operations plan."

"And what about the vans we'll need?" asked Rasid.

"We'll need to be on the road for a few hours until we get to our exit point, and that puts us in jeopardy once the authorities start looking for the missing girl."

"If all goes well, no one should be looking for Schiff for quite some time," added Assad. "We should be out of the country by the time the authorities get involved, but we need to guard against any unforeseen possibility. That is why we will need two vehicles. Rasid will be in Vienna a week before the abduction date scouting around as usual for a van to steal. That will need to be done in the very early hours of our extraction plan, and it will be our abduction vehicle. However, as Rasid correctly pointed out, we'll be on the road for several hours and cannot be in a vehicle police will have identified as stolen. Sulayman, therefore, will be in Vienna to help us organize our ski outing in Innsbruck."

He heard muted laughter from his colleagues. "Yes, we will travel to Innsbruck as a group of skiers, and Sulayman will legitimately rent a van, buy some ski equipment including large bags to hold skis and something else.

"Sulayman and Rasid will find someplace where we can abandon the stolen vehicle and move the girl to the rented van. Then we'll all drive to Innsbruck and our flight back to Dubai. The rented van will be returned to the agency at the airport after all its cargo has been placed on the plane. All very open and aboveboard and no one looking for a van that was a legitimate rental."

There was agreement all around, and Zayed was instructed to put together a draft operations plan including dates for his return to Vienna to fine-tune the abduction scenario.

* * *

Zayed stayed that night at the villa with Hazem and was awakened the next morning by the shrill ring of the phone he used for his contacts with Khalid bin Mohammed in Vienna. *What the hell can he want?* thought Zayed trying to shake the cobwebs out of his head. "*Marhaban*"—hello, mumbled keeping the conversation in Arabic as usual.

"Salaam, my friend," replied Khalid. "It is done."

"First, I am not your friend. You provide services for me for which you are handsomely compensated. And what is done?" Zayed asked, sitting up in bed and swinging his legs over the side.

"Claudia Schiff," Khalid answered. "She has been taken care of. It was easy. Each day, she leaves her residence at the Kabelwerk apartments on Gertrude-Wondrack and runs in the Meip Geis Park. At the area where there are woods, I took care of it."

"What are you talking about?" demanded an agitated Zayed, as Hazem entered Zayed's bedroom.

"She is dead. I did the work for you."

"Are you mad?" screamed Zayed. "I didn't want her dead! Who said I wanted her killed? You fool! What have you done?"

"Only what I thought you wanted," stammered Khalid. "You had me follow her and trace all her movements. I thought you wanted to assassinate her, make her, her family, the university, and the country suffer for how they treat us."

"Praise be to Allah. May he give me the strength," muttered a bewildered Zayed, looking at Hazem. He rose and walked to the front window tightly squeezing his phone and staring out but not at anything. "Tell me, has anyone seen you this morning? Were there any people near the park? And how did you kill her?" Zayed rattled off the first thoughts that came to his mind.

"Killed her?" exclaimed Hazem.

"No, no one at all saw me," Khalid said. "It was still almost dark, and I just came out of the trees, came up behind her, and stabbed her three times in the back very quickly, and then I fled. I was back in my apartment in no time."

Zayed's stomach ached and his head throbbed as he tried to make sense of the catastrophe. "You said you stabbed her. What did you do with the knife?"

"It is in the Vienna sewer system blocks from the park," Khalid replied very nervous from the reaction of his contact. "I of course wore gloves, so there would be no fingerprints."

"And your gloves?" asked Zayed. "What did you do with them?"

"They are with yesterday's garbage. There was a sanitation truck on Otto-Bondy Platz, and the Pakistani workers were at the buildings retrieving the refuse bins. I simply threw the gloves into the back of the truck along with all the other garbage there. By now they are gone, maybe already at the incinerator facility. All is fine, I assure you. Now I must go. I have to be at the office in a half hour."

"Yes, yes. Go," said a now subdued Zayed. "Say nothing to anybody. Do everything that you usually do today. If that means going out now for exercise or jogging, continue to do it. Change nothing. Are we clear?"

"Yes of course," Khalid replied, "but I thought there would be praise from you."

"Yes, but you surprised me," said Zayed. "You were very brave to take this initiative." He did not want to rattle Khalid any more than he had. "Now go about your business as usual, and please, no more calls to me. Destroy your phone, and get rid of it where it cannot be found. I will get a new phone to you immediately, and I will call you, but only after a few days. No contact until you hear from me, Khalid."

Khalid picked up his backpack and prepared to leave for his university office. *He just didn't think I could do this*, he thought. *Now he knows I am a special asset for him, and Allah Akbar, I can do more.*

* * *

Klaus Schickhaus called Ray Kapur later that day. "Ray, it might be a coincidence, but a woman, a student, was attacked early this morning near her student residence in Vienna. The Austrian police have informed me that this was very near the area Ussman frequented last week. There's a park and a cemetery nearby, and the girl, Claudia Schiff, runs there most mornings. I'm informed that she's one of the best students at the university, top of her class."

Ray digested the information for a few seconds. "Interesting, but the people we're tracking don't kill their targets. They take them."

"I know, I know, but top of her class, among the very best students—sounds like our profile, no? Just a coincidence?"

"We know not to trust coincidences," Kapur said. "You said she was attacked. Is she dead?"

"No, not yet anyway. Stabbed multiple times, possible damage to her kidney. The fact that she was wearing a padded vest—it's still quite cold in the early morning there—may have saved her life. She's probably still in surgery. There's a first-class medical facility at the university, so she couldn't be in better hands, but it's touch and go I understand."

"I'll let the team know and see what they think. Keep us apprised. And what about the equipment needs I emailed you about?" Kapur asked.

"DHL delivery to the address you gave me possibly today."

"*Danka, mein heir*," replied Kapur.

* * *

"Now what, Assad?" Zayed asked after filling him in about the disaster in Vienna.

"Have Hazem get immediately online and find out everything about the assault. First reports will undoubtedly be from Viennese and Austrian news agencies. You know enough German to understand what they will report. Check CNN also. We have to know everything and obviously if there were any witnesses to the attack."

"We will never be implicated, Assad. The phones we used are disposable with no trace possible, and Khalid doesn't know my name, so even if he comes under suspicion, there will be no connection to me or us," said Zayed.

"I know, but this is a big loose end we do not need. Praise Allah, why would he think we wanted the girl murdered?"

"He always pushed to do more," he said looking at Hazem, "but he has to be deranged. He was too enthusiastic. I should have sensed that."

Still on speakerphone, Assad said, "You never met him and looked into his eyes. It is impossible to sense this from thousands of miles away. He's the cousin of the Iraqi contact we have in Cairo, right?"

"Yes. Can't trust Iraqis, can we? What do we do now?"

"We have no choice. I will contact the Egyptian," lamented Assad.

"The one who settled the Italian problem with Professor Raimondi?" asked Zayed.

"Yes. I believe he is in Sardinia when he's not working. It will cost us, but this has to be done very swiftly, no matter the assurances you received from Khalid. Very swiftly."

* * *

Claudia Schiff gradually recovered from her injuries but was totally unaware of what had happened and who might have assaulted her, and even more, why? Her insulated vest had indeed saved her life. The wounds were serious, but they had missed her kidney. The *Kurier*, a Vienna newspaper, carried ongoing stories about the attack of the university student and the police investigation that followed. The *Vienna Times*, an English-language newspaper, also featured a few features on the investigation, but after a time, the story just disappeared.

Then one day, a few of the Viennese newspapers—in a less prominent section of the news—reported the death of another student at the same university. Khalid bin Mohammed, an engineering student age twenty-four, had been found dead, apparently of a drug overdose. An Iraqi by birth, he had an official residence in Cairo. Drug paraphernalia were found in his apartment along with quantities of cocaine, heroin, and fentanyl, the drug that had caused his death. There was no history of the student as a drug user, and professors and fellow students were shocked at reports of that. Many thought that that was totally out of character for the young Arab. The story of his death quickly transitioned to reports of the increased use of drugs, even among the educated and affluent, and the name Khalid bin Mohammed was soon forgotten.

Chapter Thirty-Eight

Frankie and Paz really bonded with the children after the fashion show. There was laughter—something the two teachers had not heard often up to then—abounding throughout the palace, coming from the sheikh, the mothers, aides, and most important in the classrooms with the children. Omar's roaring beast continued to be the highlight for all, and reports of his antics spread throughout the palace.

One day when Mariam and Frankie were at the equestrian center, Mariam approached Frankie when the two were alone and whispered, "I know, Miss Fontana, that you are not here by your choice."

Taken aback, Frankie asked, "Mariam, why do you say that?"

"There are rumors, Miss Fontana. I hear Samira and Majid talking. In the palace with all the marble and granite, voices echo."

"You should not speak of this, Mariam. It is not good for you or me or Paz. You must not speak of this."

"It is just you and me here, Miss Fontana. I know you like us—your students—but there is a sadness in you. I see it. We had a great time with the fashion show with everybody laughing, but after that, I saw the sadness in your eyes return. I can see that you are not allowed to communicate outside the palace. You have no phones—and everybody has cell phones—even I, and your computers cannot send emails. You spoke of your family, but I don't believe you ever communicate with them, send them pictures—anything. When your Christmas passed, you were both very sad and took no joy in the coming of the New Year. You are prisoners here, aren't you?"

"Mariam, I have been made to swear never to talk of this, but you are a very bright, astute young woman. You are and will be a very special woman, but I can say no more."

"Will you please excuse me for a moment?" Mariam asked. "I have to use the restroom." As she left, she put her hand into the pocket of her vest, withdrew her iPhone, placed it on the railing they were leaning against, and walked off.

Bewildered, Frankie looked at Mariam walking away, then at the phone, and then all around her. *Alone except for the horses.* She grabbed the phone and dialed her father's number in the US. As it rang, she pleaded, *Pick up, Dad. Please pick up.* The call went to his voicemail. "This is Michael Fontana. Please leave your name and number and I'll call back."

At the beep, Frankie said, "Dad, Dad, this is Frankie. I'm okay. Paz is okay. We've been kidnapped and taken to a place called Ras al-Khaimah, part of the United Arab Emirates. We're at the emir's palace, and we were taken here to teach his children. His name is Sheikh Saud bin Nassr and something else … I can't remember. We're being treated well, but we're prisoners. I luckily got access to a cell phone, but get us out of here," she pleaded. "I gotta go before someone sees me using this phone. Love you and Mom, but get us out of here!"

She put the phone back on the railing. When Mariam returned, Frankie mouthed a soft "Thank you." Mariam nodded and put the phone back in her vest pocket.

* * *

Michael Fontana had taken his dog, Sundae, out for a quick walk— it was still cold in the hills of Bedminster—and he had simply forgotten to pick up his phone from the table in the foyer. He returned after about fifteen minutes and unhooked Sundae from her leash. He saw his phone on the table; he picked it up and noticed a missed call. The number displayed was a total mystery to him, but he saw that there was a voicemail. He hit the play button.

He ran into the kitchen. "Good God! Sherry! Frankie called!" He put the phone on speaker and played the message for his wife. She was almost uncontrollable with the news that Frankie and Paz were alive, deliriously happy, and then almost unable to comprehend that her daughter was somewhere in the Middle East.

"Where the hell did she say she was, Raz what?"

"Damned if I know, Sherry. Sounds like one of the emirates. I'll check it out, but I have to get this news to Guiness at the FBI. I don't want to use this phone again for fear I might erase this message. We have a phone number, and they can probably trace it to its source. Sherry, we have hope now. After all these months, we have hope!"

Using their land line, he called Guiness in Quantico, Virginia.

* * *

Shane Guiness dispatched an FBI agent from the Newark office to get out to Bedminster for Fontana's phone. The agent would helicopter out to Donald Trump's National Golf Club, also in Bedminster, only minutes from the Fontana residence. In half an hour, the agent was at the Fontana front door asking for the phone. "I'll get this back to you as soon as possible," he said. He was shortly back on the helicopter headed to Newark Airport, where he would take an FBI jet to Quantico.

The director called Gino about the phone message. "We'll be able to pinpoint the call as soon as the phone arrives. Then we'll have some figuring out to do. You and the Interpol agents are virtually on site but operating without Dubai or UAE sanction. Now we're talking about an abduction in a neighboring emirate—essentially another sovereign state—possibly involving a king, or emir, or whatever the hell he is, who owns the country. Shit. This has red flags all over it."

"We just set up our camera and audio surveillance equipment to monitor our guy here in Dubai. He looks to be part of the network responsible for the abduction and possibly the six others. We have to handle this carefully or risk alerting them and then never getting the other girls back," Gino said. "But Ras al-Khaimah is just next door, so to speak. I'm guessing this will be a priority after you place exactly where the call emanated from."

"Yes I know, but I'm walking on eggshells here. I'll have to bring Luxmore in on this, but I could see this going to the secretary of state and even up to the president. We have a lead to get an American girl back to her parents, which—as you know—is the FBI's primary mission here, but we can't fuck up your operation with Interpol. There'll be a ton of political shit to deal with, certainly with people in agencies who want to be instant heroes. Add to that the political fallout involving at least two sovereign states, three if you include Saudi Arabia, and who knows where else this will go," said an exasperated Guiness.

"I hate to mention it, but you or I will have to update Interpol, certainly Schickhaus," said Gino. "That's yet another agency with two of their agents on the ground with me down here. They're not going to do anything on their own considering that the other girls remain the main focus of their investigation, and we're just getting started with that part of the operation."

"Call Schickhaus, Gene. Give him the bare bones and stress that no action is to be taken. Nothing posted on their website either. Also, log into the CIA World Fact Book and find out everything you can about—what is that place?—Ras al-Khaimah. Who runs it, how far it is from Dubai, where exactly the emir's palace is, and what kind of military or security forces are in place—everything. Get everyone on your team to bone up on this and just hang tight. Continue to monitor your neighbor."

"I'll have Mercedes and Gisella get on that immediately. They're good at that."

Guiness ran his fingers through his hair. "Look. Things are coming to a head rapidly, and that's good, but there are two missions here. We can't, however, lose sight of the fact that we need to find and rescue the American and the Spaniard. Make no mistake about it—Michael Fontana is not going to sit on his hands. He will undoubtedly alert de la Cruz about this, and they are powerful, connected men who are sensing a miracle in the making. I'll talk to Fontana again stressing patience. Have Mercedes call de la Cruz and make sure he holds this news in confidence. No talking to anyone and certainly no one in the Spanish government."

"Let me also talk to Fontana," said Gino. "I've kept in touch with him over these months, and we have a good relationship. I'm sure he'll understand how close we are and won't want to jeopardize his daughter's rescue. Mercedes will call her boss at the National Police Force. No getting around that, but I know these people. They'll let us do our work, but you know how delicate this is. The Spanish feel as driven to get back one of their own just as you feel about the American."

"Fine, Gene, but understand that the last thing we need is for the Spanish prime minister to call the president of the US, wanting to take action. We have to be as stealthy as possible or the whole thing can blow up in our face. Shit, the political repercussions have to be managed. Let me start organizing things here. Maybe at one point the president will have to call the Spanish prime minister to keep him in the loop but also make sure they do nothing. Hell, they have one of their agents in the middle of this, so they're not on the outside looking in. That should calm them down."

"Okay," Gino replied. "We'll make our phone calls then get back to the surveillance on our guy. Other than that, I'll wait to hear from you."

"Done," said Guiness. "I've got a ton of shit to put together at this end. I'll get back to you when the next steps get a little clearer."

Chapter Thirty-Nine

With the Vienna debacle seemingly under control, Assad set up another conference call with the Saqr team and brought everyone up to date. The story of Khalid's drug overdose had faded from the media, and no connection had been made with the attack on Claudia Schiff.

"I want Sulayman and Rasid to come to Dubai immediately," Assad said. "Zayed has determined that the Schiff girl is recovering from her attack and that the police have made no headway on her attacker. Fortunately, this issue seems closed, but we must meet, review what went wrong, and start planning anew. I advised Azziz that there will no need for his jet to fly to Austria. He was not happy that this plan went so bad, so quickly, and he thought it would be best for him to travel to Europe himself as authorities would likely still be monitoring private-plane travel, without the principal owner on board. There was a business opportunity in Munich, and he thought he'd go there. I agreed with his thinking. In fact, I recommended that several trips might be a good idea over the next few weeks."

"That's wise," Zayed said. "Keep the prince's plane away from Austria, and have it make a few legitimate business trips elsewhere."

"But we need to regroup," continued Assad. "Let's thoroughly review our assets and their reliability before any further operations planning. We are safe, but we need to exercise caution before we put another plan in place."

"I'll get the villa stocked with provisions for the five of us and prepared for your arrivals," said Hazem.

Assad intended to drive from Abu Dhabi as he wanted time to think. The 150-kilometer trip would give him a couple of hours to do that. Sulayman would be flying in from Muscat, Oman, and Rasid from Doha, Qatar. By early evening, all five members of the Saqr team would be at the villa on Jumeirah Road across the street from Gino's surveillance location.

* * *

While difficult to operate initially, the audio monitoring equipment provided by Interpol picked up a good deal of the conversation between Zayed—apparently the Ussman individual they had tracked from Vienna—and someone named Assad. They also learned that Hazem, the leaseholder of the villa, was also across the street. The equipment was not operational at the time of Zayed's conversation with Khalid bin Mohammed despite its having arrived in Dubai under a French diplomatic shipment and had not been subject to customs inspection.

"It's obvious that this Zayed and Hazem were mostly listening, so it seems this Assad is the boss," said Rajesh Mitra, who was operating the audio disc that looked like a small satellite dish with a tube-like projection at its center. He wore earphones and managed a recording device, which he played back to the others in the villa on Jumeirah Road. "My Arabic is pretty good, but we'll need a professional translation of everything we pick up. We'll have to do that via Lyon as we cannot trust this to any service here. Nevertheless, there seemed to be some urgency in setting up this meeting." He gave them the gist of what he had heard.

"I'm guessing it's tied to the assault on the Schiff student in Vienna," said Gisella. "It's a leap, I know, but somehow I think it might be related. That's why they're bringing the others, three more of them, who are likely part of this Saqr group. That's the company that owns the house."

"Maybe," said Kapur. "Makes some sense particularly since they mentioned the prince and his plane. Schickhaus texted us that Azziz cancelled a flight plan to Innsbruck. Not that close to Vienna, but not that far away."

"I think I agree with Gisella," said Gino. "No coincidence."

"Not to me," replied Kapur.

"We need to prepare for the arrival of the other members," Mitra said. "We need to get provisions as I think we'll be spending some time together here."

"Yes," added Mercedes. "Plus, we don't know what will be required of us regarding the developments with the kidnapped women. Gisella and I will put together a dossier on Ras al-Khaimah and be ready for what happens on that front."

"You start," added Gisella. "I'll shop and get this place fully stocked with food for all of us."

Chapter Forty

Hazem ordered food for the team to be delivered that afternoon. He and Zayed planned for the meal to be something light and traditional, prepared by a gourmet food store in the commercial district nearby. After the arrival of Assad, Sulayman, and Rasid, the men set up their rooms in the villa and moved to the spacious dining room.

"Nothing fancy," said Hazem arranging the variety of dishes delivered on the dining room table. There was hummus with triangular pieces of pita bread for dipping, falafel—fried balls made from chickpeas, onions, and spices, and tabbouleh—salad greens, mint, parsley, and cracked wheat. "After, baklava for dessert with tea," Hazem concluded. The sweet pastry was very traditional in the Middle East made with walnuts, honey, and sweet syrup.

The meal passed swiftly with the men talking of things unrelated to business—traffic in Dubai, the pending World Cup to be held in Qatar, the variety of new, exotic sports cars used by the Dubai police—benign chitchat. After dinner, the group moved to what they called the office, which contained Hazem's desk with two computers, a conference table and large, flat-screen monitors, where Hazem spent most of his time. He could forward data and images to a wide-screen monitor on a wall, where three flat-screen TVs hung.

The men sat around an oval table in large leather chairs. Each seat had a leather-bound notepad in front of it on the table, and they all pulled out their iPads.

"The disaster in Vienna is a wake-up call for us," Assad said. "That and the visit by the American ambassador to Prince Azam dictates that more caution must be taken. At the same time, members of our network are demanding that we improve our output—the pace of our abductions."

"You want us to increase the number of our abductions but at the same time proceed more cautiously?" asked Zayed.

"Yes," replied Assad. "We have almost sixty members in the Saqr network. These men have been recruited carefully and are totally committed to our mission. Yet we have had relatively few auctions, seven to date. They are getting impatient. We have to improve productivity, and let us not forget the costs that go into each operation. The original membership fees—essentially our seed money—is being rapidly depleted, and annual fees may have to be increased. And yes, we have to be more careful in the selection of our assets and our extraction methods."

"Assad, will we continue to use the Saudi's plane?" asked Rasid.

"Yes, Rasid, but other planes can be available to us. At least ten in our network have mentioned that their planes could be provided. We got too comfortable with Azam's support and the use of his jet. We should also consider extraction by boat. Our friends have large yachts throughout Europe. We should think carefully regarding their use for escape."

"But our extractions have been flawless," added Rasid.

"Yes, the result of intensive planning and cross-checking all aspects of each operation, but that takes time. We have had no failures, no threats to our mission, but there have been some undesirable circumstances we have had to deal with," responded Assad. "The issue in Milan required the use of the Egyptian to ward off any potential complications, and now, we have had to again use his services in Vienna with Khalid, so flawless may be too generous a conclusion. Khalid totally misunderstood our mission and ruined a highly valuable operation, one that promised to bring probably our highest return ever. This cannot happen again. It could have compromised our entire operation."

"But there are no repercussions for us, Assad, right?" asked Rasid.

"No, none that we are aware of anyway. But this was a total ..." Assad paused for a moment. "...fuckup as our American friends might say."

"No more fuckups," added Zayed, and the group started laughing.

"Right," said Assad with a smile, "no more fuckups. Now let's get down to business on how we move ahead."

They spent the next few hours reviewing all potential targets they had identified and all the network operatives aligned for target surveillance at the universities and their coordination with their assigned Saqr contacts. Zayed projected all details on the large monitor, and each member updated the others. All used the information on their iPads, updating areas for follow-up and further action. They had only six viable targets identified—one in Rome, two in England, one in Edinburgh, one in Brussels, and one in Utrecht, Netherlands.

"Six women are barely enough," said Assad. "We've already taken two from England, and while this is our most attractive source, I don't want to go there again. At least not for a while. That leaves only four who have been vetted. But Hazem has showed us that we have fourteen operatives in place. This includes universities in Munich, Cologne, Heidelberg, Barcelona, Strasbourg, Paris, Luxembourg, The Hague, and Salzburg, in addition to the cities with the vetted targets. We need to go back to each of these operatives, first to make sure they are reliable and safe, and second to get updates on potential targets. And I must stress, no more surprises like Khalid. Any concerns, we cut them loose. Let them go to school, get their degrees, and go back to where they came from. They will be of no use to us.

"Let's break for the evening. Work on this all day tomorrow and longer if needed. I want our list of potential targets expanded. I will go back to our members who have planes and yachts we can use. Monte Carlo is one place our colleagues maintain permanent births for their yachts and Nice, Portofino, Positano, and Marbella also. I need to assess the viability of this avenue for extraction. It would be a long voyage to get to the emirates from there but not out of the question for these mega- yachts."

"One thing, Assad," Hazem said. "I keep getting update messages regarding some of the software we're using. I need to update the computers here as well as at the souk. Let me do that first thing in the morning and then I'll get to the work on assets and targets."

* * *

Rajesh and Fred fine-tuned the video and recording equipment at the villa. Gisella had bought notepads, pens, a whiteboard with markers, and other materials to help record surveillance information. By late afternoon, they had filmed the arrival of the Saqr team, one by car—a black Mercedes SUV—and two by taxi. Their images were transmitted to Interpol to compare to the images recorded at Madrid Immigration Control. The audio recording went on for several hours, and not everything was clear given the noise of passing cars and the frequent flights landing at Dubai International. Nevertheless, it gave them plenty to work with as Rajesh provided a running translation of the Arabic conversations.

"This looks to be a gold mine," remarked Gino. "It gives us everything we need. These are definitely the abductors—and we now know their names, first names anyway—of, what did this Assad imply? Eight women?"

"Plus responsibility for the two deaths, one in Milan and one in Vienna," Mercedes said.

"An auction?" commented Fred. "What the hell is that all about?"

"I couldn't get everything," added Rajesh, "but let's put up some key words on the whiteboard. Auction, network, operatives, a private plane armada, new target cities, the Egyptian, and the confirmed complicity of Prince Azam Azziz to name a few. I'm going to transmit this to Lyon. We'll need a full transcript in English as soon as possible."

"The other thing of interest is reference to a souk I believe you said. Then the need to update their software at a souk and across the street. Put that up on the whiteboard, Gisella," directed Mercedes. "Is that an opportunity?"

"Don't know," Gino said, "but if this Hazem is going somewhere tomorrow, we have to tail him." Gino asked the Interpol agents, "Do you guys have any tunics or Muslim garb at home?"

"No," replied Kapur, "but I can get some. There are all-night markets that sell the stuff and in souks by the way. Let me get some things for all of us. We may have to do some undercover work, and it would be better if we just blended in. Rajesh and I can easily pass as Middle Easterners. Gino, with his Mediterranean looks, and Mercedes could pass as well. Even Gisella with her olive Italian complexion wouldn't raise any questions. Plus, the women dressed in *abayas* and *hijabs* wouldn't raise any questions. Fred, you're too Western looking, but five of us could easily fit in if we had to. Let me go now. I'll be back in an hour."

The rest of the night was basically allowing for Rajesh to refresh his memory from notes he had been taking, tightening up some of the translation he had made, and updating the whiteboard's key words and phrases.

Gino called FBI Director Guiness with the gist of what they had heard and seen.

"Christ, you guys got it all. I don't believe it. Have that transcription sent to me as soon as you get it. Better yet, have Schickhaus send one to me directly using the secure email address I gave you. Two murders, eight abductions, and potential targets for additional kidnappings? We need to confirm who exactly the other women abducted are and compare their names with the list Interpol generated. And where they wound up."

"Yes, Director. We learned a lot about this trafficking ring, but we have miles to go. And this evidence is questionable and possibly illegal considering we're operating without UAE sanction."

"I'll worry about that later, Gino. These guys are ours. I'll deal with the legalities when I need to."

"What do we do about the two girls in Ras al-Khaimah?"

"I'll talk to you about that tomorrow, Gino. I'm meeting with the secretary of state and Martin Luxmore this afternoon and expect to have a plan of action by the end of the day. They may have to wake up the ambassador to the emirates and get him on board, but for now, you guys stay on top of what's going on across the street and think about your next steps. Think about ways to get into their computers. Make that happen. Well done, Gino. Maybe I'll have to make your temporary credentials permanent. I'll also think about getting Clark Breslau and his IRT team back on the case. You may need more boots on the ground down there."

"What I need down here is some IT help. None of us can do anything to get into those computers. I need Sean O'Casey here immediately."

"Who?"

Gino laughed. "The kid who hacked into the Moroccan and Spanish banking systems in the Zahori conspiracy."

"Yeah, I know what you guys did in Spain to bring an end to that plot, but who is this O'Casey?"

"Part of the team we recruited to expose the plot and bring all involved to justice. I got him through Danny Boggs at the Service working through one of your guys, Ernie Watson, at the Electronic Crimes Branch at Fraud."

"Sure, I know Ernie—top notch."

"Well, the kid was put into the White Deer Federal Corrections Institute after going on a hacking spree that involved changing grades of students at CCNY, but the biggie he was arrested for was hacking into the IRS and increasing refunds to random people. Kind of a Robin Hood but a big-time embarrassment for the IRS. Our activities in Granada got him a reprieve, and working with a couple of CIA tech guys from the American Embassy in Madrid, he went on a tear moving Zahori money around and out of sight. That was the critical element in bringing them down. Danny got him a pardon and enrolled him the Federal Law Enforcement training program, so he knows where he is. Eventually, he could wind up working for one of our agencies. Unless you have someone of that caliber you can get down here immediately, that's whom I want and now."

"Christ, Gene, I don't know. I'll get on it and see if that's even feasible. We'll talk."

Chapter Forty-One

After updating software and rebooting the computers at the villa, Hazem left at midmorning the next day. The others then went to their laptops and iPads to begin fine-tuning the information relating to assets at the university locations and potential new targets.

Anticipating Hazem's departure to the souk mentioned the night before, Kapur, in a tunic and knitted skull cap, prepared to follow him. The Interpol agent had his Toyota Camry in the carport as there had been no time to rent an upscale car. Gisella's and Fred's Audi was there, but the team decided to use the Toyota for surveillance.

Ray was already in his car when the garage door opened across the street and Hazem pulled out in another black Mercedes SUV. Ray followed at a discreet distance and hoped traffic would not complicate his being able to stay with the man.

Hazem traveled west along Jumeirah Road to Al-Khaleel Street and through the Al- Shindagha tunnel under Dubai Creek. The SUV exited on Baniyahs Road winding alongside Dubai Creek on its eastern side. Traffic was moderate, so Ray had no problem keeping the black Mercedes in view. He recognized that they were in the Deira district and saw the spice market just off Baniyahs Road. One block later, the SUV turned left and then right at Al-Kabeer Street, where the Deira Old Souk came into view. He found parking.

Ray drove past him and found a space about thirty meters farther on. He sat in the Toyota watching Hazem through the rearview mirror exit his SUV, click the lock on his key fob, and head toward the souk's entrance. Hazem, dressed in black slacks and a white shirt, walked with a crisp gait and was swinging a black leather case. He passed various vendors of clothing, jewelry, and tourist items without acknowledging them and occasionally dodged around shoppers.

Ray was quite inconspicuous with his white and blue-trimmed tunic with a light-blue knitted cap, something like a yarmulke, just a little fuller. He had not shaved that morning; his five o'clock shadow gave him an Arab look.

Hazem continued walking down the labyrinth of passageways, and Ray took note of shops that could serve as landmarks for the forks in the road and which way his quarry went. *Left at the old shop with the gold lace neckwear in the window, bend to the right at the shop with the antique merchandise outside and scimitars hanging in the window,* he noted and repeated to himself. He remained about twenty meters behind Hazem, who never looked around.

Nearing the end of a narrow passage lined with more antique shops, Hazem glanced at a heavy wood door on his right, and walked past the shopkeepers lounging around their wares, some smoking cigarettes and engaging in conversation. It looked to Ray that he had given them a curt nod as he slowed and fumbled for something in his pocket. Hazem stopped in front of a double set of dark wooden doors, inset with carved panels of some indeterminate design.

He withdrew a key, unlocked the door on the right, went in, and quickly closed the door. Ray saw light shining out below the doors. He paused to look at the wares of one of the vendors and snuck a glance at the closed doors. Arabic letters carved in the beam above the doors may have designated a shop number or name. Ray moved to a shop with men's and women's traditional *abayas* and tunics and held up a three-quarter-length tunic, the kind worn over trousers. He was quickly joined by a vendor who greeted him in Arabic. Ray responded to the *"Ahlan wa sahlan"* welcome greeting with *"FurSa sa'eeda,"* —Nice to meet you, some of the little Arabic he knew, not wanting to use English. The tunic appeared to be his size, and the man said, *"Saba'een,"*— seventy dirhams, which Ray immediately cut in half. He pulled out some bills from his pocket and handed the merchant the discounted amount in dirhams, approximately $10. The man smiled, took the money, and put the tunic in a plastic bag.

Ray strolled back along the passageway, content that while the vendor would not take Ray to be an Arab, he would not think he was American or English and his bargaining strategy would be consistent with what locals did. Ray determined that he couldn't just hang around in this area, so he took out his phone and discreetly kept the camera button pressed as he videoed the doors where Zayed had entered and the adjacent shops. He backtracked the way he had come in, pausing and snapping pictures of the landmarks where he made turns.

He spent more than an hour browsing the wares of shop after shop clutching his small plastic bag in one hand and taking pictures with the other. Hazem apparently remained behind those closed doors as he did not pass him on the way out. He wished he could have had even a small glimpse inside those doors as he couldn't really determine if it was a shop like the others around it or something else. If the double doors were opened, it could be a shop of some kind, the wide opening room enough to display something, but there was no large window like so many of the other shops had and no chairs or benches outside, just two solid double doors.

Ray eventually decided he had spent enough time in the souk and didn't want to raise any suspicions, so he moved toward the exit, taking pictures as he did. He thought he'd return to the Toyota and continue surveillance from there. As he walked to his car, he was shocked to see that the black SUV was gone. *How? There's no way Zayed could have passed me. There has to be a back door.*

He then began a slow foray on the outside of the souk, looking for places where Zayed could have exited. From his point of entry to the souk, Ray gauged that he had walked south in a line somewhat parallel to Al-Kabeer Street. Inside, he remembered a bend to the left and then to the right, which should still take him in an approximate southerly route, so he walked the perimeter of the souk with that in mind. Most of the building was just an adobe-like brown with no doors or windows, so he assumed that all vendors and delivery people came through the main entrance.

As he neared the end of the building, he saw a heavy wooden door, similar in size and color to the one Zayed had used to enter his chamber but without insets or designs. The door had no lock that a key would open. On a beam framing the door was a keypad. *Not good*, Ray thought. *Might be tied to some kind of alarm or monitoring system. But I'm guessing this is where Zayed had exited the souk.* He took a few photos of the door and the device and returned to his car. He called Gino and reported on his morning, which in fact had taken him well into the afternoon.

When Ray arrived back at the villa, he found a young stranger slouched in one of the living room armchairs. He looked at the man and then to Gino and the rest of the team, his eyebrows raised. Taking off his skull cap, he asked, "And …?"

"Ray, meet Sean O'Casey," Gino said. "He just got here, and we hope he's going to help us get into their computers. The FBI got him to the Al-Dhafra Air Base just outside Abu Dhabi. The US has the 380th Expeditionary Wing of our air force there, and the bureau used one of their Gulfstream 650s to get him here in record time. With the

US passport he carries, there was no problem to exit the base and go through UAE immigration. The embassy sent a nondescript car to get him here. He's a little jet lagged as you can see."

O'Casey rose somewhat unsteadily, smiled, and extended his hand to Ray. He was tall, in his early twenties, and he had curly red hair and fair skin with a few freckles. They shook hands, and the young man slumped back into his chair.

"Sean worked with Mercedes and me on our mission in Granada and was a tremendous help. I'll fill you in on that later," Gino said, "but let's get to what you found out."

Ray went to one of the laptops and began downloading the photos from his phone. "The guy did in fact go to a souk, one of the older ones not far from here."

The others gathered around Ray and took in the images as he explained what they were seeing. He scrolled back and started with the interior of the souk, where they could observe the narrow passageways and shops lining them.

"If I'm not mistaken," Mercedes jumped in, "we were there with Alex, Fred's tour guide. I recognize the layout and definitely remember that woman with her kids," she said pointing to one of the photos on the screen. "She was kind of pretty, maybe in her early forties, and I remember thinking how pretty her two girls were. That's definitely her selling those antique pieces."

"Yeah," said Fred, "antiques dating back to last year and probably made in China."

"Regardless," replied Mercedes, "we were there. It's near the spice market."

"That's right," said Ray. "The smells from there permeate the air."

He scrolled to the photos of the wood doors at the end of a

passageway. "That's the unit he entered, but I couldn't see anything inside. The door was open and closed very quickly."

"Okay," said Mercedes, "so they have to have some kind of computer set up behind those doors. Something related to what they're doing. Otherwise, they wouldn't have hotfooted it to the souk this morning."

"So we have computers for their scheme in the villa across the street and in an old souk, full of shops and shoppers."

"Ray, go back to the outside of the souk," said Fred, "and the photos you took of the back door and the keypad."

Ray scrolled some more and stopped at the photos of the outside door.

"That looks like a keypad on the side of the door," said Fred. "Can you enlarge the picture?"

The close-up of the keypad revealed the typical set of numbered keys; they made out the brand—Schlagel XL.

"Schlagel. Sounds German," said Fred as they all strained to get a closer look at the keypad.

"Sean, can you find out about that manufacturer and what kind of system that lock utilizes?" asked Gino. "See what its features are—a simple electronic lock or some kind of alarm system tied to it."

"Sure. The FBI guys who picked me up in Georgia got the staff to lend me one of their supercharged laptops, so let me set it up and get to work."

Gisella noticed that an email had arrived on one of the other laptops; it had come from Interpol, and attached was the translated transcript of the conversation from the villa across the street. "We have the transcript," she called out.

"Good," said Gino. "Print out six copies for us. Can you tell if it was sent to FBI headquarters?"

"Yes it was. Director Guiness was copied."

Chapter Forty-Two

Director Guiness called Gino. "We have a plan, Gino. I haven't fully reviewed the transcript sent by Schickhaus, as we have been focused on the situation of the girls apparently being held in Sheikh Saud bin Nassr al-Sisi's palace. God, I wish they used simpler names. Anyway, we've been working with Luxmore and the secretary of state himself and will eventually have to brief the president. Schickhaus called Madrid and briefed the prime minister. The Spaniards agreed to let us manage the operation, and he's aware that one of his officers, Mercedes Garcia, is with you. It's officially a joint operations between our countries with the FBI and the State Department, the lead agencies. That's a big deal, and the prime minister agreed not to take any separate action and will keep this very hush-hush. I know that Mercedes advised her superior at NPS. The prime minister said he'd talk to them to ensure no one does anything we haven't authorized."

"That's a lot of coordinating at very high levels in a very short time. Nice job," said Gino. "And thanks for getting Sean here. You obviously had to pull a few strings."

"More than a few strings as well as the cost of a supersonic plane flight to get him there. The FBI and State will be haggling over the cost of that for a while," said Guiness.

"He's at a computer right now earning his keep. What's the plan you came up with?"

"Very delicate and very aggressive at the same time," replied Guiness. "We talked to the ambassador to the UAE—William Atkins—who has been in that post for the past two years. He has strong diplomatic credentials in the Middle East, having held positions in the State Department in Egypt and Oman. He'll be playing a critical role—*the* critical role in the plan."

"And Atkins is aware of our team's activity here and what we've been up to?" asked Gino.

"Yes. He is of course concerned about your surveillance operation in Dubai and the complications it's likely to cause, but that's being put off to the side for now. The UAE is a very important ally of the United States. It hosts a military presence in the emirates in support of our military actions in Syria, Iraq, and Afghanistan. I can't stress that enough. But the priority is the girls at the palace in Ras al-Khaimah and getting them back. The rest of what's happening and what you've been up to takes a back seat for now. Any political and diplomatic issues regarding that operation will be dealt with later. We have enough political and diplomatic issues involving the girls to deal with first."

"On that end," Gino mentioned, "we've profiled the leadership of Ras al-Khaimah and got a lot of information about the sheikh— his background and the political atmosphere in the emirates. Ras al-Khaimah is kind of below the radar, with Dubai and Abu Dhabi being the main players in the UAE, but essentially, he owns the country. He seems quite moderate, and his having been educated in the US is a plus, but it's not every day you go up against a guy who owns a country. How do you get over that hurdle?"

"We'll know when we get to that point, Gino. Our approach now is for Atkins to ask for a meeting with the sheikh at his palace. He's met the man and some of his entourage at several functions primarily in Abu Dhabi, but he hasn't had a real one-on-one with him and certainly not in Ras al-Khaimah. He'll rectify that. The plan is for the ambassador to make an approach talking about promoting US tourism to his emirate. That should spark an interest as the sheikh doesn't have Abu Dhabi's oil or Dubai's commercial success. Tourism could create a lucrative income stream. The sheikh has spoken about increasing tourism as part of his economic goals, so he should be very open to meeting with Atkins."

"Okay, so he sets up a meeting with the guy. Then what?"

"Hear me out." said Guiness. "Atkins is the US ambassador, so he travels to Ras al-Khaimah in a secure convoy accompanied by a squad of marines. That's not unusual."

"So Atkins arrives at the palace gates or whatever they have there, in an armored Chevy Suburban accompanied by a few jeeps full of armed marines?"

Guiness sighed. "That's about it for the first phase of the operation. There will be about a dozen of them led by a lieutenant and a sergeant, and they'll also have a full colonel along for the ride. The colonel will be with Atkins in the Suburban and serve as his attaché. Whether the marines will be allowed into the palace grounds with all their hardware is an unknown. There's security at the palace but not a large contingent of Emirati soldiers, maybe a dozen or so on the grounds. Now here's where the rubber meets the road. The ambassador with the colonel at his side and you and Mercedes right behind them—"

"Whoa! You want Mercedes and me going with the ambassador to the palace?"

"Let me finish, Gino. The ambassador will introduce the colonel and then you as a Special Agent of the FBI and then Captain Garcia of the Spanish National Police Force. The law enforcement presence of you and Mercedes is important to what follows. Atkins is then going to state with no preamble or diplomatic niceties that we know Fontana and de la Cruz are being held at the palace. The US has absolute proof of this, and we demand their release to us right now. No negotiations, no obfuscation. Bring the girls to us immediately."

"Wow. If the president gave his okay on this, I admire his balls."

"This operation will require big balls and big ovaries on everyone's part. Like you said, the guy owns the country. But the ambassador will have a full squad of armed marines behind him, and while not voicing any threat, a threat will be there. The secretary of state has basically said, 'Diplomacy be damned.' We have role-played all the scenarios from denial to confrontation, but the carrot the ambassador has is a big one—no repercussions."

"You mean turn the girls over and life goes on? No consequences for kidnapping and sequestering two women all these months?"

"That's right. That's the deal we want to offer him. With the FBI and the National Police Force present, we want him to understand that this is more than a diplomatic discussion. Crimes affecting two sovereign nations have been committed, and Spain and the United States will not let that go. But as you said, life goes on. Give us the girls and nothing further is said. No salacious news stories. No confrontations between governments. We leave with the girls and the sheikh goes back to his business."

"At some point, if this goes well, we might have the leverage to learn more about how the sheikh acquired the girls," said Gino.

"You mean that Saqr network?"

"Yes. It would be nice—more than nice—if we could learn how this whole thing works. How far these people have infiltrated governments and for what exact purpose. I'd like to have that discussion with the sheikh. As part of the deal of us keeping quiet, we should try to get more from him," replied Gino.

"Agreed, but we won't draw that line in the sand—and there's plenty of sand out there, isn't there? We want the girls in the back seat of that

Suburban. That's phase two of the operation. Then we'll see. We hope that the sheikh sees that this is a big win for him—not being implicated in a human trafficking ring on the front pages of newspapers across the globe—and perhaps he'd be amenable to some information sharing. That however is an international matter. Our priority—that of the FBI, the State Department, the president—is the return of an American citizen back to her family and the Spanish girl back to hers. Interpol and all the other European agencies take it from there regarding the other abductions. We don't know how deep this conspiracy goes in the UAE hierarchy in Abu Dhabi. Then there is the issue of the Saudis, a real mess that will have to be dealt with. Your team and Interpol are closer to this than we are back here."

"Got it. Getting the girls back is the priority. Anything else is gravy. When's this going down?"

"Not sure. We want to make sure that Atkins is primed to pulling this off. Then we organize all the support he needs and particularly the military assets. State has apprised the Defense Department, and word has gone out to the Middle East Command to respond to Atkins's direction on this. Then he has to get that appointment with the sheikh. We'll have to wait on that, but when the timetable is established, you and Mercedes need to get to Abu Dhabi and join that convoy. I have a team going over the transcript we got from Interpol. We'll bring the CIA in on this as well, and after it's scrubbed and laid out, Schickhaus and I will talk."

"It's good that we may have a little time before we confront the sheikh. You got O'Casey down here, and many thanks for that. He's looking into some of the security systems these guys have, at least at the souk."

Gino gave Guiness a quick summary of Kapur's surveillance of Hazem al-Sawai at the old souk. "They may break up their meeting soon and return to their residences. If that happens, it could give us an opening to get into their systems either across the street or at the souk."

"Fine. Your team can continue to record what goes on at that villa and see what else that reveals. Whatever you do with this O'Casey, just be sure it in no way compromises the plan to get the girls back, Gino."

Gino returned to the dining room, where the group did most of their work, and summarized the plan to recover the girls. "No one talks about this, guys. Ray and Rajesh, nothing of this to your superiors. Guiness will discuss this with Interpol, but nothing comes out of here, clear?"

Both agents nodded.

"Mercedes," Gino said, "as to the Spanish authorities, this has been discussed between our president and your prime minister. He was very pleased that Spain would not be left out of this rescue effort thanks to your being here. He will take care of briefing your boss in Madrid, and he's committed to assuring no leaks. Fred and Gisella, you've done this long enough to know what not to do, and you have no one to tell anyway."

The FBI assets in Dubai laughed.

Gino turned to Sean, who was nose-down into his laptop. The young man looked up and smiled. "Been through all this secret stuff working with you guys in Granada, so no problem."

"Okay. Let's see what we can get done before Mercedes and I are pulled out of here. Fred, what's the fastest way to get to Abu Dhabi when the call comes?"

"I'll drive you and Mercedes there. I can use the Audi or one of our agency's SUVs. It will be less than two hours, by far the quickest way to get there. You guys pack a bag, and when you get the green light, we can go immediately."

Chapter Forty-Three

Sean had moved to one of the rooms in the villa that was set up as a small office. Away from the others, he was able to concentrate better and begin his search. Rajesh was busy manning the recording equipment. He would activate the video surveillance only when there was any activity outside the villa. The others had their laptops and iPads on the dining room table, but things were quiet there for the time being. Gisella ran out for more food for breakfast, and they would order in food for their other meals, not unlike what the Saqr group was doing across the street.

"Schlagel is a German security company with all sorts of locks and security systems for homes and businesses," O'Casey yelled from the other room. The group moved to the office area and gathered around the young man. "The Schlagel XL unit is a simple keypad lock. Push in four numbers and it opens or locks. No alarm system at all."

"Great news," said Fred. "We just have to get the right numbers."

"There's a spy shop here in Dubai that sells everything," said Ray. "It has all sorts of hidden camera and recording devices, lock-picking tools, and devices to unlock or detect code numbers on electronic keypads. We could have obtained equipment similar to what we are using here at the villa from them, but it was better to have it shipped in without alerting anyone. Getting these other devices and tools shouldn't be a problem. Plus, being in the spy business, they keep things pretty confidential."

"No questions asked?" inquired Gino.

"No. In Dubai, you can find anything, and this spy store even has its own website. A crazy name, La La Systems. It's run by some Chinese, and a few of the salesmen are Indian," Ray said. "I've been there once or twice for some items but nothing in the way of what we need."

"Let's visit that website and make a list of what we think we need," Mercedes said. "Lock-picking tools for the doors in the souk and a device for that keypad outside. Maybe even some cameras and recording devices we can place there or at the villa if we can get inside. And for sure, two-way communication sets preferably the ones that fit in your ear. What else?"

"Sean, bring up that La La website," Gino said. "Maybe they have an infrared device that can determine what numbers are used on the keypad, you know, something that can pick up fingerprints on the number buttons. Fred, did you have experience with this kind of thing at the bureau?"

"I did, but that was some time ago. Technology is light-years ahead of what we used then."

"We'll have to unlock their computers also. User names, passwords, and what if this is all in Arabic?" asked O'Casey. "I might be able to do something with user names and passwords using the laptop and software I brought with me from the States, but I can't read Arabic."

"There are few PCs and Macs with keyboards using Arabic characters. Software in Arabic is just developing," Ray said. "Any text will probably be Arabic but using the Roman alphabet."

"Shit," said O'Casey. "When we hacked into the Moroccan banking system, most of the stuff was in English, though some of the targeted accounts did have names in Arabic. If this is all in Arabic, notwithstanding the use of our alphabet, we'll need it translated."

"You hacked the Moroccan banking system?" exclaimed Fred.

"That's a story for another day," Gino said. "And Sean, Rajesh can handle any translations to English. For now, however, let's focus on what we need from La La Land."

"Systems." Ray laughed. "That's La La Systems."

"Right," said Gino. "How are we coming with that list?"

"Let me play a bit more on their website," said O'Casey, "but one thing we'll definitely need are flash drives to download the data. Sixty-four gigabytes each. One will likely be enough but let's get three or four."

"You and Ray browse the website and compile a list," Gino said. "Fred, help out with that. We also need to know what kind of security the souk has. What time it closes and whether there are night watchmen inside and outside."

"Damn right," said Fred. "Don't want to unlock that outside door and find us face to face with armed guards."

"We'll need to get someone there tonight. We can find out what time the souk actually closes, check out the exodus of vendors, and see what happens at the main entrance. Do guards come in after they lock the doors? Are there guards posted out front? In the back? And then we have to determine if any guards are inside walking around. Is there a check-in system the guards use when making their rounds, like they do in department stores and offices? Still lots of questions."

"The souks generally close at ten. Some close between one and four for lunch and then open again until ten, but I'm not sure what time this souk closes," said Fred. "I'll check that out with one of our tour guides. They will know." He went to the other room and made a call. He came back and said, "Midnight. Somebody's going to have a late night."

"That'll be me," said Ray. "I'll easily fit in with my new clothes. I can hang out at the Abra Station. *Abras* are those small boats that cross and tour Dubai Creek," he explained. "Many will use the abras when leaving the souk, so it will likely be quite busy even at midnight. From there, I can walk around and see what kind of security the souk has. At least I hope I can."

"I think you should be inside at closing time. That way you can see if any guards are already there. Stay near the jewelry stores. They're most likely to have guards patrolling them. And you may want to rest up before you venture out. Take a nap or something," said Mercedes.

"Or have a few coffees at the Abra Station," added Fred, causing the others to laugh.

"Gino, I've also been thinking about our need for translating Arabic," Mercedes said. "We used two tech analysts from the US Embassy in Madrid for the Zahori operation to work with Sean. Men from Evans's CIA in-station group. I'm sure we can get someone who can handle Arabic either from the embassy in Abu Dhabi or the consulate in Dubai. We don't want the CIA interfering in our operation, but maybe, through Guiness, we can get a message down here to lend us someone as they did in Madrid. Rajesh needs some help. He can't be doing this twenty-four seven and we definitely need someone in the souk with Sean."

"Great idea, Mercedes," said Gino. "No way is Guiness going to use a Gulfstream 650 to fly another body down here. Tapping into local assets makes sense. Guiness can get Ambassador Atkins to get someone here ASAP. I'll call him now. Plus, you gave me an idea of an alternative source for the equipment we need."

Gino got the cooperation he needed from Guiness, and he received a call from the CIA Station Chief, Peter Dascenzo, at the US Embassy in Abu Dhabi. Dascenzo had been alerted by the ambassador of their plan to rescue the women in Ras al-Khaimah. He had also received a directive from Washington to assist "as needed by the ambassador," so he was open and willing to provide support to the group in Dubai as well. He had also heard how Ray Evans, his counterpart in Spain, had worked with Gene and Mercedes in taking down the conspiracy to return that nation to an Islamic monarchy, so there was not going to be any political infighting on the mission. Cerone and Garcia were somewhat legendary particularly in regards to how they emptied the conspirators' bank accounts and deposited the money temporarily in a safe CIA account in Geneva.

"Gene," Dascenzo said, "I'm sending you someone from the consulate in Dubai, Nina Darvish," he told him. "She's an Iranian-American born in the States of Iranian parents who fled that country in the midst of the revolution. Both parents are professionals, the mother a physician and the father a professor of physics at Georgetown. Nina graduated from Georgetown and then got an MA at their School of Foreign Service, including two years of cybersecurity studies and—long story short—was recruited to our agency. Nina is fluent in Arabic and Farsi, the language of Iran. This is her first foreign posting, but she's worked as an intelligence analyst in DC and has gone through our training program, so she seems perfect for your needs."

"Peter, before you go—"

"Pete. Call me Pete."

"Okay, Pete. I hate to be a pig about this, but at some point, we're going to do some B&E around here. My group is perusing a local spy shop website seeing what tools and equipment they might have that we'll need. When I worked with your counterpart in Madrid, he gave us a few toys that proved invaluable in video surveillance, audio recording, and GPS tracking. Great equipment."

"Don't laugh," Pete responded, "but we heard about you and what happened to Evans's favorite toy, that Rolex Submariner with the voice transmitter and GPS system. It somehow went off a cliff in Spain with the bad guys."

"Christ, am I on some CIA social media network?"

"No," replied Pete, "but word does get around. Tell you what—send me a list of the things you need. Use this secure email …" He gave Gino the details. "… and I'll see what we can do. I'll look in our own spy store," Pete said laughing as he hung up.

By the end of the day, well before Kapur was to set out for the souk, Nina Darvish was ringing the doorbell at 9528 Jumeirah Road.

Chapter Forty-Four

Nina Darvish was a striking young woman of medium height with long black hair and penetrating dark eyes, framed by long black lashes and contoured eyebrows. Her complexion was also medium, neither fair nor dark—something akin to a light suntan. Quite beautiful.

"Nina, come in. I'm Gino Cerone, special agent of the FBI. Pete gave you a rundown of what we're doing here and what we need?"

"Briefly," Nina replied. "He said this is a human trafficking operation with you and your team doing surveillance on the suspected traffickers."

"That's basically it," said Gino. "We'll give you a full briefing shortly."

Introductions were made. "Wow," said Nina. "FBI, Interpol, Spanish National Police Force. Impressive. And I missed Sean's affiliation."

"Sort of Secret Service. We pulled him out of his training program, but he's a computer wiz and maybe your cybersecurity and intelligence analysis background can help him out. We'll also need your translation skills once we get access to their operation, the guys across the street that is."

"I'm all in. Just point me in the direction you want me to go."

Mercedes sat with Nina and within twenty minutes had brought her up to date with the surveillance operation as well as the plan to rescue the two women being held in Ras al-Khaimah. Nina then sat with Rajesh going over his audio recordings with him, and he explained his process of taking notes on what was said before a translated transcript was received from Interpol in Lyon. Rajesh and Nina could probably do a full translation, but it was decided to continue to use Interpol so the transcript could be forwarded to the FBI and State Department. They had a full organization there and technology that could create translations rapidly.

"We have that same technology at the station in Abu Dhabi. It's straightforward translation software. Probably could do it here as well with that same software," Nina said.

"Good point, Nina," said Gino. "You guys weren't in the picture when we got started, so we never thought of that. However, let's stay with Interpol. They'll be taking center stage on this investigation." He nodded at Ray and Rajesh. "And with emails, it doesn't take much longer than doing it here. Nevertheless, why don't you get that software from the embassy and have it downloaded to our computers. Can't hurt. Thanks."

After a dinner of Chinese food they had ordered in, Gino asked, "Fred, is that list of spy store needs complete?"

"Yes. I have it here," Fred answered holding up a sheet of paper. "Flash drives, automatic lock-picking gun, traditional lock-picking implements, keypad deciphering tool, fingerprint powder, fingerprint recording tape, evidence bags, flashlights, camera and voice recording equipment, and ear-bud telecommunication devices. Is that it?" Everyone said yes. Fred said to Ray, "Ready to roll?"

"Hold on, guys," Gino said. "I got big help from the CIA guys in Madrid on our last operation. Pete Dascenzo, station chief in Abu Dhabi, agreed to look at our list and see what he has in inventory. That may enable us to keep a lower profile on this."

Gino took the list from Fred, went to one of the laptops, and sent the list to Dascenzo.

In twenty minutes, Gino's phone rang. "Got a pencil?" Dascenzo asked.

"Shoot," replied Gino.

"We have some very unobtrusive, state-of-the-art video and audio recording equipment of UK origin that can't be traced back to us. The software will transmit to cell phone or computer—just need to activate. We also have a device that can—in effect—pick that Schlagel keypad. It has a magnet that attaches the device to the keypad and with the press of a button, electronically unlocks the unit. I'll also send you a Brockhage electronic lock-picking gun for cylinder locks. The box of goodies will also include six two-way ear-bud communication units. They need to be programmed to the same frequency, but that's easy. They have a range of about five miles and battery life of a week depending on usage. I'm including plenty of batteries—very expensive state-of-the-art batteries I might add—for these units. They beep twice when batteries are running low giving you half an hour of operation. Communications from those units can be fed right into your computer. Fingerprint powder and tape may not be necessary as the keypad device should be all you need. Have someone go that spy shop, La La Systems, anyway. Get a standard, stealth nanny cam system with audio as backup. Everybody has these nowadays. And pick up a standard lock-picking tool set. They'll also have small, powerful LED flashlights. That's not very suspicious. Flash drives too, though you can get them anywhere. Same with evidence bags. Get some gallon zip-locks at a supermarket. Some black Sharpie pens too."

Gino gave the group the good news. A parcel delivery van would be at the villa in two hours. Ray and Fred ventured out with a much shorter shopping list.

* * *

Ray and Fred were at La La Systems in fifteen minutes. The shop wasn't large, but the walls and counters were filled with all sorts of equipment including stealth camera equipment visible behind a counter. The clerk, a tall, portly Indian gentleman about forty years old, was the only salesperson there. The man introduced himself as Ratnakar Singh.

"Dev Chopra," said Ray, extending his hand to the clerk, "and my associate, Anthony." Fred nodded to man behind the counter.

"And how can I help you?" asked Singh. "Cameras and recording devices are our most popular items, and we have every variety you can think of. Tiny cameras you can place in the eye of a doll, others you can mount on a wall. Anything you need."

"That's primarily what we're looking for," said Ray. "Something small, not easily visible that also features audio capability."

Little by little, the countertop filled up with all kinds of possible selections, and Ray and Singh discussed merits, drawbacks, and prices. After a selection was made, Ray asked about lock-picking implements, and again, the counter was laden with all sorts of kits. A Goso brand kit was selected, and Ray also asked for three sixty-four-gig flash drives and four LED flashlights with an infra-red feature.

Singh presented Ray and Fred with a piece of paper on which he had written the cost of each item and the grand total.

"A thousand euros?" Ray asked in feigned surprise. "You must think I'm a rich sultan from some exotic land. That will not do."

"Mr. Chopra, I am giving you my best price, rock bottom I promise you," Singh said.

"Please! A few hundred euros is all these items are worth. The nanny cam system is even more than you have posted on your website," Ray countered.

The bargaining went on for ten minutes, with

Fred—Anthony—watching in silence. Eventually, €375 was agreed upon, and Mr. Singh started wrapping and bagging the purchases.

"I want you to throw in batteries, Mr. Singh," Ray said as he was counting out the money.

"That's fifty euros alone! I am making no money on this."

"I think you are making quite a bit of money," answered Ray. "And all of these items better work as promised or we'll be back."

"That will not be necessary I promise you. Just remember to program the recording equipment with your phone or computer. The instructions to download the software are quite clear, and you should test it out before you place it. Everything else is straightforward, as I explained."

"More promises," said Ray. "I will hold you to them."

The men shook hands, and Ray and Fred went back to the Audi with the packages.

"Always bargain," said Fred.

"Yes, it's a disease around here no matter what you're buying. Generally, what they ask for is more than double a fair price. Gino gave me a thousand euros, but no way was I going to give our Mr. Singh anywhere near that. I am Indian, but there is a reason so many Indians run retail businesses. Check out all the gold and jewelry stores all with Indian salesmen. They can be ruthless."

"The next car I buy, I'm taking you with me," said Fred.

As they returned to Jumeirah Road, Fred said, "I hope we have time to get this operation rolling before Gino and Mercedes are called to Abu Dhabi for their trip to Ras al-Khaimah. We have yet to lay out just exactly how we're going to get into the souk and that room Hazem had entered. I'd like Gino around when that happens."

"As do I," said Ray. "Much will depend on what I find out tonight, but regardless, this will be very risky. Very."

Chapter Forty-Five

"You did what?" exclaimed Paz.

"I called home. I called my father," whispered Frankie.

"How?" a wide-eyed Paz asked.

"Mariam left her cell phone on the railing at the stables. I'm sure she did it on purpose. She wanted me to make the call."

"Whom did you speak with? Did you tell them where we are?"

"My father. Quiet. Not so loud, Paz. Unfortunately, the call went to voicemail. He usually has it with him."

"Mierda!" Paz muttered. "What did you say?"

"I told him everything. That we're okay, where we are, being held in the palace of the sheikh of Ras al-Khaimah, Saud bin Nassr al-Sisi. I said we're being treated well, but we're prisoners, kidnapped and brought here to teach his children. I gave him all essentials quickly. I put the phone back on the railing where Mariam left it for me. The look she gave me told me she knew … and she was okay with it."

"Dios mio." Paz sighed. "Now what do you think's going to happen?"

"My father will move heaven and earth to get us back. So will yours. But who knows how and when. We're on the other side of the world in an Arabian desert surrounded by sand and our sheikh owns the country. But I feel free for the first time since we've been here. We now have hope, Paz. Our fathers will get us out of here."

* * *

The days that followed were back to the full schedule of lessons with the children. Mariam and Frankie often locked knowing gazes quietly acknowledging what had transpired between them.

The teaching aides—Fatima and Latifa with Paz and Jumilah and Farah with Frankie—were becoming quite proficient in organizing the daily lesson plans for each child, and their demeanor was friendlier. The fashion show had loosened up things for everyone.

It was back to business for Frankie and Mariam at the equestrian center, caring for and training their steeds. Nothing was ever said about the phone Mariam had set down for a while, and Frankie seemed to have gathered a new level of spirit and confidence working with Aladdin. Mariam continued with Saladin working in a more advanced program under the direction of João Carvalho.

When back at the palace and generally during dinner, the two women wondered what was happening with their rescue. They seemed resigned to having it take some time, but they controlled their anxiety well.

"What's the first thing you're going to do when you get home, Paz?"

"Besides giving my mother and father a million hugs and kisses, I want to go to a good *tapas* bar. *Jamón Jabugo, tortilla, pulpo gallego*, all those little plates of delicacies with a nice Ríoja wine. And you?"

"I'll join you for tapas. I love that stuff, but once I get back to New Jersey, a rare Porterhouse steak, French fries, roasted red pepper at Sammy's in Mendham. I'm drooling thinking about it. Maybe Kentucky fried chicken too."

"We really can't complain about the food here. Typical Arabian, very healthy, and not bad," said Paz. "Maybe I'd like to add sushi and a big meal of Chinese food—wonton soup, egg rolls, chow mein, lo mein. Yes, that too."

"You're making my stomach growl, Paz. God, I just thought of spaghetti and meatballs. I'm adding that to the list. But for now, eat your hummus and pita. No more torturing ourselves."

Chapter Forty-Six

Ray Kapur set out for the souk at eleven. Gino thought it would be wise for Nina to accompany him given her greater proficiency in Arabic, though according to Fred, English was widely spoken in the souks. Both put on their local garb, Nina an *abaya* and head scarf but no facial veil. They inserted the ear-buds and practiced with each other and with Mercedes and Fred, who would be monitoring the action at the villa using the base module. Transmission range was about ten kilometers—six miles—according to the equipment manual. Gino asked that Ray and Nina continuously talk to each other while walking in the souk and make observations that Fred and Mercedes would note.

Once inside the souk, the pair strolled all the way to the back end, relaying the level of security they encountered. There was surprisingly very little, even around the gold shops. Nina bought a head scarf at a small shop exhibiting traditional clothing. Ray stopped at a sports store for some running gear—black pants and black, long-sleeved tops, some with hoods—in different sizes for men and women—along with five black fanny packs. He thought these acquisitions might come in handy for the night operations to follow.

At 11:45, a bell alerted customers that it was near closing time and all had to exit. Many shopkeepers had already started moving their merchandise inside their shops to be locked away. Many others, however, those selling T-shirts and inexpensive clothing, left their wares on the benches and low shelves outside their shops.

Nina and Ray slowly sauntered back toward the entrance studying what level of security was deployed inside. They saw nothing except for an elderly gentleman in a gray tunic who sat about half-way in arranging colorful cushions on a chair. Perhaps he was making himself comfortable for some kind of surveillance after closing, they thought. He had a small plastic bag at his feet—*food?*—and a liter bottle of water.

Ray and Nina were among the last to leave the souk; they were hurried along by men dressed in gray security garb but with no weapons. They noticed that the gold shops had cleared everything from their windows and had locked their wares behind heavy wood doors. Vendors slowly emerged from the entrance some toting boxes and others with large plastic bags containing merchandise, they guessed.

Nina and Ray moved to the Abra Station, where vendors were still offering varieties of snacks, tea, and coffee. Both opted for coffee, and they sat and watched the exodus of shopkeepers until all was quiet. They could see inside the souk and observed that most interior lights were turned off.

Two security guards lingered at the exit, closed the large double doors of the souk and appeared to lock them. Then they sat on either side of the entrance looking bored and disinterested.

"No guns apparent with the two guards out front," reported Ray, "and I never saw that old guy we noticed inside emerge. Maybe he's inside security, but I bet he'll be asleep in ten minutes. The guys outside look like they'll soon be taking naps as well."

Fred said, "Stay there for another few minutes and then stroll along outside the souk toward the back where that other door is. You parked your car in that area, right?"

"Yes," replied Ray. "We'll finish our coffee and work our way back to the car checking on security outside, besides the two guys out front."

A short time later, Ray and Nina walked slowly along the outside wall of the souk toward where their car and the back door were. The area was deadly quiet and dark. There were apartment houses farther down the street, but there was no activity in the immediate area. The small shops on the other side of the street had been closed and shuttered for hours. There were no street lights though the souk had some small light fixtures on the outside wall, dim, very few, and far between. As they approached the door with the keypad, they saw a small light overhead, a single light bulb, dim and yellow like the others.

"Dark and quiet out here," reported Ray. "Nobody around, and the light above the back door can be knocked out with a peashooter. Better yet, Nina, come here." He quickly gave her a boost and instructed her to turn the light bulb until it went off. "All dark now," he reported.

"Good thinking, Ray," Gino said. "Now get out of there."

Ray and Nina walked to the Toyota and drove past the front of the souk to see if there had been any changes in security and saw just the same two guards slouched in their chairs. One man's face was lit up by his cell phone on which he seemed to be playing a game. The other guard just stared into space.

Ray and Nina got back to the villa. Fred said, "The communication devices worked great. All was very clear."

"And apparently security seems to be very light," commented Mercedes. "The only question is what about that guy inside. Do you think he strolls around or just sits there?"

"There's almost no crime here in Dubai," Rajesh said, "so maybe they just set up a few people around for show. No one robs stores or banks or anything like that. First, because most people are doing very well and second, because penalties for such crimes are very severe—like losing a hand—so definitely not worth it. And as for those indebted laborers, well, they're pretty much confined to specific housing areas, and they have no means of transportation."

Ray produced the jogging outfits he bought. "These might come in handy when we decide to carry out the break-in. The black clothing will make us virtually invisible back there. Bought these fanny packs also for our tools."

"Well done, Ray," Gino said. "Let's get some sleep. It's almost two. Tomorrow, we'll set up the plan of action."

As all members of the team went to their rooms, Gino approached Rajesh. "Did you send that last bit of conversation across the street to Lyon?"

"Yes, just after Ray and Nina took off to the souk. Not a lot of activity as we have observed all day. They all seem to be working updating their data, vetting their operatives. They're all working with their computers or iPads, very little talking. I know Assad was going to make some calls, but he went to another room, and I couldn't hear anything."

"It would be nice if we could get a look at those phone numbers," said Gino.

"Between the CIA and Interpol, we have the technology to get into PBX Systems Dubai, the carrier around here, but without the number, we can't do anything."

"Put that up on the whiteboard," said Gino. "PBX access. We'll think about that later. As for now, are you and Ray going to bunk here or go back to your apartments?"

"We'll go home tonight," said Ray, "and come back in the morning. We need to gather a few things in case we do have to camp out."

"I may not have mentioned it," Rajesh said, "but before she went to the souk, Nina installed that translation software onto my computer just in case. It's on her laptop as well."

"Great. Go home. We'll talk in the morning. You bring the bagels," said Gino.

"You got it." Ray laughed, and the two left.

Gino went to the whiteboard. They had made progress in some of the key words: network, operatives, souk, private planes, Saudi prince, and target cities. Rajesh had added PBX access, but target cities still needed to be fleshed out more, as the Saqr team updated their data. He looked at the other key words: auction, the Egyptian, and software and computers, knowing there was still a lot of work to be done. He hoped they would be able to shed some light on those last key words when they got into the souk and Hazem's back room. *Tomorrow,* he thought. He went to bed for a short night's sleep.

Chapter Forty-Seven

The call came at nine the next morning. Gino was awake and dressed and was having coffee. After Gino talked to a secretary at the US Embassy in Abu Dhabi, Ambassador Atkins got on the line.

"Special Agent Cerone, we're going to take that trip to Ras al-Khaimah tomorrow. The sheikh has confirmed our appointment, and all is a go. We'll need you here today along with Captain Garcia to brief you on the operation, which is not very different from what Director Guiness explained to you. You and the captain need to be up here as soon as possible. The name of our mission is Operation Retrieve, kind of innocuous, but our CIA folks like to tag everything."

"We'll be on the road in thirty minutes, Mr. Ambassador, and be there before noon."

Ray and Rajesh had not arrived. Gino first advised Mercedes of the news and then got everyone up and around the breakfast table. "Good news bad news, guys. Mercedes and I have to be on the road very shortly to Abu Dhabi. Fred, I want you here, so please call one of your tour guides to drive us."

Fred left the room to make the call and returned shortly. "Someone will be outside in fifteen minutes, Gino," Fred said as he walked back to the kitchen for coffee.

From downstairs, they heard a door open. Ray and Rajesh came upstairs. They couldn't have had very much sleep, Gino thought, but they were carrying sleeping bags and a bag of warm bagels, whose aroma quickly permeated the room.

"Thanks to Interpol, we have a great breakfast, and you've arrived at the perfect time," Gino said. "Mercedes and I are heading to Abu Dhabi. Operation Retrieval—that's what they're calling it—has been green-lighted for tomorrow."

"Wonderful," exclaimed Ray. "Wonderful but scary."

"Everything we're doing is getting into scary territory now," said Gino. "I don't, however, want to delay getting into that souk. Things are relatively quiet across the street, but who knows when activity will start to pick up and they go running off somewhere."

"That could be positive and negative," said Fred. "If everyone takes off for other places, that leaves the villa unoccupied, and probably Hazem doesn't return to the souk."

"I agree, but it's hard to pinpoint where any of this will take us. You know, strike when the iron is hot, is generally a good thing, but the issue is, can you guys get into the souk without Mercedes and me around? Remember, that redhead at the end of the table stuffing a bagel with cream cheese into his mouth needs to be on that mission."

"Shit," said Sean wiping cream cheese from his mouth, "I can always dye my hair. I'd be very handsome with black hair."

"Yes you would," said Gisella, "but then, there are those freckles …"

Everyone laughed.

"Listen. This is serious," said Gino. "The way I see it, Nina and Fred have the background in things like this. Sean has had some training, but he's still in training, and we need him to get into those computers at the souk. Once inside, he does his thing, but our ability to get inside that souk is the key issue. Breaking and entering, undetected, is our challenge."

"We don't do much of this stuff at Interpol and certainly not here in Dubai," Ray said, "but our training is solid and extensive. We're investigators primarily, and that investigation requires many methodologies. Plus, I'm your guide to the souk—been there, done that."

"Do you think it's feasible for tonight, given what we know?" asked Mercedes.

"Yes, but Nina, Sean, and Fred will have to go ninja," said Ray.

"You mean dress in those black leotards?" asked Fred.

"Probably, if we're going to go dark."

"Okay, okay," said Gino. "Fred, Nina, Ray, and Sean—and why don't we dye his hair? Maybe you too, Fred."

"Oh good. He'll finally look Italian," said Gisella.

More laughter all around.

"I'm still running a travel agency, and my guys would wonder why I'm dying my hair," replied Fred. "I'll just use the hoodie on one of those jackets. That's perfect."

"Fred, I'd like you to run this. With the FBI, you've had more experience in this kind of operation than anybody. You and Nina will manage the equipment to get into the souk and then into that back room. It looks like there will be little security inside, but use caution if that old man in the chair is still about, or if tonight, there's a more alert guard. Whoever is there must be silenced if he hears anything and starts to investigate."

"Chloroform. We need to get some chloroform today. That's probably how those guys silenced Paz and Francesca when they abducted them," Mercedes said. "If it's the old guy, I doubt he'll be much of a threat, and if we incapacitate him and put him back in his chair; he won't know anything happened."

"I'll get the chloroform," said Gisella.

"Sounds good. The devices we got from Dascenzo should get us into both rooms. Once inside, wedge something in the doors so they look locked. If you have to make a quick exit, I don't need you to be fumbling with unlocking devices, especially with that keypad door. And once inside, Sean goes to work. You'll have your laptop with you?"

"Absolutely. That will allow me to hack into their system."

"Once inside, we have to make sure there are no surveillance or alarm systems in place. Look for cameras and any wires around that door. The flashlights have an infrared light that will let us know if there are any laser beams that could be set off. Use them when you open that door to the room. Anything like that and you abort. Clear? If you can't diffuse it, leave. We regroup and figure it out later."

All nodded.

"Gisella, you and Rajesh will be back here with the telecom base unit monitoring what's happening the whole way. I'll keep my phone on, so keep me apprised of any issues and what you are able to achieve inside. Don't worry about the hour. I want alerts as to what is going on. Got it?"

"Got it, boss," said Sean, and the others nodded in agreement.

* * *

Mercedes and Gino were picked up by one of Fred's drivers, and they set out for Abu Dhabi. At the villa, the team continued to practice with the equipment. Fred and Nina tested the lock-picking gun on the outside door at the carport with no difficulty. They locked the door and opened it several times flawlessly. They already knew the two-way communication system worked well, given Ray's and Nina's experience. Sean and Fred practiced with the ear-buds in the villa, and their units performed equally well. Fred and Nina also tried on their black outfits. The countdown to midnight had begun.

By early afternoon, Gino called Ray advising him that he and

Mercedes were at the embassy and would be meeting shortly with the ambassador and his support team. First stop, however, was to meet Pete Dascenzo and thank him for the toys he had sent over.

"You're a godsend, Pete," Gino said after introducing himself and Mercedes to the CIA station chief. "That equipment will be invaluable for getting us in that souk."

"Not a problem, Gene," replied Dascenzo. "You have state-of-the-art stuff, and none of it costs what Ray Evans's Rolex did … fortunately."

"Yeah," said Gino. "Sorry about that, but it was unavoidable, and it did the job, but you know I paid him back big-time. Transferred all the Zahori holdings to the agency's Geneva account, so he shouldn't complain."

"He didn't," Pete said laughing. "We know he got the okay to donate almost all of it—anonymously of course—to that pediatric cancer hospital your bad guys were supposedly financing in Madrid."

"Right. That was supposed to be their entrée into the hearts and minds of the Spanish people, en route to their plan to take over the government and convert it to an Islamic monarchy. In the end, it worked out well for Spain."

"Let's hope Operation Retrieval works out as well. It's a bold plan the ambassador worked out with the intelligence and diplomatic hierarchy back in DC," commented Dascenzo. "We'll be monitoring the whole thing here, with you, Captain Garcia, as well as Ambassador Atkins and Colonel Sanders—Yeah, I know, no fried chicken comments please—all miked up. You all will be wired, and there will be a transmitter in one of the marine vehicles sending everything back here. Sanders will also be wearing eyeglasses with an embedded video recording device—another one of our toys—so nothing will be missed."

"Shit," said Gino. "I should have held out for a set for us as well."

"You'll be fine. Have you determined when your guys are going to get into that souk?"

"Tonight, well after midnight. Fred Leamington, ex-FBI and freelance contractor for the bureau, will be running the show along with your Nina Darvish, a local Interpol investigator, and the young man who got Ray Evans all that money, by hacking into the Zahori bank accounts. Hopefully, once inside, he can get into the Saqr computer system and get what we need to track down the other women who were abducted and get the evidence to stop them and put them away."

"Stopping them and getting evidence to put them away are two distinct issues. Operating here with no jurisdiction, no warrants, and technically no authority, has you out on a tightrope with no net. I hope all goes well. Give the guys monitoring your operation my number in case anything goes awry. Have them commit it to memory. No paper trail. I'd really prefer your team didn't take any action until we got our girls back, but I understand how critical the timing is."

"I'd like to be there with them, but no one will be carrying any incriminating IDs, so the operations shouldn't conflict with one another. By this time tomorrow, hopefully, both missions will be successfully completed."

"Your mouth to God's ears," sighed Dascenzo. Looking at his watch, he said, "Showtime. Let's meet with Atkins and Sanders now and lay out the plan."

Chapter Forty-Eight

By the time midnight came around, Sean O'Casey was a handsome, raven-haired man with freckles. He, Fred, and Nina wore their black ninja outfits, and Ray was back in his Arab garb. The plan was for Nina and Fred to get into the souk and once inside and in the back room to alert Ray and Sean, who would be waiting in the Toyota nearby.

The four of them left the villa at half past one, drove to the side street adjacent to the souk, and waited. There was no one around on the dark and quiet street, but they waited and watched until two o'clock before turning off the car's dome light and venturing out wearing their blue, nitrile surgical gloves. Nina and Fred moved to the wall of the souk and slowly crept about twenty meters to the side door. The light bulb Nina had unscrewed the night before remained dark, but there was just enough ambient light for Fred to locate the keypad, attach the decoding device, and push the button to start its analytics. Fred cupped his hands over the unit as it showed blinking yellow lights and then a green light as each password digit was decoded. In less than a minute, four green lights appeared and then a click. The door popped open a few inches.

"In," said Fred. "Remain in the car until I get through the next door," he said to Ray and Sean. He put the decoding device back in his fanny pack. He slowly opened the door, and they silently slipped inside. They closed the door. Fred used masking tape to hold the lock open and wedged a piece of cardboard between the door and the frame, before closing it. The two waited inside, not moving for about two minutes as their eyes got accustomed to the dark.

"Nothing," whispered Fred. "No one around I can see." He and Nina waited a bit longer. Off to the left, they saw a very dim yellow glow from some light fixture farther down the passageway. None of the glow carried to where they waited. Nina crouched and silently worked her way toward the glow staying close to the wall and checking for any sentry. She returned quickly and reported, "No one around. If the guy we saw in the chair last night is still around, he's deeper into the souk."

They moved to the right until they were in front of the wooden doors that Zayed had entered. Fred felt all around the door for wires that could be part of an alarm system. He removed his flashlight from his pack, adjusted it to a pinpoint beam, and traced the sides, top, and bottom of the door. Nothing. No cameras either. He withdrew the lock-pick gun and inserted its filaments into the door lock. Slow, steady pressure on the trigger activated the mechanism; it clicked away, searching for the tumblers that would unlock the door. Fred asked Nina to go back a way into the souk to see if the noise had attracted any attention. To Fred, the clicking was deafening, but in reality, it was relatively quiet until the lock clicked open. Nina returned and joined Fred at the door. They slowly, very slowly, pushed it open. Again, Fred used the flashlight, this time pushing the red button on the barrel to activate the infra-red light to scan the area inside for any laser alarm beams. Again, nothing.

They moved inside. Fred again taped the lock in open position and wedged another piece of cardboard he extracted from his fanny pack to keep the door in a closed position. They found themselves in a small room with stacks of carpets on either side of the door. Off to the left was a counter not more than two meters wide with pads of paper and two small calculators on top, but nothing else. At the back of the small antechamber was another door. With the front door closed, they used their flashlights to scan the door again looking for any alarm wires but found none. Fred tried the door, but it too was locked. The lock gun was again inserted into the keyhole, and after a series of familiar clicks, it opened. Nina went back to the front door once all flashlights were doused. She peeked out to see if there was any activity, but all remained dark and silent.

After another sweep with the infrared beam, they entered the other room quietly closing the door almost all the way before turning on their flashlights. They were in a much larger room with a high ceiling. They saw four flat-screen monitors on one wall. Below and in front of the monitors was a small circular platform, not quite a foot high and partially covered with a rectangular oriental carpet and a simple chair at its center. On the other side of the room were tables with a computer terminal at one end farthest from the door and chairs behind the tables. They saw several fluorescent light fixtures hanging from the ceiling, and they eventually located a light switch near the door where they had entered. The lights would remain off as the pair continued to survey the room with their flashlights.

"There's our computer," whispered Nina also noting a printer on the floor below it and a couple of remote-control units on one of the tables, possibly for the video monitors. A tripod with a video camera mounted was at the far end of the room with some cables hanging from it leading to the computer. There were a few more carpets strewn around behind the chairs but little else, except for a small refrigerator near the carpets and a door that led to a small restroom, housing a toilet and sink, but no towels. She related what they saw to the others through her ear mike and then said, "Sean, time for you to get in here. I'll meet you at the back door and lead you in."

Fred added, "Ray, you remain in the car and keep your eyes on the street." He took out his cell phone and began taking pictures of the room, every nook and cranny of its layout and close-ups of the computer and television monitors. He sent them to Rajesh's computer at the villa, and once receipt was confirmed, he deleted all the photos from his phone.

Sean had left the car and was slipping on his rubber gloves as he walked and was quickly at the side door. Nina had removed the wedge and slowly opened it for Sean to slip inside. She closed the door and reinserted the wedge. Quickly, they moved to the double doors, and Nina brought him inside silently closing the door. She navigated through the small antechamber and into the larger back room, ostensibly the control room of the operation.

"Nina, as we discussed, you work with Sean. I'll set up a couple of cameras where they won't be seen and then slip outside and keep tabs on any activity," Fred said, keeping his hoodie in place. "You guys check out this computer and see what you can do."

Sean took a seat in front of the computer terminal, opened his laptop beside it, and flexed his fingers backward. He was ready to play. He booted up his laptop and hit the power switch on the Dell computer in front of him. Lights on both machines blinked yellow and blue as they powered up and lit the room with a soft glow. They were in luck. The keyboard was using the Roman alphabet in Arabic rather than Arabic script. Windows had devised an Arabic-character keyboard and software, but it was not extensively used in global businesses. Nina would work that computer.

The sign-on screen on Hazem's computer popped up, and Sean began typing on his laptop. It was now a waiting game as Sean went through his process to get through the computer security. Nina transmitted to Rajesh and Gisella what was going on while Sean worked his magic. Fred, in the meantime, texted Gino, "We're inside."

Sean clicked away on his agency laptop, its hacking software searching for an opening into the adjacent computer. It eventually deciphered user name and password, which turned out to be Saqr##5. Immediately an icon screen displayed a variety of symbols and descriptions. Most were in the Windows English text, but one was a circle with a falcon at its center, and the one right below it, "Habduja Bank," caught his eye. The task bar at the bottom of the screen had symbols for Word, Excel Spreadsheet, PowerPoint, Google Chrome, and g-mail.

"I'm gonna try this Saqr icon," he said to Nina. He clicked on the symbol, and a gateway to an apparent website appeared. It exhibited a black falcon. Around the falcon were phrases in Arabic. "Nina, can you open this on their computer? We're in, but it has to be your game now. Fred, are you getting this?" Sean asked.

"Got it," Fred replied. "I'll text Gino. See what you can pull out of that unit."

Sean turned to Nina and noticed that the Saqr website was on the Dell screen. "Nina, here—take this flash drive and see what you can pull out of that site. Download anything and everything you can."

"Shit, Sean. There's another log-in screen here. Can you break it?"

"Sure, but you may need to peek over here if I get bogged down with the Arabic. There doesn't seem to be any sophisticated security on this computer, like thumbprints or eyeball readers, so it'll just take time and effort."

After another fifteen minutes, the website indicated that there could be multiple sign-in access codes. "Looks like this is set up for multiple users, each with his own sign-in code," said Sean. "I'm going to open up just one to get inside. Then you'll see what it offers us."

Nina explored the website and translated some sections to Sean. She clicked on *sabaa'm*—clients—and a list of names appeared. "Look at the names here, Sean. They're laid out by country— Saudi Arabia,

Qatar, Dubai, Abu Dhabi, many countries and many names and some obviously royalty. Look, Ras al-Khaimah, with Sheikh Saud bin Nassr al-Sisi, the guy who has the American and Spanish girls."

"Click there," directed Sean.

The screen opened with pictures of the two girls with a euro amount below each picture—€800,000 for the de la Cruz girl and €1,000,000 for the American.

"Do you think that's what was paid for each girl? They sold them for those amounts?"

"Maybe," replied Sean. "Download all this stuff, the lists of clients, and see if you can pull up anything on the other girls. Then open all the other portals and download them as well."

"I saw a portal *banaat,* meaning girl. Going back, the term was *banaat/faaresa,* girls/prey in English." *Prey of the falcon?* Nina asked herself. She opened that portal, and a full list of the kidnapped students appeared with their university and dates. *Dates of their abductions?* Camille La Monde, Sorbonne, Paris, December, 2012; Gabriella Santini, Politecnico, Milan, November, 2013; Elizabeth Mills, Claire Windsor, Jana Weigel, Greta Mulder, Paz de la Cruz, Francesca Fontana. They were all there, their schools and the dates abducted. No further details in that portal, but it was a breakthrough, and all went onto the flash drive.

They worked for two hours doing more downloading than reading. In the Excel spreadsheet were more details of the operation and profiles of the abducted women: ages, areas of study, honors received, home residences, school residences, profiles of activity, what they did, where they went. Under "local asset" was a name, presumably the person who had coordinated the abduction with Saqr. At the bottom of each girl's profile were details of the transaction—the sale of the women, to whom, destination and cost/benefit for the operation. All went onto the flash drive.

Sean clicked the Habduja Bank icon. Saqr, Ltd. was the account, and with the agency laptop, Sean hacked into the system, gained access to the account, and downloaded what was there.

Fred popped in. "Time to close-down and go, guys. Put everything back as you found it and let's get out of here. We're pushing our luck. Ray, all clear outside? Okay to come out?"

"All clear, Fred. I fought to stay awake all this time as it's dead quiet on the street. The most noise will be me starting the car and driving away."

The three silently exited the operation center and removed the masking tape and the wedges. As they were traversing the anteroom and about to enter the souk, Nina said, "Wait."

They huddled behind the front door while Nina peered out of a crack. "Shit. Someone with a flashlight. Maybe that old guy from last night. Quiet."

They waited. Their hearts pounded. One minute. Two minutes. Three minutes. Four minutes. She cracked the door and peeked out. She smelled cigarette smoke wafting through the opening. She saw the beam of the flashlight moving deeper into the souk. The guard took his surveillance walk enjoying a cigarette, and he was returning to his post.

"Now," Nina whispered. They filtered out of the front door again taking the tape and wedges. They moved to the side door and retrieved the tape and wedge.

Fred said, "Ray, still clear?"

Ray had heard what had gone on inside and was relieved that their incursion and exit were without incident. "All clear. I'm starting the engine."

Quickly one by one they slid along the wall, Nina leading, Sean behind her, and Fred taking up the rear. They all entered through the back door of the Toyota, with Nina scrambling over the front passenger seat while Sean and Fred slid into the rear. The Toyota moved slowly with lights out until it was at the end of the block. Ray turned left, put on the headlights, and headed back to Jumeirah Road. On the way, Fred texted Gino, "Goods obtained. We'll see what we got later today," It was four forty a.m.

Ray drove into the carport with headlights off. Rajesh opened the door for them, keeping the hall light off. He had followed Nina's and Sean's conversation and was eager to see what they had found.

"No more tonight guys," Fred said as they entered the living room. "A few hours of sleep and then we dig into those flash drives and put together a dossier. What was Gino's operation called, Operation Retrieval? We'll call ours Operation Discovery, okay?"

"I'm very optimistic that we've blown this thing wide open," Sean said. "Later, I intend to play with their accounts at Habduja Bank and see if I can work more magic. Night, all," he said as he headed to his bedroom.

* * *

Gino slept lightly that night; checking his phone each time the message function beeped. Fred's texts were purposefully somewhat cryptic, but he knew that they had gotten the data. *They'll have a busy morning as will I.*

Chapter Forty-Nine

Knowing that the US ambassador would be coming to Ras al-Khaimah by car, the sheikh had considerately set up the meeting for noon; he planned to entertain his visitors with a lunch as they talked about tourism to his emirate.

At nine thirty, the caravan set out from the embassy. Ambassador Atkins and Colonel Sanders were in the second seats of the oversized Chevy Suburban with Gino and Mercedes in the third row. The squad of marines traveled in three military jeeps and another Suburban; two in a jeep in front of the caravan, two in a Suburban behind the ambassador, and nine in the two trailing jeeps. The Suburban with the two marines also contained a transmitter that would record and transmit the conversation at the palace to Pete Dascenzo and his agents. Colonel Sanders's camera glasses would forward a video feed to the embassy basement as well.

Light conversation took up the travel time; the key players got to know each other better. Atkins was a slightly portly man with fair skin, thinning red hair turning gray, and a gray moustache with red highlights. He was a career diplomat with the State Department and was in Abu Dhabi with his wife. His children were back in the States. His daughter was studying at Duke University in North Carolina, and his son was a Wall Street investment banker.

Sanders, in his late fifties, was a tall, light-skinned black man with

237

short-cropped hair mostly gray. He looked elegant in his dress blues, his chest festooned with medals from his time in the Gulf War, two tours in Afghanistan, and one in Iraq. He was stationed at the new US embassy there. Iraq was his first embassy support assignment; he has been in Abu Dhabi for two years.

Gino and Mercedes recounted their work in Spain uncovering the conspiracy of the Zahori family and their plans to convert Spain into an Islamic monarchy. Dascenzo had given Atkins and Sanders a briefing of that incredible mission and how Gino and Mercedes had pulled it off with a ragtag team of talent Gino had put together, independent of the US intelligence and investigative agencies, but with a lot of under-the-table support, notably from the CIA group attached to the Madrid embassy. Atkins and Sanders had many questions for Gino and Mercedes regarding that operation and marveled at how they had stopped a five-hundred-year-old conspiracy.

Traffic was light on the modern highways in the Emirates. At eleven forty-five, the caravan pulled up to the front entrance and was directed by palace guards into the grounds; they stopped near the looming statue of Midnight. The jeeps with the marines were directed to shaded areas where they would wait. Majid Khan was beside the fountain waiting to greet the emissaries as they exited the lead Suburban. The second Suburban moved off to where the jeeps were. Majid introduced himself and led the four visitors to the palace, where they ascended marble steps to the main building. At the top of the stairs and standing just inside huge, heavily decorated wood doors at least twenty feet high, was Sheikh Saud bin Nassr al-Sisi, splendidly bedecked in a full, flowing, white robe and white headdress with a thick red and white *agal* circling his forehead.

"Welcome to my home," the sheikh said beaming to his visitors.

William Atkins swallowed hard. "Thank you so much for meeting with us, your highness." He extended his hand to the sheikh, who warmly clasped it in his own. "Let me introduce Colonel Thomas Sanders, United States Marines, attached to our embassy." The colonel stepped forward and shook hands with the sheikh. "And Special Agent Eugene Cerone of the Federal Bureau of Investigation, and Captain Mercedes Garcia of the Spanish National Police Force."

"The FBI and Spanish National Police?" the sheikh queried. "For a meeting to discuss tourism to this emirate?"

"It is more than that, your highness. I am here to demand that you immediately release Paz de la Cruz and Francesca Fontana to our custody. We have incontrovertible proof that you are holding these women against their will, after their abduction from the University of Madrid in November. Incontrovertible evidence. Hand them over to us now and it goes no further. No diplomatic incident, no headlines in the world press, no criminal charges for human trafficking against you or your regime. Give us the girls, and as far as your involvement is concerned, the incident is closed."

The sheikh's smile had faded. His mouth was agape. Seconds passed in silence. He blinked and turned to Majid Khan, who stared back, his eyes round and his eyebrows arched as if asking the silent question, *How do they know?* The silence continued. No one moved. All eyes were on the sheikh.

Shaking his head slowly and staring at the marble floor, the sheikh released a sigh. He raised his head and looked one by one at the visitors behind the ambassador and then to Atkins. "Mr. Ambassador, I am at a loss for words. This is really not what it appears to be," he stammered.

"It is exactly what it appears to be, Sheikh Saud!" Mercedes blurted out. "The girls were kidnapped and taken here, to your palace, for your pleasure, or for what other purpose, I do not know. They need to be brought to us now."

"For my pleasure? By Allah no. They have been treated well, as part of my staff. They have become magnificent teachers, mentors to my children, who truly love them. That is the pleasure I get, seeing these wonderful women instill knowledge, leadership, and confidence in my children, who will someday lead this country and perhaps the entire region out of its Middle Age shackles."

"Very commendable, your highness," Atkins said, "but you know full well that this cannot be the way to achieve your vision, not by emulating that slave trade from the Middle Ages you so detest. You were educated and welcomed in my country and you resort to this abomination? It would be interesting to learn why and how you chose such a devious means to an end, but not today.

"Bring us the women and we will be on our way. This does not have to go any further. Not to Sheikh Shehzad bin Sultan al-Nazari, the head of the UAE. Not to anyone outside this tight circle of those involved in the investigation, who have documented that the women are here. Now, your highness. Now," demanded the ambassador, emboldened by the conviction and determination of those standing behind him—and the marines in the courtyard.

"Majid, instruct Samira to bring the girls to us now," the sheikh ordered. "Say nothing to the children or their mothers."

Majid lingered a moment, then turned and left.

The sheikh said no more, and the contingent from the embassy did likewise. Five people, standing rigidly, looking forward, saying nothing.

Shortly, Samira and Majid emerged from the deep hallway, leading the women by their arms to the palace doors, where they incredulously looked at the gathering before them and noted the rod-straight soldier with medals on his blue jacket and a white hat pulled down close to his eyes. *An American soldier!*

"Miss de la Cruz and Miss Fontana," the sheikh began, "these people have come to take you home. Please accompany them. I thank you for what you have done for my children. You have made a contribution I will always be grateful for, and I am truly sorry for any hardship we have put you through. *'Ila l-líqaá.* Goodbye."

Majid and Samira released Paz and Frankie, who, bewildered, moved swiftly to the group before them. Mercedes hugged them and led them from the palace.

Gino said, "Your highness, you know how we feel about what you have been a part of, but I detect sincerity in your words and demeanor. You apparently are not a bad man, and I would like to know more of your vision to escape the entrapments of the Middle Ages, though this palace hardly looks like an entrapment. Why and how this came to be intrigues me. Would you allow me the honor to hear more of this from you?"

Atkins, Sanders, and especially Mercedes turned to Gino trying to understand the curveball he had just thrown.

"Let me sit with you and try to understand this. We still have time set aside for a meeting. My colleagues will leave with Francesca and Paz. I hope you and I can learn more about each other, especially in regard to your vision. I can return to the embassy later," Gino said.

"Well—what is it, Special Agent from the famous FBI?—I had arranged for us to meet over lunch. No need for that food to go to waste. We can talk," replied the sheikh.

"Give me a minute, your highness. I think I surprised my friends." He moved to his colleagues, who had halted their exit.

"What are you doing, Gino?" Mercedes asked more perplexed than the girls were.

"We will never get an opportunity like this again. We have six other girls to find, and if I can get more details about how this scheme works, it will help us enormously."

"You'll be on you own, Gene," Ambassador Atkins said. "Our work is done. We got the American girl back with her Spanish friend. I want to get out of here with no diplomatic blowups."

"You were great, Mr. Ambassador. This is an incredible win for all of us, but there is more to be done. I have my team here in Dubai working with Interpol. We can take it from here. They're working with data they extracted from a Saqr computer, and maybe I can help by getting whatever I can from the sheikh. There's nothing to lose.

"Mercedes, the ambassador and Colonel Sanders have a plane waiting to take the women to Spain. Go with them and make sure your government stays quiet about this. Your guys should liaise with the FBI. Better, try to take the lead in working with Guiness. We have to get our stories straight when the girls get back. What did you say, Mr. Ambassador, so there is no diplomatic blowup? We don't want a blowup back to the sheikh, and we don't want to alert the other abductors about this. This is vitally important. Everybody clear on that?"

Ambassador Atkins and Colonel Sanders replied almost simultaneously, "Got it," and Mercedes said, "*En acuerdo,*—I agree.

"We have to get going, Gene," said the ambassador. "Operation Retrieval is closed. An incredible success all around. Let me know if there's anything more I can do, and let me know what you get from the sheikh. I'll leave one of the Suburbans and a driver here. Good luck."

Atkins and Sanders shook hands with Gino.

Mercedes approached Gino. "Call me," she said kissing and hugging him. She left arm in arm with the confused but smiling women.

Atkins will leave the Suburban with the transmitting equipment in it, Gino thought. *Dascenzo will be get the whole conversation.*

Chapter Fifty

The sheikh led Gino down a marble hallway with mosaic floor patterns, passing marble pillars and gilded archways. Polished, wood, double doors on each side of the hallway were studded with stars, horse heads, and crescent moons, all decorated in gold.

"Eugene Cerone and Captain Mercedes Garcia," the sheik said. "Didn't I read something about you regarding an incident in Spain a few years ago? Something about a conspiracy to take over the government that was thwarted? You and the captain were involved in that, no?"

"Yes, we were part of that, your highness, but many very good people were involved in that effort, including many from the Spanish government itself."

"You apparently are very adept at such investigations, Mr. Cerone. Were you also responsible for determining these girls were brought here? How did you accomplish that?"

"That I cannot tell you, your highness, but all the investigative bureaus in the US and Spain never rested in searching for them. Interpol played a large role also, and as always, a little luck was part of it too," Gino replied smiling.

The two arrived at an elaborate dining room with table settings for four at one end of a long, beautifully grained wood table that could have held at least a dozen more place settings. "I did not know that Ambassador Atkins was bringing guests. I anticipated myself, Majid, the ambassador, and an aide, but the food will not go to waste," he said with a laugh.

The sheikh moved to the chair at the head of the table and gestured for Gino to take the seat to his right. At each place setting was a plate of white china trimmed in gold and embossed with a golden horse in the center of the plate, in the same pose as the statue in the courtyard. Tea was poured, and two servants, women dressed in white-, gold-, and red-trimmed *abayas,* with no head coverings brought in a series of small plates and served portions to the diners.

"I am both embarrassed and somewhat relieved at this turn of events," began the sheikh. "What began as admittedly a terrible thing soon evolved into something, wonderful. My greatest hopes for my children were being achieved with the presence of those two women. Such leadership and strength and strong spirits. Just what I hoped for my children, especially the girls."

"With respect, your highness, you have three wives. Hardly an example of strength and independence of your women in your household."

"Touché, Mr. Cerone. Yes. Hypocrisy on my part. Traditions die hard in this part of the world, and you fall into the trap of doing what is expected. But I can promise you that none of my daughters will be part of any harem and my sons will not make that mistake either. It was that strength of character we were working toward. My family will be devastated by this loss. After lunch, I will sit with them and give them the sad news. I will have to concoct something plausible, but Mariam, my oldest, will take this hard. She and Miss Fontana were becoming very close."

"For your children, I am sorry, but we have had many months of sorrow with the families of Miss de la Cruz and Miss Fontana. The sorrow you feel now is balanced by the joy their parents will soon experience, holding them in their arms again."

"I am aware of that. We got caught up in the audacity of the plan and the ingenuity of those who put it all together and carried it out. Taking these women out of their universities, their countries, totally undetected and transporting them thousands of miles, in this case, to the middle of a desert. To accomplish this and to keep it going for years is incredible. But ultimately, our selfishness fed their operation."

"For years, your highness? You mean there have been other abductions?" feigned Gino.

"Ahh, I have said too much. I promised to share with you the rationale for what I did, however unworthy of who I really am—and I have. I should say no more. If you and your investigative colleagues can locate these two women out here, you undoubtedly will find the others. How many? I have no idea. Several for sure, but I fear that those young, idealistic men behind this may have met their match."

The two men picked at their food and sipped tea in silence for a few moments. "I ask of you only one thing, your highness. Those '*young, idealistic men*' behind this scheme should not be alerted to what has happened here today. We said we would not hold you accountable in the face of the world. There will be no repercussions for you or your government. We will keep silent, but you must also. If you break that silence, I promise nothing."

The sheikh was silent for a while. "All right, Mr. Cerone, we will say nothing of today. Only Majid and Samira, my closest aides, know what happened and will be sworn to silence. My wives as well. But when the girls arrive home, the world will want to know what happened to them. Where have they been for these months? I trust you to keep my name out of it, Mr. Cerone, but those behind the operation will know and will look to me for answers. A can of worms has been opened. I remember that phrase from my days in California. It will be hard to put the lid back on."

"We have a plan to contain this on the other end, your highness. That is critical."

"Ahh, but this is the Middle East, Mr. Cerone. No one here can keep secrets for long." The sheikh rose and extended his hand to Gino. "We will both do our best, Mr. Cerone. Majid will come and show you out."

* * *

As Gino was being driven to Dubai, he called Dascenzo. "How much of that did you get, Pete?"

"Pretty much all of it, Gene. I'll have a transcript sent to you in Dubai. Nice job. Nice job all around. Mercedes called Spain and New Jersey to let the parents know she was bringing them back to Madrid. Fontana's parents will fly to Madrid immediately. Both parents have been cautioned to say nothing to anybody. Atkins informed the secretary of state and Undersecretary Luxmore, and they'll debrief the FBI director and of course the president, who will call the prime minister of Spain. They will create a cover story that all will have to adhere to, but I fear the cat will likely be out of the bag soon, and alert the Saqr guys. Can't see any way around that. Gotta hand it to you though. Atkins too. What balls going in there and getting the girls out. If you ever want a job in the CIA, you got it."

"Ha! Getting a lot of job offers lately. But still much to be done. We move from Operation Retrieval to what my guys have termed Operation Discovery, and Nina is doing a great job helping us out. Unless we keep the cat in the bag, Saqr will be alerted and alert the others. Can't let that happen."

Gino then called Fred in Dubai about what had happened. He

directed Fred to put their operation into high gear anticipating they didn't have a lot of time before Saqr would find out. He made a quick call to Mercedes and let her know he was en-route back to Dubai. He then closed his eyes and napped. He had gotten very little sleep the previous night.

Chapter Fifty-One

Mercedes and the women arrived in Abu Dhabi and were driven to the airport, where a private jet was waiting to take them to Madrid, perhaps the same Gulfstream that had brought Sean to Dubai. Mercedes would record her debrief of the women with equipment Dascenzo had provided. Interpol, the Spanish police, the State Department, the FBI, and CIA wanted details of what had happened starting at the university parking lot. *We promised to keep the sheikh's name out of this?* Mercedes thought. *Maybe Gino can come up with another playbook.*

* * *

"Okay, guys," said Gino after accepting congratulations from all, "we need to fly." He filled them in on his conversation with the sheikh that had confirmed additional kidnappings carried out by Saqr. "From what I understand, the flash drives should give us the evidence we need, but let's focus on the most important issues. One, confirmation of who the other abducted girls are. We have a pretty good idea from the work by Interpol, but some of that was speculative. We need to know for sure. By the way, Ambassador Atkins was to inform all the key agencies in the States. Do we know if Schickhaus was informed?"

"Yes he was," replied Rajesh. "We got a congratulatory call from him a little while ago. Director Guiness filled him in. Schickhaus is waiting for the next steps from us based on what we got from the Saqr computer. He will be maintaining silence."

"Okay, good. So first, we confirm the girls kidnapped and where they are. Then, who has them? How do we get them back? What the role of Interpol will be? Substantial I would guess. To what degree—if any, and when— do we bring in the local police agencies, the ones who have been working on the investigation since we put all this together? When do we involve the foreign secretaries of the European countries, as we did with the State Department? The women are here, somewhere in the Middle East. That was implied by Sheikh Saud and by the involvement of Prince Azam Azziz. So make some space on that whiteboard, Gisella. Write down;

The girls

To where?

By whom?

Retrieval/confrontation—Interpol? Local police agencies?

Involvement of foreign secretaries and local ambassadors.

Middle Eastern government or police involvement."

"We've made a lot of progress on this Gino," said Nina. "From the data we pulled from the Saqr computer, the girls are exactly those we identified previously, and we know who has them and where they are. It was all laid out on a spreadsheet we downloaded complete with their photos. Gisella, add this to the whiteboard;

Camille Le Monde, Paris—Prince Azam Azziz bin Turki, Riyadh, Saudi Arabia. That son of a bitch was the first one to get an abducted girl.

Gabriella Santini, Milan—Ammaral Said al-Nabi, Manama, Bahrain.

Elizabeth Mills, London—Akram Zaatari, Abu Dhabi, UAE.

Claire Windsor, Oxford—Yasser Ali, Doha, Qatar.

Jana Weigel, Heidelberg—Mahmoud al-Mabhouh, Dubai, UAE.

Greta Mulder, Amsterdam—Waled Shaldubi, Riyadh, Saudi Arabia. We should also put down de la Cruz and Fontana, Madrid—Sheikh Saud bin Nassr al-Sisi, Ras al-Khaimah."

"So we have two Saudis, three in the emirates—Dubai, Abu Dhabi, and Ras al-Khaimah, one in Qatar, and one in Bahrain," said Gino. "Great work." He chuckled. "Atkins will have to teach his diplomatic counterparts the speech he gave to Sheikh Saud. What do we know about these guys?"

"Mahmoud al-Mabhouh in Dubai is a big-time developer," Nina said. "Half of those cranes you see in the city are from his company. No doubt he's connected to the royal family. He wouldn't control all that real estate if he weren't. But we don't know if he's directly tied in with Sheikh Mohammed bin Sa'id al-Masaari, the vice president and prime minister of the UAE. Haven't found anything on that yet. His connections could also be at any other level of the ruling family. It's a nightmare to try to figure out the family tree.

"Zaatari in Abu Dhabi is a director in the State Banking and Investment Ministry. That's a big, big post, and for sure he has connections—family or otherwise—with Sheikh Shehzad bin Sultan al-Nazari, who is head of the entire UAE.

"Waled Shaldubi is another cousin among hundreds in the Saudi royal family. Can't figure out if he's a prince like Azam Azziz, but he holds a very prominent position in Aramco. He and the crown prince were exploring taking the company public, but that seems to be on hold for now.

"Yasser Ali is way up there in al-Jazeera, Qatar's telecom giant, and he was heavily involved in getting Qatar to host the World Cup in 2022.

"Ammaral Said al-Nabi is a director in the Finance and Investment Ministry in Bahrain, the tiny island kingdom off the coast of Saudi

Arabia. Bahrain is supposed to have one of the fastest growing economies with a highly educated population, and it has been broadening its economy into banking with many of the largest financial institutions having a presence in Manama, its capital. He played a big role in diversifying beyond oil and natural gas production. Ties to their king and the Sulimani family? Don't know yet.

"And of course we know all about Price Azam Azziz bin Turki and his lend-lease Gulfstream jet," Nina concluded.

"You guys get any sleep at all?" asked Gino. "Terrific work. We need a sixth point on that whiteboard. Gisella, add Saqr. We have the first names of all the operatives. Their leader is a guy named Assad. Do we have their full names?"

"Yes," said Fred. "Nina and Sean pulled it out of the computer. The boss is Assad al-Amin. The others are Zayed Falaj, Hazem al-Sawai, Sulayman al-Raja, and Rasid bin Seray. Don't know very much about them other than they're all across the street right now. We also have a list of the assets they have in place across universities in Europe including the guy who died of an overdose in Vienna, the one who attacked Schiff. Why did he do that? No idea, but let's come back to that asset list later, hopefully as part of a cleanup. For now, as Gino said, we tighten up those key points remaining and most important come up with an action plan for recovering the girls."

"Yes, and that will be as complicated as Hades. Six European governments, actually five, and an equal amount of police agencies. Then there's Interpol, probably the lead agency in this, and what is it? Four other Middle Eastern monarchies?"

"Five," said Nina.

"Five," said Gino. "And how long will it take for the rescue we pulled off this morning to hit the press? We have to move at the speed of light to organize six rescues. I'll call Dascenzo and see if he can patch me through to Mercedes. I have a thought about how to keep this as stealthy as possible, at least in Spain."

A connection to the aircraft was swiftly arranged.

"Mercedes," Gino said, "you have to buy us some more time before the press gets wind of the rescue. Don't bring the girls to the de la Cruz apartment in Madrid. Either with your superiors in the National Police Force, or certainly via Ray Evans, come up with a safe house where the families can be reunited but kept secluded. You need more debriefing time with the girls anyway, and we cannot alert Saqr, and more important, the men who have the other girls. If this hits the fan, they can simply make those girls disappear. I'll ask Guiness to have the president make that clear to the Spanish prime minister. Then maybe we'll have time to put together something like we did with Atkins with the European foreign secretaries and their local country ambassadors. Get it done, Mercedes. Your role is vital."

"*En acuerdo, mi amor. Buenas suerte.*" She ended the call.

"Rajesh, get me Schickhaus in Lyon. He has to pull this together with European diplomats and the involved police agencies. Maybe we'll need the head of Interpol to take the lead on this, but get me Schickhaus first," Gino directed.

* * *

Klaus Schickhaus immediately brought Richard Lee, secretary general of Interpol, in on the planning after Gino's phone call. He explained to Lee how the Atkins confrontation had been managed, and the secretary general directed his staff to set up immediate teleconference calls with the foreign secretaries of France, Italy, the Netherlands, the UK, and Germany. If possible, the heads of the national police of those countries should be included, or at least the lead investigators who had been involved in the kidnapping investigations. Under the authority of the president of the United States and the US secretary of state, it was agreed that Atkins would lead the teleconference and relate exactly what had been accomplished in Ras al-Khaimah, with the hope that they could pull off the same thing in the other countries. It was recommended that Interpol agents and heads of the European national police forces accompany the country ambassadors in the confrontation with the suspected—the documented—kidnappers.

Local ambassadors would have to arrange meetings with the abductors. Unlike in Ras al-Khaimah, the meetings would have to be at the business offices of these men with Interpol agents stationed outside of the residences to take the released women into safe custody. Atkins would tell them that their demand had to be, "Release them now." It was deemed too complicated to have the local ambassadors included in the teleconference—far too many locations—but a videotape was being made for the foreign secretaries to take the ambassadors through the roles they would have to play.

Germany's and the Netherlands's foreign secretaries wanted to advise their counterparts in the countries involved and perhaps even the heads of state regarding the confrontation they were planning. It would be proper diplomatic protocol, they argued.

Gino, who was introduced to the group at the outset of the teleconference, strongly objected. "That would complicate and jeopardize the entire operation. We couldn't be sure that alerts would be given to the targets. Further, this way, we keep them clean. We attribute the kidnappings to an international human trafficking ring and keep their princes and business bigwigs out of the press. No diplomatic scandals for the world to see. We can tell them later, if necessary, and apologize afterward, but the more their counterparts don't know, the better it is for them and their image to the world."

That seemed to quell the unrest, but the UK foreign secretary voiced a different objection. "You want to commit to no repercussions for the perpetrators? They get off scot free? How is that justice?"

"If it could be done another way, I'd support it," replied Gino with Interpol Secretary General Lee nodding. "We want the girls back, no strings attached, and we want them back immediately. If we were to pursue this as a criminal matter, it would drag out forever in whatever courts we could prosecute them in, and it's quite probable that the girls would no longer be around. They'd disappear, and what would we have achieved? In these governments, not the most democratic of societies, rumors spread and these individuals become damaged goods. Things will likely take care of themselves eventually. But never lose sight of the fact that our primary objective, our only objective, is to bring the girls home."

That seemed to have brought unanimity within the participants. The only thing left was to alert and brief the local ambassadors. Their primary mission was to get appointments with the targets feigning some sort of important issue to discuss only with them and quickly. The goal would be to have meetings on the same day across the countries involved. Three days hence was set as Retrieval Day. It also gave time to have Interpol agents dispatched to the cities if no presence was already there, and get European police investigators down there as well.

Gino sighed in relief that all had gone well. He hoped that the appointments could be set up in time and that the actors would be well rehearsed for their confrontations. The balls—or ovaries in some cases—to make the confrontation with conviction, determination, and authority was the other unknown. They were diplomats used to being diplomatic, not necessarily forceful. *Fingers crossed*, he thought, but based on the palpable anger displayed by the foreign secretaries, they seemed up to it in Gino's mind.

Walking into the kitchen for a beer, Gino asked, "Where's Sean? I don't think I've seen hide nor hair of him since I got back."

"He's in his room," answered Nina. "He said something about a raid by the Berbers."

Walking into Sean's room, Gino saw the now black-haired young man hunched over his laptop oblivious to Gino's presence. "What's this about Berbers?" Gino asked. "That rings a bell."

"Yeah," Sean responded smiling. "That's the name we took—the CIA analysts and I—in Madrid when we hacked into the banks with the Zahori money."

"And …?"

"The Berbers ride again. I was able to get into the Habduja Bank in Dubai and link to Geneva. Saqr has funds locally, but most of their transactions—the money they got for the girls—is in Geneva. If Evans can give me his account number again, I should be able to engineer a transfer and route it to a few places until it gets to his— the agency's account—which also happens to be in Geneva, but at a different bank."

"He's gonna love that. I'll have Dascenzo pave the way unless he has an account number he'd like us to use. Keep on it. When I get the number, I want you to be able to just press a button."

Chapter Fifty-Two

Appointments were set up with the abductors, the ambassadors using whatever pretense they determined would entice their targets to meet without delay. The meetings spanned a range of three hours, but all on the same day. Simultaneous confrontations was the ideal, but Gino suspected that was not likely and felt relieved that they would at least be on the same day.

As two women were taken from the UK, the UAE ambassador, John Forsythe, would handle the Mills abduction in Abu Dhabi and the UK ambassador to Qatar, Henry Wilcox, would be responsible for Claire Windsor. Saudi Arabia was somewhat more complicated with two women taken to the same country and city, albeit from different European cities. The Dutch ambassador, Walter Ridyke, would confront Waled Shaldubi at Aramco headquarters on the kidnapping of Greta Mulder, and the ambassador from France, Brigit Deneuve, would meet with Prince Azam Azziz regarding Camille Le Monde, the woman who had been detained the longest. The ambassador from Germany, Erika Adler, was set to meet Mahmoud al-Mabhouh at his office in Dubai, and the ambassador from Italy, Bruno Ventura, with Ammaral Said al-Nabi in Manama, Bahrain, on Gabriella Santini's abduction. It was a veritable attack by the European Union on the richest and most powerful men in the Middle East. Representation from the police agencies of the countries involved were dispatched and already in place at the in-country embassies, as were Interpol agents. NATO could not have had soldiers in places as quickly.

While Frankie and Paz were secluded with their parents in a villa outside Madrid, the countdown for the rescues began; the plan was dubbed Operation Retrieval-EU, for European Union.

Three confrontations began at eleven o'clock. The French ambassador—Brigit Deneuve—along with Klaus Schickhaus and Claudine Montand of the Police Nationale met with Prince Azam Azziz bin Turki. Because of the prince's active role in facilitating the abductions, Schickhaus wanted to be there. At the same time, the UK ambassadors to the UAE and Qatar, reinforced with Interpol and national police representatives, began their confrontations in Abu Dhabi and Doha. The meetings with the UK ambassadors to both countries went according to script, but the meeting with Azam Azziz was more difficult. Schickhaus had to take the lead in documenting the presence of the prince's plane at all the abduction locations, as well as evidence from the Saqr computer including how much the prince had paid for Miss Le Monde.

"Incontrovertible," Schickhaus asserted.

"Camille has been with us for five years," Azam Azziz blurted out. "She enjoys a freedom we never anticipated. She is almost like one of our family. She may not want to leave."

"Let her make that decision. If she were not a prisoner, she could have gone back to Paris when she wanted and returned to Riyadh if she loved being here," said Schickhaus.

"But you did not permit that," Ambassador Deneuve said. "Release her now. If she wants to return to your employ—if you can call it that— she will. Do we need to bring this debacle to the attention of King Ali bin Assad? Think of the diplomatic and criminal consequences that would cause. Would Crown Prince Mohammed bin Hassan welcome such notoriety? I think not. Make the call. We have agents outside your residence waiting for Miss Le Monde."

Azam Azziz reluctantly picked up a phone.

The next two confrontations took place at noon. The ambassadors from Germany and the Netherlands went into their meetings in Riyadh and Dubai simultaneously each accompanied by Interpol and national police agents from their countries. Neither target was intimidated at first, but both showed shock. In Dubai, Carl Mittemaier of the German BKA got the impression that the Dubai royal family—or at least someone in that circle—would not have been surprised by the allegation, but the promise of no repercussions eventually closed the deals. Calls were made to release the women to the Interpol agents.

By early afternoon, five of the six women were discretely at their country embassies and a blackout of the news prevailed. Each embassy was told that it couldn't release the rescue information for fear it might compromise efforts underway elsewhere. Not even the parents of the kidnapped women would be advised until all were safe and the cover story established. That basically meant until the Saqr group was neutralized.

* * *

Ammaral Said al-Nabi, second to the Minister of Finance and Investment in Bahrain, was also a previous director of BAPCO, Bahrain Petroleum Company. He was a middle-aged man with thinning black hair combed straight back and a large salt-and-pepper moustache. He was dressed as a civilian, blue suit—impeccably tailored—white shirt, and a blue and gray necktie. His demeanor was somewhat sullen; he was undoubtedly perturbed that his busy day had been interrupted by a meeting with the Italian ambassador and couldn't fathom why the ambassador was accompanied by someone from Interpol and a detective from the Guardia di Finanza, Maria Marzano. His secretary had said nothing about that when setting up the meeting.

The Italian ambassador, Bruno Ventura, was about six feet tall with unruly, shiny black hair flowing over his shirt collar. He had a healthy-looking tan, great teeth, but barely a smile, and his stature conveyed an image of someone in control, likely due to his many years as a commander in the Italian navy. All three visitors were directed to chairs in front of al-Nabi's massive desk.

Sitting between detective Marzano and Giancarlo Marino, representing Interpol, Ventura immediately went to the script regarding the abduction of Gabriella Santini, almost five years earlier from Politecnico di Milano. Ventura accentuated his words with almost an orchestra conductor's hands; making his points and then slamming the desk with the words, "Incontrovertible proof!" of the executive's role in the girl's abduction and imprisonment.

A long silence followed the ambassador's charges and demand that Gabriella Santini be immediately released.

"And what if I deny any knowledge of this?" asked al-Nabi

"Then this goes public," replied Ventura. "Every news agency in the world will be presented with the evidence against you, and demands will be made to your king for your criminal prosecution. With Bahrain's spotty record on human rights—to say the least—it will be a black eye the regime would surely not welcome. Not now, when the kingdom is saying it is making improvements. Release the young woman. We have agents outside your home to receive her."

Ammaral Said al-Nabi sighed. He rose and looked out the window behind his desk overlooking Manama. "I no longer have the Sabatini girl," he said in a barely audible voice. "I haven't had her for more than two years now."

"What do you mean you don't have her?" demanded Detective Marzano.

"She never accepted the role we established for her. She fought us at every turn and refused to work with my children. She destroyed her residence and at times refused to eat. My staff was extremely patient with her for almost three years, years in which my children's education was totally forsaken. We had to bring in new tutors to catch up to where they should have been. She was an uncontrollable firebrand. We indulged her, hoping she would accept her role, but she didn't; so she had to go," replied al-Nabi still looking out the window.

"Go where?" Marzano asked.

More silence. Ammaral Said al-Nabi walked back to this desk, put his hands on it, and leaned forward. "Sold. She was sold."

"Sold?" exclaimed Ventura. "She was kidnapped, bought by you in some hideous scheme, taken to your home, and then you sold her, a human being? To whom?"

"Many organizations in the Middle East are very adept at moving people."

"You're talking about human traffickers, you scoundrel. You sold her to a trafficking ring?" Marino asked almost not believing what he was hearing. "Let me make something clear, Mr. al-Nabi. You will contact the people you sold Miss Santini to. You will find out where she is. You will move heaven and earth to work with us to get her back."

* * *

The joy felt by the other European ambassadors and their police and Interpol colleagues at the release of five kidnapped victims—apparently unharmed—was severely tempered by the tragic occurrence in Bahrain. It took only a few days to track Santini's whereabouts, as she had never left Bahrain. Ammaral knew the consequences if he didn't direct those involved to locate her immediately. He made it clear that failure was not an option. It was swiftly ascertained that the girl had been sold to someone in the royal family tree—Farhaj bin Tariq Ahsan—who had made her, in essence, part of his harem. It was discovered that at times she was administered drugs to make her compliant with this sultan's demands, but she never stopped fighting her imprisonment. Her fate was despicable but far better than winding up in a sex-trafficking ring and shipped off to somewhere in the Philippines, Hong Kong, or wherever, and ensconced in a bordello run by the lowest of animals. Without question, Sabatini had been sexually abused by her captor, something she might never recover from, but she was found and was going to be returned to her family in Italy.

When Gino heard the news about the Santini girl, he placed a call to Dascenzo in Abu Dhabi. "What do you think, Pete?" Gino asked.

"There needs to be some retribution, Gene. Our promise to keep this whole conspiracy quiet really sticks in my craw."

"Yeah, we did make a deal with the devil—several devils—but at least we got everyone back. I wasn't sure we could pull it off."

"That doesn't make the pain go away. I was talking about this with Al Rivera, my counterpart at the embassy in Bahrain. He was really upset. He told me that the fury at the Italian Embassy was almost uncontrollable. They would love to find a way to deal with him, that al-Nabi bastard."

"Yeah," Gino replied, "and that fat prick of a sultan—Farhaj bin Tariq Ahsan—or whatever the hell he is, made her part of a harem; the way they did a thousand years ago."

"Maybe not so long ago, Gene. This shit still goes on around here. Human trafficking continues in this part of the world. It's like an import/export business run by those who can present a legitimate veneer over sleaze and corruption."

"So that's it?" asked Gino. "Case closed?"

"Maybe, maybe not," said Dascenzo. "You know we have contact information for that Egyptian."

"Yeah. I thought that Interpol was going to follow up on that. They even hinted at my pursuing it."

"Stay away from it for now. We traced that phone number to a guy, Gamal Faruk, living in Golfo Aranci, Sardinia, somewhere in the north of the island. This guy got rid of a risk in Milan, that professor, and the kid who assaulted the Schiff girl in Vienna. Nice and clean. No trace."

"So what are you saying, Pete?"

"We now have a lot of money sitting in Geneva thanks to your guy making a withdrawal."

"And?"

"Maybe some of that money can be used productively. Closing things that need to be closed," answered Dascenzo.

"I get your drift. No need to say any more. This is more your area than mine, but retribution would be a very nice ending to this all."

"Leave it to me, Gene. We'll see what we can work out."

Chapter Fifty-Three

Klaus Schickhaus got back to Gino later in the day with the news and details of their sweeping successes, notwithstanding the horror of the Santini situation in Bahrain, but at least they got her back. While promises were made by the perpetrators not to communicate with Saqr, there was no guarantee that that would hold for very long. Nor could they maintain an extended blackout on the embassies involved in the recovery. A leak was bound to occur and alert the team across the street. There needed to be swift police action taken against the trafficking ring, but no one in the villa had any authority to move on that front.

The observation by the German BKA agent was passed on to Gino, and it got him thinking that the regime in Dubai had perhaps been turning, at least a blind eye to the Saqr operation. Three abductions to the UAE could not have been kept so secret. As the girls had been taken to Dubai by private jet and had passed through immigration without incident, nor any record, there had to be a support network they hadn't uncovered, Gino was sure.

Gino, Mercedes, and the others explored their options. They considered going directly to Sheikh Mohammed, ruler of Dubai, and imploring him to close down Saqr forever. In Dubai, as with Ras al-Khaimah, the sheikh owned the country and virtually all in it. A word from the sheikh and the members of Saqr would disappear without a trace. They also thought about going to the head of the police in

Dubai. Ray and Rajesh knew the man and several of his officers, but ultimately, something so explosive had to be brought to the sheikh. And there was the issue of the sixty or so- supporters of the Saqr operation, those who had provided Assad and his crew with financing, not to mention the assets Saqr had placed in the European universities. Those assets could be rounded up easily by local police and Interpol. The men who financed Saqr and awaited their opportunity to acquire their own kidnapped student, however, would need a powerful voice to direct them to find another way toward modernity and leadership development. Their network and all operations tied to it needed to end.

Gino discussed the issue with Guiness, who explored options with the State Department. Getting a green light from the president, they developed a plan. As they had done in Ras al-Khaimah, there would be a meeting with Sheikh Mohammed bin Sa'id al-Masaari advising him of what an Interpol investigation had uncovered. It was important to use Interpol as those were the kind of investigations they did all over the world. Without going into all the details, those meeting with the sheikh would explain that this trafficking ring—Saqr—had been traced to Dubai and that immediate police action was required to ensure their capture and detention. There would be no mention that Saqr was essentially crippled as their funds had been transferred to the Cayman Islands and then to Hong Kong and finally to a secure CIA account in Geneva.

Ambassador Atkins would again lead the effort to confront, no, *advise* the sheikh, with Gino, Colonel Sanders, and Raymond Kapur, representing Interpol, attending. As expected, with the US ambassador to the UAE, requesting an urgent meeting with ruler of Dubai, who was also vice president of the UAE, was compelling and expeditiously arranged.

* * *

The blackout of the release of the kidnapped girls continued, so everything relating to the Operation Retrieval-EU remained secret as Atkins led his group into the sheikh's palace. Escorted by two aids, they walked through rose-colored marble and granite halls, not unlike the splendor they had seen in Ras al-Khaimah. They stopped in front of two massive, elaborately carved, dark, wooden doors. One aide opened the doors pushing meter-long bronze handles on each and gesturing for the visitors to enter. The salon reminded Gino of what the Oval Office looked like. A large desk toward the back stood in front of windows looking out on the Persian Gulf. A large seating area was in the middle of the rotunda, all French provincial furniture, with three plush upholstered sofas and a large armchair obviously for the sheikh. A large, rectangular table—granite top and ornate gold provincial legs—sat in the middle with a very large oriental carpet of what may have been of Emirati design—definitely not Persian—extending a meter or so beyond all the furniture.

The sheikh moved from his desk to greet the visitors. He was bedecked in a traditional white *thobe*, a red and white *ghutra* covering his head, and a black *agal* cord just above the forehead, holding the head scarf in place. He also wore a white *bisht*—cloak—trimmed in gold. He was a tall man, light- mocha skinned with a neatly trimmed black beard and black eyes. He was handsome and seemingly quick to smile, something that might have come easily to the man who directed the miracle of Dubai. Two staff members entered from a door off to the side of the room. They were introduced, but no function was mentioned, and none of the visitors would remember their complex names.

The ambassador introduced his entourage and their titles. With the mention of Interpol and FBI, Gino detected a slight movement of the headscarves covering the host's forehead. *Maybe eyebrows rising*, he thought.

The sheikh directed the group to sit. A woman entered with a tea service and filled cups for the men without asking if they wanted it or not. Tea was the instrument of conversation in the Middle East, so it went without saying that everyone partook of it.

"You said this was urgent, Mr. Ambassador, and you insisted that you could give no details," the sheikh said. "Curiosity kills the cat, they say, but nevertheless I am intrigued. More so now that you have brought with you an American FBI agent and an Interpol agent. Are you here to arrest me?" he said with a big smile. The group responded with polite laughter. The sheikh lifted his cup of tea, took a sip, and said, "Seriously, Ambassador Atkins, the stage is yours."

Once more, the ambassador confidently and deliberately divulged the result of an almost world-wide human trafficking investigation that had brought them to Dubai. The sheikh's demeanor showed neither surprise nor anger. His features remained placid—although his staffers gave each other quick glances—while Atkins related Saqr's well-documented activities.

"I don't know if or how deep this trafficking operation has penetrated your administration, and I'm not sure I want to know, your highness. It is possible that these five men have acted entirely on their own, but undoubtedly they spread money around. We know of their ingenuity, their brazenness, and their incredible attention to detail. They are tactical geniuses, but it has all caught up to them. They must be stopped and Saqr destroyed. All elements of it. Our investigations have taken us here to Jumeirah Road in the city and a souk in al Deira. Now this must become a police matter, a Dubai police matter. We have no authority to take it further, but the image of Dubai must not be besmirched with such a horror."

"I am not sure what authority you had to take this investigation so deeply into my country," the sheikh said. Atkins started to speak, but the sheikh raised his hand. "But that is of no consequence. I want nothing of this nature to taint what we have built and what we are building in Dubai. I am aware that many in the emirates, and elsewhere in the Middle East, want more for us and our people; stronger and more-modern leadership. That is what I and my Emirati brothers are building toward, but some want it faster, at all costs. I am not aware of this Saqr unit, but I would not be surprised if others were. No, what you have described is not the way to bring us forward. There is no way I can condone what has happened here, not very far from this palace. I will immediately direct my chief of police to go over with you the evidence you have developed. If this is true, we will close down Saqr and all things related to it."

"Thank you, your highness," replied Atkins. "If it meets with your satisfaction, I will leave Special Agent Cerone and Agent Kapur at your disposal, but time is of the essence. We need to ensure that Assad al-Amin and his team do not get wind of our rescues. We can keep this quiet for only so long. We cannot risk their fleeing. Then we will have to work to control any fallout especially here in Dubai but elsewhere as well."

* * *

Cerone and Kapur spent the afternoon in an operations center one level below where they had met with the sheikh. Chief of Police Mizar Hussain was accompanied by four high-ranking officers and an IT officer who worked with the flash drives Cerone had brought with him. On several occasions, to the question, "How did you …?" Cerone and Kapur gave little details other than that someone on their team had hacked into the Saqr network.

As each new piece of the abduction puzzle was uncovered and documented, the Dubai police officials broke out into animated conversation in Arabic. One officer took copious notes. A copy of the flash drive was left with them but without the banking connections. Chief Hussain told Cerone and Kapur that when it was completed, they would present their plan to Sheikh Mohammed for his approval. He offered to have a car take them back to their residence, but Gino had arranged with Ambassador Atkins to have a car wait for them at the palace. The last thing he wanted was to have a police car take them back to Jumeirah Road and possibly be witnessed by someone across the street.

* * *

"Did you share with the cops any of the transcripts we recorded?" asked Fred.

"No," replied Gino. "I essentially kept this place out of it. I want you guys to start disassembling everything here. Get this stuff back in boxes and in closets, out of the way. I want this to look like a plain old rental villa in two hours."

At dawn the next day, Jumeirah Road was suddenly filled with blue and white police cars. Nina Darvish was on surveillance duty that morning—without the video and audio recording equipment—just eyes- on, and quickly alerted everyone in the villa. Discreetly from the windows facing the street, they observed some Ferraris, Porsches, at least one Mercedes roadster, and several Mercedes SUVs, all emblazoned with the traditional blue and white colors of the Dubai police force, pulling up in front of the Saqr residence. Armed officers alighted from the SUVs and swarmed the villa across the street. They also noticed a number of female officers wearing their royal-blue *hijabs* taking positions at each end of the street and essentially closing it down.

"Somebody get the coffee going," said Fred. "This is wild."

Doors were smashed open. The officers, all carrying automatic rifles, quickly entered. Gino and the others heard shouting but no gunfire. The cops had obviously caught everyone asleep. A blue van came down the street weaving around the assortment of sports cars the Dubai police routinely used and stopped in front of the villa. It was a little confusing with so many officers in and around the villa, but they saw men being roughly pulled from the house and pushed into the van. A few were wearing T-shirts and shorts, most likely their normal bed clothes. In a short time, the van pulled away and most of the sport cars with it. The SUVs moved in closer, and officers carried out computers, laptops, and boxes, loading them into the vehicles.

"Do you think they're doing the same thing at the souk?" asked Nina.

"I'm sure of it. We were very clear about what we believed was going on there, and they'll soon know more than we do."

A forensic van pulled up; four people in white carried large black leather cases inside.

"Guys, I want you out of here," Gino stated. "When things quiet down across the street, Ray and Rajesh should get back to their apartments. Load up your car with the equipment, and check with Lyon on what they want to do with the stuff they sent down. They may want it rerouted through the French Embassy. Find out."

"I might just want to keep it down here," Ray replied. "Might come in handy one day."

"Okay, your call. Fred and Gisella, time to get back to the travel business though I'd like Fred to close out our lease on this place. You can say Mercedes and I were called back to Spain for a family emergency.

If there's a penalty—which I doubt—just take care of it. Nina, you can go with them when they leave. They'll drop you off wherever you like, but I'd prefer you stay in case I need some assistance. Sean, I'll call Washington and see how they want to get you back to the States. I'll check into the Sheraton again, but let's hold tight for now and keep watch on what's happening."

* * *

Things remained relatively quiet the rest of the day with police tapes stretched across the front door and garage.

The next morning, local newspapers carried a story, far from the front page, that arrests had been made of individuals—never stating how many—who had been trying to set up a human trafficking ring out of Dubai but that an ongoing police investigation had stopped it.

"Interesting, Gino," said Fred. "We've been watching and listening to these guys for days but we have only snippets of their faces. I'd love to interview them."

"So would I," said Gino.

"And we also never learned who the Egyptian is though his number is somewhere in the data we appropriated," remarked Fred.

"He's obviously some kind of contract killer. Eventually, Interpol will follow up on that," added Ray.

"I hope so," said Gino not mentioning the conversation he had had with Dascenzo. "But I'm quite content with where we are and what we've achieved. I worked with such a great team in our conspiracy investigation in Spain, but you guys are easily their equals. I'm very proud of the work you've done here. You're not going to get much credit for our success, but you know how vital you've been in getting those girls home and closing down Saqr."

"Gino, will the blackout be lifted?" asked Gisella.

"I'm told yes, soon. Interpol will take the lead. They'll attribute the abductions to an international human trafficking operation and try not to go much further than that. The girls were taken, kept as prisoners, and forced into some kind of service. They were taken for their brains and not put into some white slavery kind of thing. No sex trafficking, no harems. That will be a hard sell, but Interpol is committed to keeping the bigwigs out of it, as we promised. But rest assured, one day, some pain-in-the-ass investigative reporter is going to dig into this. Then who knows?"

* * *

The next day, Gino called to Chief Hussain hoping to get information beyond what the newspapers were reporting. The chief had given Gino his card with a direct line to his office, but Gino, nonetheless, needed Nina's Arabic skills to wade through the office staff to reach him.

"Special Agent Cerone, you have given us more intrigue than we have experienced in the past year. Maybe even longer than that. A nightmare for Dubai. We are making great efforts to contain the ramifications. We are building the case against Saqr and delicately trying to close down the network they built. About sixty men, business leaders and various levels of royalty, have supported this scheme across half a dozen countries, quite a few in the emirates."

"Yes, I know. A herculean task I imagine. I read the story you engineered in the newspapers and hope you will be able to keep it at that," added Gino.

"That will not be a problem in this part of the world, Agent Cerone. We have a way of controlling the story."

"Are the men you brought into custody opening up on their operation, Chief?"

"Yes, the four we arrested at the house…"

"Four? There were five of them!"

"Yes I know. We took four into custody from the raid on the villa, but Hazem al-Sawai wasn't one of them."

"Hazem escaped?" gasped Gino. "He's the one who runs their whole data system. He's the IT guy. He controls everything!"

"Yes, we are aware of that from our discussions with you, but apparently, he was up at the time of our assault. He undoubtedly saw our cars lining up outside the villa and decided to make his escape just before we entered."

"So he got away?"

"No. He donned one of the black *burqas* the group had used when transporting the women and went out the back, through the garden and pool area. He scaled a wall and slowly walked down the street and away from the villa. An astute officer, a woman by the way, noticed that the *burqa* was a bit short for this woman's stature and stopped to question her. It soon became clear that he was no woman, and our officer drew her gun and detained him. She called in the situation and in no time, al-Sawai was surrounded by other officers and taken into custody. He had no weapons, so the arrest proceeded without incident. We had him remain in the *burqa* throughout the day, even after processing him. He is currently in a Spartan cell here at the station. He hasn't talked very much yet, but he will. All of their operation went through him, and he will assist us in extracting what we need from the computers from the villa and at the souk."

"Praise Allah as you say," sighed Gino.

"Yes, praise Allah." The chief laughed. "But based on the evidence you gave us, Assad al-Amin is the brains behind the operation. He runs everything. Hazem only records it. Between the two, we will ascertain who the others who support their network are—the immigration and customs people who looked the other way when the girls entered

Dubai, the people who provided the array of false passports these men used when traveling, the assets in place at the various universities in Europe—all those who facilitated Saqr's operation. You mentioned a nightmare, and it is, but it will be taken care of I assure you."

"Thank you, Chief Hussain, and thanks also to Sheikh Mohammed. I am impressed at how quickly you have closed down this abominable criminal operation."

"The thanks go to you and Interpol, but do not be surprised if you read nothing more about this in the newspapers. Things will be taken care of."

Chapter Fifty-Four

Mercedes remained with Paz and Frankie and their families while they waited for the finalization of the cover story regarding the abductions. They were settled in an old hunting lodge of King Philipe, not far from Aranjuez, dating back to before the Spanish civil war. It had seven rooms, so they were comfortable. Rodrigo de la Cruz and Michael Fontana were very opposed to creating this fiction, but they relented when they were assured that the Saqr abductors would be taken into custody and more than likely would be convicted without trial. Most likely, they would just disappear. Middle Eastern justice. The women and their families had to remain silent on exactly where they had been taken and by whom. The story would be that Frankie and Paz did not know where they had been taken—into the desert someplace. While in captivity, their roles were menial like those of servants, babysitters, and at times tutors, an enigma. Obviously due to the trauma of the ordeal, there would be no press briefings or interviews.

While thrilled beyond belief to be back with her parents and basically in her home away from home—Madrid—Frankie nevertheless felt strange being pulled away from the children she had bonded with. If anything, they too had been pawns in this calamity, and she felt especially sad about Mariam, whose generosity and compassion were responsible for their rescue. Frankie really liked the girl, soon to be a woman, albeit a princess. Yet there she was, out in the desert in a massive palace, being taught by hired tutors, and then Paz and Frankie picking up the reins of her and her sisters' and brothers' education. Rarely had she interacted with others of her age. *No friends. Sad.*

"Captain Garcia, I need you to do me a favor," Frankie asked.

"Yes of course, *Señorita* Fontana. What do you need?"

"Frankie, Captain. Call me Frankie. What I need may confuse you, but you know I wouldn't be here were it not for one of the sheikh's children leaving her cell phone unattended—on purpose."

"Yes. That call to your father changed everything."

"I want you or Ambassador Atkins—someone—to give me the phone number of that call to my father. If necessary, contact the sheikh for an email address for Mariam, the oldest of his children. The one I owe everything to. I would like to text or email her from time to time. But I don't want to get her in trouble. That's why going through the sheikh might be safer. Our love of horses was also something we shared, and I'd like to keep in touch. Sound crazy?"

"No, no, Frankie, not crazy at all. From what I've learned in our debriefing with you and *Señorita* de la Cruz, it is clear that you enjoyed your time with the children. That perhaps preserved your sanity during this ordeal. You believe Mariam will not reveal that you used her cell phone to make that call, so that should remain a secret. Even if contact with her is established, it should never be repeated. I will call Gino, the FBI agent who remained in Dubai. He is also my partner. After we left, he spent some time with Sheikh Saud, so maybe he can make the inquiry. We have access to that phone number in any case. We'll see what we can do."

* * *

All the surveillance equipment had gone to Ray's apartment. The Interpol agents got Schickhaus to agree to let them keep the equipment in Dubai. The toys Dascenzo had lent them for their penetration of the souk were also back in their boxes, and through the Dubai consulate, Nina was having them returned to the embassy in Abu Dhabi.

Sean O'Casey was not going to get another Gulfstream 650 ride back to DC, but Colonel Sanders had arranged for him to be on a military flight that evening out of the Al Dhafra Air Base, the same air base he had arrived at. He and Nina exchanged phone numbers and email addresses.

Fred and Gisella were back at their office booking tours for vacationers. Fred had closed the leasing agreement with Victoria Westbury, who, while disappointed that Gino and Mercedes had been called away, was very satisfied with the financial arrangements that essentially let her agency keep the fees for the full term of the lease.

Gino was left to close out the bank account in Dubai and spent a few hours compiling a ledger of sorts for the expenses incurred during the operation. With so much cash involved, a thorough reconciliation was necessary. Once back in Madrid, Gino would meet with his old friend Ray Evans and work out what they would do with the Saqr funds sitting in a CIA account in Geneva. Letting Interpol divide it up and send it to the victims of the abductions was logical. That might also incentivize their families to "stick to the script."

Chapter Fifty-Five

Some weeks after the police action in Dubai, Ammaral Said al-Nabi was in Brussels attending a conference with a number of EU ministers and directors responsible for investment strategies for member states. Sometimes, such meetings proved useful, but that day, bureaucrat after bureaucrat seemed enamored with the sound of his voice. Al-Nabi set up some side meetings with individual country representatives later in the day. While listening to someone from France drone on and on, nature called; he advised his aides that he was going to the restroom. As he was wearing Western clothing—a tailored, bespoke navy-blue suit and matching tie—he intended to use the restroom down the hall from the conference room. Most of the time, his Middle Eastern brethren who dressed in traditional garb preferred to return to their rooms because managing a billowing, floor-length *thobe* in a public restroom stall or at a urinal was out of the question.

The hallway was quite wide; a number of people were milling about—journalists, aides, and others just congregating. Long tables were set up on the far side of the hall where participants could check-in and get briefing materials and conference badges.

As al-Nabi neared the men's room, he was bumped ever so lightly, by a relatively tall man, also dressed in suit and tie, but his Arabic features were enhanced by his neatly trimmed beard and moustache.

In British-tinged English, the man apologized for not paying attention to where he was going. al-Nabi smiled, nodded, and entered the men's room.

While at the urinal, al-Nabi began to feel flushed, and his heart began to beat rapidly—too rapidly. He stumbled backward, the zipper of his trousers still undone, falling to one knee while trying to stabilized himself. He collapsed on the white tile floor, his penis exposed and his trousers wet with urine.

The neatly dressed gentleman who had brushed against al-Nabi was by then out of the building and walking in a relaxed manner to his BMW rental in the parking lot. He removed the badge he had deftly swiped off the registration table, wiped it down with a handkerchief, and tossed it into a trash barrel.

As he neared the BMW, he fished a narrow plastic cap out of his pocket and put it on a small syringe he was carrying, hearing it snap into place. He would dispose of it later. The Egyptian would have liked to see his quarry succumb to the injection of potassium chloride, but al-Nabi was certainly dead by now, he was sure. Sudden cardiac arrest the physicians would undoubtedly conclude. The Egyptian liked potassium chloride because it generally gave him a minute or so to distance himself from the scene, without drawing attention. The device he used was like an enema bulb but smaller and with a needle attached to it. The bulb was easily concealed in his hand with the needle protruding between his index and middle fingers. As he neared his target, he would discreetly slip off the plastic cap to expose the needle. Then a small bump with his hand, generally at thigh level and, simultaneously squeezing the bulb; the fluid entered his target. The pinch of the needle was never felt.

That went nicely. He slid into his BMW and headed to the airport. The next day, articles in all the Bahrain Arabic and English-language newspapers reported the death of Ammaral Said al-Nabi, director of the

Finance and Investment Ministry of Bahrain, who had suffered a heart attack while attending a business conference in Brussels. Al-Jazeera also reported the untimely death throughout its worldwide network, and long editorials followed for days extolling his contributions to diversifying Bahrain's economy and making it one of the most dynamic economies in the Middle East.

* * *

Farhaj bin Tariq Ahsan, unlike Ammaral Said al-Nabi, was a solitary man who rarely left his residence. Al-Nabi, the consummate businessman, was often out of the country, and his itinerary was relatively easy to ascertain, given that it was often reported in local newspapers and ministry websites. The Egyptian merely had to go to a location and look for an opportunity. If that didn't work out, he'd go to the next destination, even if it was in Bahrain, and try again. He would use different passports to travel, change his looks, and reconnoiter.

That tactic would not work with Tariq Ahsan, whose gated residence was in a very upscale section of Manama, but not grandly palatial, as might be the case with the residences of more-connected cousins. He had adopted the title of sultan, which had no official significance at all, but it lent the man an air of aristocracy. His stipend from the monarchy indeed allowed him to live a life of luxury, but of no significance. In his sixties, soft and overweight, he enjoyed good food, lounging by the pool, reading or being read to, and daily massages by a bevy of woman who were part of the household. In days gone by, his harem.

The Egyptian's surveillance noted a recurring series of services to the gated estate, generally carried out on the same day and at the same time. Refuse was collected every Monday and Friday morning by one or two men entering the grounds via a service gate, and someone serviced the pool every Tuesday morning, entering through the same gate. Also predictable was the arrival of a landscaping crew every Wednesday morning at nine, spending up to two hours there. They—Ahsan Landscaping Services' four men—typically carried or wheeled-in equipment with them, but not lawn mowers. Apparently there was no grass in the front or rear of the property. At first, the crew worked in the front of the estate, trimming and clipping the various shrubs, palm trees and massive red and pink bougainvillea. What went on in the back was probably more of the same, as he saw the men wheeling debris from the back, to their van. The Egyptian determined that the gate was unlocked on the days and times such services took place. *If this so-called sultan doesn't leave his residence*, the Egyptian thought, *I'll have to find a way inside and past his servants and attendants.*

Disguised with dark auburn hair—not uncommon in the Middle East—and a light beard, the Egyptian paid a visit to Ahsan's landscaping company's offices with a simple, though unusual story. His father wanted him to learn a good trade, and considering the need to maintain all the horticulture amid a desert environment, year round, he thought that the landscaping trade would suit him well. He asked to work with a crew and follow the lead of the supervisor as just an apprentice, but preferably in an upscale neighborhood—*like the one where Tariq Ahsan lived.*

Hamza Mustafa, the manager of seven landscaping crews, was not an affluent man, simply a competent manager for the owners, who rarely got involved in the business. Mustafa had been university educated and took immense pride in the work of his crews, but he saw all the money going right to the owners. He sensed an opportunity when the Egyptian told him that his father would be willing to offer 200 dinars a week, about $540, for an apprenticeship. Mustafa considered this an under-the-table windfall and agreed to the proposition; he said he wanted a month's payment in advance, in case the apprentice decided to quit after a few days. The Egyptian agreed and handed the manager 800 dinars, which Mustafa quickly slid into his desk drawer.

For three weeks, the apprentice worked at a few dozen residences, some more opulent than others. He had been on Tariq Ahsan's grounds three times clipping shrubs, climbing palm trees to trim fronds, picking up debris and dead branches, and even planting some rose bushes. Each time, he had seen Tariq Ahsan on a patio by the pool with several women attending to his needs—food and drink mostly. The man also entered the pool with stone lions spewing fountains of water at the far end. Considering his size—quite corpulent—he merely waded in the low end, wearing a ridiculously tiny black bathing suit that disappeared under the folds of his stomach. He waded back and forth for fifteen minutes before emerging and sprawling on a lounge chair and falling asleep.

The Egyptian decided that for this assassination, he would use something with a more immediate effect. After his first visit, on the days he worked the property, he brought a device similar to the one he had used in Brussels, but filled with succinylcholine. As was potassium chloride, the drug was quickly metabolized leaving no trace for physicians or coroners. Once administered, the target would be immediately rendered immobile due to the drug's neuromuscular paralytic effect. All organs would shut down, and the target would stop breathing. If he administered it when his prey was sleeping, he would remain reclining in his lounge chair, as if asleep.

On the fourth week of his apprenticeship, an opportunity presented itself. Tariq Ahsan was fast asleep as the Egyptian passed by him. He barely had to lean over to reach the man's upper arm, where there was less fat to penetrate. A touch. A squeeze. It was done. The Egyptian moved from the pool area and continued to work around the grounds until the crew left for another residence.

The Egyptian, his apprenticeship and assignment completed, packed up and prepared to leave Bahrain at about the same time newspapers reported the death of Farhaj bin Tariq Ahsan, a distant relative of the monarchy. The sultan, as he was referred to, had been obese and had been in poor health; he had quietly passed away at his residence.

Dascenzo received a text from an unknown caller with one word: "Done." The CIA man had appropriated a bit of the Saqr funds in Geneva, and the Egyptian had become part of a black ops operation, on call as needed, but now, committed to a new and exclusive employer.

Looking at the text, Pete thought, *Retribution.*

Chapter Fifty-Six

The weeks that followed the return of the women were filled with jubilation and complexity as the news of the abducted students' release was made known throughout Europe and the world. An international human trafficking ring had been exposed, and its victims had been returned safely to their families. That was the story, but the clamor for details was deafening. The stealthy offer of monetary compensation for the victims' ordeals was well received, but no amount of money could ever erase the trauma the girls and their families had suffered. But for the time being, the families agreed to respect the deal with the devils. They had gotten their daughters home, and that was most important, but the quest for more information continued daily.

Frankie and Paz would forgo their semesters at the university and resume again next year. Paz returned to her apartment with her parents in Madrid, and Frankie went home to Bedminster, New Jersey. One of the first things she did was to see Wicked and Sultan. She especially appreciated the majesty of Sultan particularly after spending time with the magnificent stallions at the Pegasus stables. "You could be right there with them. You'd be just as fine as Midnight, just as beautiful and just as regal," she whispered to Sultan as she snuggled his muzzle. Walking to the next stall, she pulled Wicked close to her saying, "And you're not so bad either. Really missed you both."

While Paz intended to continue her law studies, Frankie was

wavering. She had really enjoyed teaching the sheikh's children, and she would never forget the fashion show and how all the children had poured themselves into the fairy-tale characters. Even Omar, in his number 7 Real Madrid uniform, had been splendid with arms in the air as his shot on goal soared through the door at the back of the room. Joy—that's what she had seen in their faces. She would never see such joy as a corporate lawyer. No, education would be her career path. She went online to see what Princeton had to offer. *Mrs. King would have been proud of me.*

* * *

Mercedes and Gino were back together in Madrid; she started heading up a special counterterrorism investigative unit, and Gino was putting the finishing touches on winding down Operations Discovery, Retrieval, and Retrieval-EU. He had offers from the FBI, and Evans and Dascenzo kept making the case for a career in the CIA. However, Gino was content and comfortable in Madrid with Mercedes and instead accepted an offer from Klaus Schickhaus to become an Interpol investigative agent based in Madrid. More important, however, was that Gino and Mercedes decided to make their relationship official. They would wed in the fall.

* * *

"So what do you think, Mariam?" Frankie asked showing her young friend around the stable facilities in Bedminster, both women dressed in riding gear.

"Wonderful, Frankie," she replied, no longer using the Miss Fontana appellation.

"It's not Pegasus, but Wicked and Sultan are treated royally here—our version of royalty, not yours—and the woods around here have excellent riding paths for when we're not doing dressage training."

"Surely not like riding in the desert," Mariam added, "but there is so much more to see. How wonderful. This is something I never thought I'd experience, and to get away from the summer in Ras al-Khaimah, where it's forty degrees centigrade, is a pleasure."

"Do you think you can manage Sultan?" Frankie asked.

"You bet," replied Mariam enthusiastically already latching on to some Americanisms.

"Let's go."

Acknowledgements

A story that ventures into the heart of the Middle East; touching on its past, examining its present and speculating about its future is an ambitious task, and one not taken lightly. In my novel, *The Seventh Treasure,* which took place entirely in Spain, I often referred to the magic, majesty and mystery of that country, with each region offering its own unique character and history, certainly shaped by its almost eight hundred year occupation by Muslim invaders from Arabia and North Africa (Moors).

The Middle East and the multitude of countries that fall under that heading even more aptly fit the magic, majesty and mystery description. Civilizations that go back thousands of years, none more impressive than ancient Egypt, the precursor of the great Greek and Roman empires to follow. The many desert kingdoms and tribal dynasties occupying these lands for millennia were ultimately and haphazardly transformed following World War I by British and French bureaucrats into the countries we know today. But the magic and majesty of these lands cannot be denied.

Hollywood has taken us back to those times with cinematic spectaculars and even now, stories of that ancient era are seen on Broadway and in animated features that seem never to lose their popularity. We are enthralled with that magical history and the mysteries that surround it.

One of my reference materials that found a place in *Prey of the Falcon* is Tales of the Arabian Nights, or One Thousand and One Nights, as these works are referred to in earlier versions. Originally, many of these tales were set in India, which is believed to be the source of its origins, in the eighth or ninth century, or earlier. Stories were passed on by word of mouth, with Persian and Arab contributions added over the years. The storytelling traditions of these lands embellished the tales as they were passed on to one another, and as their popularity grew, the tales began to be organized. Over the next five centuries a number of manuscripts were created in several languages and a variety of versions, soon becoming a piece of classic Arab literature.

Ultimately European translations followed, first in French (Antoine Galland, 1701, 1704-1717), and the best known English translation by Sir Richard Burton was published in sixteen volumes in the late 1800's. The tales of Shahrazad, and how she beguiled a king with a labyrinth of stories within stories, were the original basis of One Thousand and One Nights. Over the centuries, the exploits of Sindbad the Sailor, Ali Baba and the Forty Thieves and Aladdin and the Magic Lamp followed, and today, it is perhaps the most widely read piece of literature after the Bible, despite having no authors, only translators.

I mention this to illustrate the concept of the magic, majesty and mystery of these lands and how many of us grew up, enthralled with stories of boys on flying carpets, genies granting three wishes, magical palaces and beguiling, young heroes and heroines. The children of today are experiencing the same delight thanks to a major entertainment and cinema studio dominating the landscape with animated features, live action movies and transitions to blockbuster Broadway plays that run for years. This, in the midst of the turmoil and uncertainty that color this region and its future.

In between how stories from The Tales of the Arabian Nights delighted the children all over the world, highlighted by the movies of the 1950's, and now, once more in the 21st century, are two important developments that serve as background for today's environment. The first is the birth of Israel (1948), partitioned out of British-controlled Palestine and vividly chronicled in *Exodus*, the spectacular Leon Uris novel depicting Israel's struggle to survive against overwhelming odds. A giant movie by Otto Preminger in 1960 brought the news reports to many more millions all over the world. The magical stories we grew up with took on a new perspective as the formation of Israel gave birth to perpetual conflict and terror endemic in this region today.

The second most influential media event was the 1962 David Lean majestic epic, *Lawrence of Arabia*, the story of T.E. Lawrence, who unites warring Arab tribes into a guerilla army that defeats the mighty Ottoman Empire that ruled these desert factions. While this event preceded the formation of Israel by thirty years, this history was brought to life for all to witness in the David Lean movie. The Middle East, as we know it today; Saudi Arabia, Iraq, Iran, Oman, the United Arab Emirates, Kuwait, Qatar, on and on, was born at the end of World War I, following the victorious campaign led by Lawrence. And then came the oil and things changed again.

So, growing up in this fairy tale environment—beguiling tales of magic, majesty and mystery—is followed by the harsh reality of where we are today, much of it the consequences of the Iranian revolution, exacerbated by the tragedy of 9/11 and all that has followed. My own travels to this area, specifically, Egypt, Israel, Morocco, Tunisia, Turkey, Oman, Jordan, the Emirates, still gives me hope, despite the schizophrenic politics and policies of these desert kingdoms. The main perpetrator in *Prey of the Falcon*, Assad al-Amin, wants something better for this region, a fair and equitable—and safe— environment for these people, especially its women. There is no magic lamp and he just goes about it in a heinous way.

* * *

Thanks to my wife Terry, who I depend on for that first read-through and my daughter George for her editing and valuable, creative input. And thanks to Sansing McPhearson who I never properly thanked for her first draft edits and input on The Seventh Treasure.

Thanks also to Alex of Sharaf Tours who showed us around Dubai and shepherded us to Ras al-Khaimah, where we spent several enlightening days in this desert kingdom.

Printed in the United States
By Bookmasters